Dear Mom:

Thank you again for the generous gift of a week-long cruise in Tahiti. It's not your fault the ship sank. Instead of all those years of computer science courses, I wish I had paid more attention to reality TV shows about turning bugs into breakfast.

I'm sure I'll be fine, and when I get home you can bet I'll listen to the rest of your advice about what I ought to do with my life, since this has worked out so well.

Love, Marissa

P.S. I don't think I'll make it home in time for the club's summer ball.

P.P.S. Please make my apologies to the blind date I'm sure you arranged.

P.P.P.S. I'm a lesbian.

Finders
Keepers

Karin Kallmaker

Bella
BOOKS
2006

Bella Books, Inc.
P.O. Box 10543
Tallahassee, FL 32302

Printed in the United States of America on acid-free paper
First Edition

Editor: Anna Chinappi
Cover designer: LA Callaghan

ISBN 1-59493-072-4

For Maria, who watched me inflate and deflate, and pointed out the efficacy of sweatbands.

Dedicated to all the women who struggle, and those who encourage, especially MJ, Reese and Romy for their examples of determination, and the denizens of Thud, where seldom is heard a discouraging word.

Nineteen, on the edge

About the Author

Karin Kallmaker, the author of more than twenty romances and fantasy-science fiction novels, began her writing career with the venerable Naiad Press and continues with Bella Books. Her works include the award-winning *Just Like That, Maybe Next Time* and *Sugar*. Short stories have appeared in anthologies from publishers like Alyson, Bold Strokes, Circlet and Haworth, as well as novellas and short stories with Bella Books.

All of Karin's work can now be found at Bella Books. Details and background about her novels and her other pen name, Laura Adams, can be found at www.kallmaker.com.

She and her partner are the mothers of two and live in the San Francisco Bay Area. She is descended from Lady Godiva, a fact which she'll share with anyone who will listen. She likes her Internet fast, her iPod loud and her chocolate real.

For more information about the health, fitness and nutrition resources used while researching this novel, go to Kallmaker.com and visit the page for *Finders Keepers*.

Part One

Chapter 1

"This is our manifesto: there is someone perfect for you out there."

Marissa Chabot paused to tuck a stray lock of streaky blond hair behind her ear. The crowd filling the meeting room was thoroughly mixed, with over-fifties and under-thirties, skin colors ranging from ebony to hothouse mushroom and hair styles screaming "het soccer mom" and "baby butch." The all-female audience was Marissa's favorite kind.

"That someone isn't at the coffeehouse. Not hanging out at the library. Not at your job or just down the street. That someone is on the Internet. Like you, works long hours. Like you, has no time to go hunting for a date who could turn out to be the worst mistake of their life."

She didn't really need the note cards she'd arranged on the lectern. She'd given this speech so often in the last two months she knew it by heart.

"Your perfect someone is there. Like anything in life, your perfect someone is worth looking for. Why not look smart? Why not let technology help? Antony found Cleopatra in a social circle of less than a hundred—and that didn't turn out that well, did it? Today you're meeting and considering possibilities with *thousands* of potentially compatible people. Your lives are busy, your jobs take energy and who has the time to figure out if that intriguing person is genuine?" She clicked the first slide of her PowerPoint deck and watched as their company name formed out of a splash of shooting stars.

"At Finders Keepers, we believe in love. We believe in romance. We believe in first meetings, second dates, third anniversaries and relationships that can last a lifetime. In the next ten minutes I'm going to explain why our questionnaire and statistical analysis has resulted in a three-out-of-four chance that the match we find for you will still be in your life in the best possible way three years from now."

She clicked steadily through the slides, pausing briefly when she realized her dangling earring was making contact with the microphone boom.

"Ninety-seven percent of our clients will match up with a high degree of compatibility with four to seven other clients. That means most of our clients complete their questionnaire and get a profile back that looks like this."

Using the laser pointer she highlighted the paragraph that summarized their personality and then the list of fictitious names grouped by their compatibility match scores, starting with the 98s. "Ninety-nine percent matches are rare, so most people get one or two names in the ninety-eights, several more in the ninety-sevens or sixes, and a few more in the ninety-fives. The report stops at ten names maximum, as we've found more than that can leave clients feeling overwhelmed."

The audience was engaged and she fielded cautiously excited questions when she concluded her ten-minute spiel. She made a note in her mental Palm Pilot about the size and time of the presentation. She wasn't used to being on commission like the other sales people. Even though she and Ocky argued about money all the time, it was only fair that she was compensated the same way everyone else was for doing direct sales work.

After the last question, she stepped back with an inclusive gesture. "Thank you, everyone, for your attention and kindness, and many thanks to the organizers of today's Women's Forum. I've got business cards galore here at the front, with a note on how to get a discount on your set-up fee. Thanks again."

The applause was polite but abbreviated as women gathered up their belongings. Marissa lingered near the podium, first slipping her earring back on, then packing up her laptop as she chatted with women who came to the front to get business cards. It was a low-key sell because that was their style. Finders Keepers wasn't about pressure. One of the first things they told clients to do was simply relax.

The next sessions got under way and Marissa escaped to the parking lot with her laptop case slung over one shoulder. Dappled sunshine warmed her face and for just a moment she heard the hiss of surf spreading on hot sand. She shook the sound out of her head. It was just as quickly replaced by the low question, "Is this what you wanted, Marissa?"

She made herself think about the unusually warm winter weather, about her shoes, about statistical regression—anything to silence that memory. She was enjoying the record high temperatures for January, she told herself cheerily. San Francisco, over the hills and on the water, was also setting records.

The San Ramon Ranch Conference Center was not far from the FK office and she had elected to walk for the exercise. It was only five minutes and she wasn't going to get in a run until tomorrow, after all. Sunny, beautiful day. Who needed a tropical paradise when the Amador Valley would soon be green with spring while the rest of the country still froze?

"It went great," she told Heather as she collected her messages at the reception desk. "There were probably two dozen cards taken, so we'll see six contacts or so and might sign three."

"Good work." Heather brushed back her hair with a long hand. "Octavia left for that marketing association thing and said the servers are slow again."

"She thinks lightning is slow. Your hair looks great, by the way."

"Thanks." She brushed it back again. "I think I need a clip or something, though."

"The price of fashion," Marissa quipped. "My underwire is piercing my armpit right now." She took her leave as Heather laughed in sympathy.

The soft, deep purple carpet of the reception area gave way to a more durable gray as she punched in the code and passed through the double doors to the main farm. Cubicles occupied the center of the large space. She dropped off her laptop case at the overflowing desk in her office and removed her rings and the chunky gold necklace and earrings that matched. Another set of codes gained her entrance into the server room and she gratefully sank down at the administrative workstation. She'd always found the chilled air and steady hum calming.

Her fingernails clicked the keyboard as she typed in the first diagnostic command. Time for a trim, she realized, then pouted as she added the To Do to her mental Palm Pilot. As the diagnostic tallied service statistics she expanded on the note in her head.

Dear Self,

Don't forget to record the presentation code for your commission and trim your nails. While it's depressing that the nail trim is for the keyboard and not because you're avoiding giving someone an ouch in bed, there's no need to whine. This week is a No Whining Zone.

Love, Marissa

As usual, the service stats were fine. She printed the report to silence Ocky's complaints and went back to her desk where a stack of questionnaires waited to be entered manually. She was going to personally find and dismember the guy who sold them that piece-of-garbage optical scanner. Maybe she could get a temp. Maybe the temp would do it right. Maybe California and Hawaii could become their own country. Right.

She pushed aside last night's empty take-out salad container and a large pile of accounting reports joined their predecessors on the floor. Ocky had left several yellow squares stuck to her monitor.

Dear Octavia M. Zant,

Put another sticky note on my screen and I will personally bad sector your writing hand.

Love, Marissa

One of these days she'd really tap that message out and send it.

The office had stilled when she finished the last questionnaire. So much for the prestige of being part owner of the fastest growing Internet matchmaking service in California. Her arms were cramped and all she could think about was some dinner and maybe a trip to the gym. A door slammed and she heard a familiar rustle combined with the rhythmic crackle of headphones. Ocky was back.

From a nonchalant pose at Ocky's office door, she watched her business partner put her notebook back in the slot where it belonged, stow her briefcase and set her phone and Mp3 player on their chargers. She waited until Ocky looked up before saying, "How'd it go?"

"Great. You look tired."

"Questionnaires. The service guy is here tomorrow morning. There's nothing wrong with the servers, by the way." Marissa wished she hadn't taken off her earrings. "You look tired too."

"Late night. And not a great one." Ocky kicked off her sandals and curled back into her desk chair, legs tucked under her. "Tell me one more time why I don't fill out my own questionnaire and get myself a real lover?"

I could run a thousand miles a day, Marissa thought, and not have her slender, toned legs. "Because you can't afford to tell the truth should you end up the one-in-four who doesn't find a good match through our system." She didn't want to admit at that very moment that she herself was now a Finders Keepers client. It wasn't the right time to break that news to Ocky.

"So I'm stuck with mismatch after mismatch using my own hunter-gatherer skills. At least the sex is great. Well, it wasn't last night but it usually is."

Marissa didn't let herself think too much about what did and didn't work with Ocky's long string of short-lived girlfriends. Octavia liked them tall, blonde, lithesome and temporary, all things Marissa would never be. Not that her own dating record had any more success. Accidents and twisted fate had played too large a role in her love life. She was hoping her future, with guided assistance from statistical analysis and algorithms she'd written herself, would improve.

As they chatted about finances, Marissa again heard the hiss of distant surf on warm sand and the quiet but intense question, "Is this what you wanted, Marissa?" Maybe the memory persisted because of the sunshine today. Just nostalgia.

Tomorrow would be one year to the day but who was counting? A vacation romance was an unreliable thing. Passion at the time but no real connection. Tears at parting, a promise she would be in touch as soon as possible—Marissa told herself she'd been a fool to believe any of it. She was over it, just as she was over her crush on Ocky. Fussing about Ocky's girlfriends and how she looked when Ocky was around was a habit she was trying to break.

"So when your next trust payout comes along, I think we'll be able to expand the office site and roll out some national advertising." Ocky tapped at her keyboard, rapidly reading and responding to messages. "Those cash infusions have been great for the business."

"It's the last one," Marissa said slowly, "since I'm turning thirty-five this summer. We need to talk about it because I really should get myself out of renting and into a condo or something."

"We should be in for some big withdrawals as partner bonuses within five years," Ocky said. She glanced up with one of her confident smiles.

Marissa didn't want to give in, not this time. They'd had this discussion five years ago. She'd invested a lot in the business and things were really going to start paying off, it was true, but she didn't want to be forty and still paying rent in one of the most expensive real estate markets in the country. "We're going to need to talk about it. There may be other ways to finance what we need to do."

"Let's go have a hot fudge sundae or something. I could use the pick-me-up."

Thinking longingly of the gym, Marissa said, "I can't be that indulgent today."

Ocky frowned. "Still dieting?"

"This isn't temporary. Our ancestors spawned in different oceans and I got the oversized genes."

"I can't even get you to split a pizza these days."

Marissa didn't say, "Splitting a pizza means I eat two-thirds, gain three pounds overnight while you have the metabolism of an atom bomb." Instead she said, with a gesture at her tummy, "I'm trying to make up for twenty years of indulgence here. Maybe we could have coffee instead of ice cream? You can always get one of those brownie things you like."

Ocky agreed with poor grace and they went about locking down the office. A few minutes later they pulled into adjoining parking spaces close to the door of the Village Roaster.

Though the desserts were arranged in the display case as seductively as possible, Marissa knew the calories, fat and carbs for each item. Knowledge was power and she was inured to their charms. She ordered her coffee iced with skim, no cream and stirred in no-cal sweetener and a dash of cocoa powder while she waited for

Ocky to join her. Even though she didn't want the large brownie and the whipped mocha with real sugar that Ocky was going to consume, she still felt a pang of resentment over the matter of genetics. It wasn't fair but whining didn't burn calories.

"So I really think we're going to be able to pull out a quarter of our capital each by the end of the next five years. Plus increase our partners' draw. Finally make a real living after all our hard work and investment." Ocky bit off a substantial chunk of the brownie and licked chocolate sprinkles off her lip.

"Thing is, in five years condos are going to cost that much more, Ocky. You already have a place."

"With a second mortgage on it for the business."

"I know," Marissa conceded. If she had to, she would point out that Ocky's condo had appreciated double in the ten years she'd owned it. Patiently, she said, "If I use my trust payout this time I can get into one of the complexes about three miles from work. I could run to work, in fact." The idea of being able to combine her need for regular, consistent exercise with her commute suited Marissa's sense of symmetry.

She took a large swallow of her iced coffee before adding, "It's ideal. The mortgage payment will be more than rent but I'd get the interest deduction and come out ahead. It makes such good financial sense for me right now."

Ocky licked an errant bit of cream from her upper lip. "I understand that but we've been planning your capital investments since almost the start."

"I know, but the last year has been so good I thought the business could get a real business loan instead of Bank of Marissa's Dead Grandmother."

Ocky frowned. "This is all out of left field, you know."

"We talked about it five years ago. I know I said I'd be willing to invest, so yeah, I'm changing my mind." Marissa wanted in the worst way to add, "Haven't you noticed that I've changed?" But she took a deep breath instead and watched Ocky's fingers drum the table, even as a small part of her realized she wasn't all gooey-hearted at the sight of Ocky licking her lips. That, at least, was something.

"Are you sure you don't want a bite?" Ocky abruptly leaned forward with a large chunk of brownie on her fork.

Marissa reared back as if stung. "No, but thanks."

"Really? They're good today."

"It's like crack at the moment, Ocky. One bite and I'm ten pounds up." How often do I have to say it, Marissa wondered.

"You're obsessed about calories."

Sharply, Marissa answered, "I have to be." It's gotten results, she could have said too. But maybe—and the thought was simultaneously a slap and a comfort—Ocky really didn't notice how she looked. More calmly she added, "Better to be obsessed with what I won't eat than what I will."

Ocky shrugged. "Seems like an obsession either way, but you're the one with the nutritionist and the new friends."

Was Ocky jealous of the women at the gym and her weekly weight bitch session? "Maybe. I just know I'm healthier."

Ocky had moved on. "It's not like I haven't invested, though I know you've put in more."

"I know—for the first five years you did all the public contact. You were the front woman for it all. I know that. We both worked hundred-hour weeks. And you've put in capital too. I know you've got as much at stake as I do. It's not about that. I just need a place of my own. I want to put out my own welcome mat." She sipped her iced coffee, savoring the chill and bitter edge.

"Are you seeing someone?" Ocky leaned back with a considering look. "You've been dressing to the nines lately."

Okay, it was pleasing to know that Ocky did actually see her in detail and not just as a vague outline labeled *Marissa*. "I've been doing lots of presentations. And . . ." She shrugged. "And discovering there are things I like about myself now. Better than before. I like shoes." She cracked a smile. "Nearly as much as you."

Ocky finished the brownie. "You didn't answer my question."

Instead of "What's it to you?" Marissa said, without mentioning

11

the ten women listed on her personal Finder's Keepers analysis as Highly Compatible Profiles, "I'm dating a little bit. But if I wanted to, I'd like to live somewhere I'm proud to invite people in. And my apartment complex—you know what the place is like."

Ocky sighed. "Yeah, I do. I guess I shouldn't be surprised. We'll get a loan or something."

Relief welled up inside Marissa, so much so that she thought she might drown. She rarely won these kinds of arguments with Ocky. "Thanks for understanding. I really was going to bring it up at our next sit down."

"This counted."

Watching her friend's face, Marissa said again, "You do look tired."

"Last night—jeez. Major crying jag and I never the hell knew what it was about. I hate that."

"Had she been drinking?"

"No." Ocky cast her gaze heavenward. "There might have been something about me not being around enough but it's not like I'm not up front about how much I work."

The tale sounded all too familiar to Marissa. "Perhaps you should get involved with women who are themselves workaholics."

"Easy to say." Marissa tried not to watch as Ocky's tongue wetted her lips. "They don't often have legs that go from here to Argentina."

Glancing down at her own legs—which merely stretched from her hips to the floor—Marissa hid her inward sigh.

They parted at the door and Marissa turned toward the gym, finally. She was suddenly restless and anxious. A workout would make her feel better.

The steady *thud thud* of her running shoes was only apparent when Marissa turned down her iPod. It made her booty move. Her booty wasn't dead, oh no. The workout last night had felt great but she was even happier to finally get into a full sweat.

Swerving into the complex where she'd lived for the last twelve years and would be so happy to leave behind, she slackened her pace as she crossed the patch of oil-slicked asphalt that separated the buildings. The morning was cool but the brilliant sunrise promised more winter warmth.

At the common mailboxes she slowed to a halt, willing her breathing to return to normal.

"Damn!" she swore quietly as stinging sweat pooled into the corners of her eyes.

Straightening, hands pressing into the small of her back, she walked toward her front door, realizing as she got closer that there was someone waiting there. At this hour? A small alarm trilled inside but she discerned it was a woman, which allayed some of her fear.

It was a tall woman with dark hair down her back. And when she turned around her eyes were brown.

In her head Marissa heard, clearly as the night it had been said, "Is this what you want, Marissa?"

Now she also heard her breathless, adoring answer. "Yes. Please, yes."

The smile Marissa had tried to forget. The charm she'd tried to deny. The memory of those hands, that body, everything she'd tried to erase from her consciousness, rushed back into vivid reality.

One year since the moonlight and kisses. It had taken months for her heart to finish breaking when each day brought silence and more silence. She didn't want to go back in time. One year since the vacation of a lifetime had changed her life, for the worse and for the better.

Fighting for breath, but no longer due to exertion, Marissa willed herself to meet the sparkling brown eyes with a chilled stare of her own. "What do you want?"

"You," Linda answered.

Chapter 2

(One Year Earlier)

"Abandon ship! Proceed in an orderly fashion to your assigned lifeboat station. Abandon ship! This is not a drill!"

Jolted out of sleep, Marissa's first thought was that she was trapped in a nightmare but when the message repeated in what sounded like Italian, logic asserted that she did not have nightmares in languages she didn't speak.

The small cabin had no clock and she'd been so exhausted on arrival she'd not unpacked her own. Dull blue lighting had sprung up near the door and she pushed herself upright, trying to shake off the jittery fog of sudden awakening.

French, possibly, then once again, in commanding but modulated tones, "Abandon ship! Proceed in an orderly fashion to your assigned lifeboat station. Abandon ship! This is not a drill!"

Her cabin mate had likewise sat up and they stared at each other in confusion. With a shuddering gulp of air into lungs cramping with fear, Marissa scrambled out of the narrow bed and nearly fell as she fumbled for the clothes she'd left folded at the foot of the bed. Socks. Shoes. Backpack from the airplane, not yet unpacked. She hopped across the tiny space to the broom closet bathroom for the small toiletry bag she'd pulled out earlier so she could brush her teeth. Her purse she stuffed into the last spare inches under the zipper before slinging the pack over one shoulder.

"Abandon ship! Proceed in an orderly fashion to your assigned lifeboat station. Abandon ship! This is not a drill!"

Her cabin mate—Angela something—was chanting a phrase that included *dios* every fourth word or so. Their lack of a common language had been a barrier from the moment they'd nodded and smiled greetings some twelve hours earlier. They exited the cabin at the same time and all Marissa could think about was how much less expensive the lower berths had been and how many more flights of stairs were between her and the lifeboats as a result. The corridor was crowded with other passengers and getting tighter by the second. Every face she glanced at reflected what she felt: disbelief and panic. The weird emergency lighting made blondes look as if they had blue halos, but the effect was something out of a horror film.

They'd had a lifeboat drill just after embarkation, but maybe this was another test. A two a.m. test. Maybe this was all a precaution and they'd stand on deck for a while, the same way kids stood outside classrooms during fire drills, knowing the time for the gift it was. Sailing on the warm South Seas was pleasant circumstances for a middle-of-the-night drill, if not for the fear and terror thing.

Grim-faced crewmembers encouraged speed and calm, pointing the way. She climbed flight after flight, not sure if her cabin mate was still behind her. She slipped once, and tried not to fancy that the ship was listing to one side. Because of the pressure of people behind her, she couldn't stop to rest. Her heart felt as if it would burst.

Rain lashed the deck—they'd been warned of a middling tropical storm that would pass them in the night. Nothing to worry about, the cabin steward had said. Strong lamps illuminated the gathering places, particularly markings that showed which cabin groups lined up where. The lifeboats were uncovered and crew members were already assisting people aboard them.

Gulping for breath, she struggled to fasten her life vest. It wouldn't click shut. During the earlier drill they'd found her a larger one, but no one was trying to do that now. One of the features of this cruise was the small vessel and passenger complement, allowing for enhanced customer service and access to more out-of-the-way ports of call. Cozy, intimate, blah blah blah, Marissa thought. *I can't get this damn thing on.*

After struggling and fighting tears for several minutes, another woman said, "Here, let's swap. This one is too big for me."

The exchange was made and the new vest was marginally larger. She was able to get the main belt secured. She felt like a big piece of meat, trussed in an orange casing for roasting. The damp, humid air didn't help.

Hardly able to breathe, she waited in the line, trying to decide if it was appropriate to yell or shriek in fear, the way someone further down was. Perhaps the shaking that seemed to start in the pit of her stomach was the right response. She couldn't help tension-filled tears and the vest made it impossible to wipe her eyes.

She saw Angela, her now ex-cabin mate, being helped into the life boat next to the one where she was queued. Then her turn came. As she threw her leg over the edge of the lifeboat all she could think was that everyone was assessing every extra pound on her body and predicting she'd reduce their chances of survival.

She clutched her backpack to her, took the empty spot next to a whippet-faced woman and tried hard to be small.

"I know we send the, uh . . ." Gregorio, the senior of the two crew members in their boat, snapped his fingers as he scrunched his eyes in concentration. "Ah, distress. Tracking beacons, uh . . . work. They know where to find."

It wasn't the first time he had said those broken words of comfort but every few minutes one of the eighteen passengers would ask how long until rescue came. The younger crew member looked as scared as the rest of them. Gregorio tried to exude confidence but facts were facts. The tropical storm's winds were scattering the lifeboats, and the lights of the ship were slowly fading from their sight. Marissa couldn't tell if that was because they'd drifted or if the ship really was sinking. She wasn't going to ask either.

When the muffled explosion sounded in the distance, Marissa clutched the woman next to her, who clutched her right back. Gregorio said something that sounded like *decompression*. Marissa was sure if she spoke Italian, she would understand. Whatever it was, it went *boom* but Marissa could see nothing. The rain continued and there was no sign of the lights from the other lifeboats.

Marissa was pretty sure the situation was dire. Panic might be called for, even. But she was too numb to feel fear but not so incoherent she didn't know numbness was a blessing.

The sea pitched them up and down but at least they didn't seem at risk of swamping. The rain had eased but everything was wet through and through—her backpack, ballcap, shirt, shoes. She wondered if her CD player would survive and if the M&M's somewhere in the depths of a pocket would be edible.

She wished she hadn't wasted time yesterday morning shaving her legs. Like that mattered. She mourned the swimsuit, the hoard of chocolate and rum and the fifteen spanking new books in her suitcase. It really was a crying shame about the books.

Right now she supposed it was time for early breakfast. She'd been told that cruise food was good. Certainly dinner the night before had been tasty. She wished she'd eaten more of it but she always felt as if people were watching her eat and deciding that was why her waist was bigger around than her hips.

The sun rose fully, the wind died and the rain slowed to a mist, leaving the air heavy and thick. Marissa didn't think her heart had stopped beating fast but she was suddenly so tired her head bobbed. A man at the front of the boat took some pictures of them all but Marissa couldn't find more than an annoyed smile. Settling her bulging backpack on her lap, she wrapped her arms over it and tried to doze. It seemed the only thing she could do that didn't add to the fear and tension in the boat.

She drifted for a few minutes then found herself writing a letter in her head, something she'd always done when stressed. They were letters she would never send.

This one began—like lots of others—with "Dear Mom."

> Thank you again for the generous gift of a week-long cruise in Tahiti. It's not your fault the ship sank. Instead of all those years of computer science courses, I wish I had paid more attention to reality TV shows about turning bugs into breakfast.
>
> I'm sure I'll be fine and when I get home you can bet I'll listen to the rest of your advice about what I ought to do with my life, since this has worked out so well.
>
> Love, Marissa
>
> P.S. I don't think I'll make it home in time for the club's summer ball.
>
> P.P.S. Please make my apologies to the blind date I'm sure you arranged.
>
> P.P.P.S. I'm a lesbian.

If I get home again, Marissa told herself, I'm sending that one.

"Hey," someone behind her shouted. "Isn't that land?"

People actually stood up. The boat rocked violently, and they all sat down again. Marissa craned her neck and saw the low white cloud in the distance.

"Great. I always wanted to be in an episode of *Lost*."

She didn't realize she'd spoken aloud until several people near her gave her annoyed stares.

You'd think she'd said *shark* or something. Marissa muttered to herself, "I'm not the only one thinking it."

Seated in the row ahead of Marissa, a tall woman glanced back at Marissa as she said, "I sure as hell was. But I'd rather *Gilligan's Island*." Her expression was surprisingly calm and they shared comrades-in-twisted-humor half-smiles.

Gregorio was trying to settle the handful of men who wanted to Take Action. One older Brit kept saying he didn't understand why they weren't trying to get to land until the tall *Gilligan's Island* fan said, firmly, "It's farther than it looks. Rowers need water and we don't have a way to get more. The beacons were on and with the storm cleared a search will be quickly underway." When he would have argued, she added, "I'm just the translator."

Marissa tried to shift her position enough to ease her back and again Whippet-Face looked annoyed, the way people did on airplanes when they realized some of her was going to possibly come into contact with some of them or their seat. The woman said something unhappily in Italian to the man next to her, or maybe it was Greek or Russian—why hadn't she studied languages spoken by people instead of those spoken by computers? Whatever it was, it didn't flatter her; whining sounded the same in every language, she thought.

Unable to stand the discomfort any longer, she unsnapped her life vest and took a full, deep breath. She was able to straighten in place and roll her neck. It helped, but all of that activity—the full range of what she was able to do in the space she was allotted—had taken about thirty seconds. Now was not the time for an attack of claustrophobia. The clouds were moving off and the sky rapidly cleared. The limitless blue soothed her until she began to think about how far that sky stretched, how big the ocean below it seemed, and how very, very tiny their lifeboat was.

The sun was only halfway out of the water. She wished for sunglasses. Someone said it was six-thirty. Then it was six-thirty-four. Every two minutes someone new took out their cell phone, muttered, stared up at the sky and put it away again.

Dear Dad:

I'm glad you spent the three months of chemo sharing all those great movies with me. I don't think I appreciated how good Lifeboat was until now. It might have been a different movie if there had been twenty or so characters to keep track of, and possibly a lot less interesting if none of them had been able to do more than stretch once in a while.

No one here looks like Tallulah Bankhead, with or without her panties.

Love, Marissa

P.S. Still waiting to hear from you about how heaven really feels about homosexuals.

P.P.S. Think I'll tell Mom. I expect it to go about as well as when you told her that you were gay.

The sound of her backpack zipper turned heads. A lot of people had either backpacks or small cases but she was the first to seriously open up. She took out the paperback she'd finished on the plane. People were looking daggers at her, as if trying to distract herself was letting the team down.

She read. Nothing in the book seemed familiar but then the flight seemed months ago instead of yesterday. She turned the page, could recall nothing from the previous one but kept going anyway.

After the water and food rations had been shared, the men demonstrated how much easier it was for them to pee—discreetly, of course. Around ten-thirty they thought they saw another lifeboat on the horizon but there was no answer to the flash of their signaling mirror. Their boat had drifted substantially closer to the low, white cloud. It must be a land mass of some kind, Marissa thought. After all, New Zealand was the "land of the long white cloud." It said so in her paperback. She wished now she'd gone to New Zealand instead of Tahiti.

Gregorio, surrounded by the Muscle Guys that had all moved to the front of the boat, continued to insist that rowing was not in their best interests. Marissa was inclined to agree—for now. But if they were still here by nightfall she was going to have to pee and she really didn't want to use the Emergency Latrine. The E.L. was a Tupperware bowl and it would be just her luck to drop it overboard when she emptied it out. They'd vote her off the lifeboat for sure. She suspected, given that only one woman had used the facilities so far, she wasn't the only one hoping to make it to the privacy of darkness.

The island didn't seem to get any closer, until, by early afternoon, it was clear they were in a current and being drawn that direction. Gregorio insisted that rescue planes and boats would have been dispatched. They would be found. They were only nine hours of sailing out of Papeete, after all.

Muscle Guy Number One, who seemed to think his English was easier to understand if he added an Italian accent, insisted, then, that the island was likely to be populated. It could even be Huahine.

A heated argument ensued. Marissa thought she heard the *Gilligan's Island* Woman in front of her say, "It's the same the world over," but she wasn't sure.

Finally, Gregorio shrugged and didn't protest when Number One directed Numbers Two through Four to get out the oars. Marissa had nothing against guys with muscles—obviously, they had their uses and she would be eternally grateful to them if they found solid ground and a place for her to pee. Marissa thought it wise to re-buckle her vest and she zipped her book inside her pack again where it was hopefully safer. If they were stuck on a deserted island for long, a paperback might be a valuable commodity for barter.

The woman next to her smelled of suntan lotion and sweat. Marissa imagined she didn't smell much better but she was glad of the long pants she'd struggled into and the light long-sleeved denim shirt she had smashed into her backpack after arriving in Papeete.

Now that they were doing something other than waiting, couples that had previously only murmured between themselves began to talk to those around them as if the energy could finally be spared. The man with the camera took photos of the rowers and the approaching land. Most people didn't speak English, something she'd figured out at dinner the night before. That could devalue her paperback should she need to trade it for chewing gum, she thought dizzily. The boat made its first directed surge through the waves and Marissa put her head down on the backpack again, letting the voices swirl around her.

"So," someone said nearby, "Did you have friends who made you watch the *Poseidon Adventure* before you left home?"

She glanced up and realized that *Gilligan's Island* Woman had turned around on her bench so they were knee-to-knee. Recalling her bon voyage party, Marissa admitted, "I have a friend that warped but she chose *Titanic*."

"I have the weirdest urge to sing—"

"Oh, please, not that song. Any song but that."

The other woman's lopsided smile made Marissa feel oddly better. "What's it worth to you?"

"Depends on if you sound at all like Celine Dion."

"I sound more like Celine Dion's chain-smoking brother."

Marissa laughed and then felt a rush of tears.

"It's okay," the other woman said. She brushed the front of her pale green T-shirt, which sported a cute cartoon dog wearing snorkeling gear. "It's just tension."

Nodding, Marissa struggled for composure. She shifted in her place and was glad that the vest blunted Whippet-Face's pointy elbows. "I'm Marissa Chabot. California."

"Linda Bartok, Boston, Massachusetts. What part of California?"

"Danville, San Ramon, Pleasanton?" Linda looked blank so Marissa added, "About forty minutes from San Francisco, to the east."

Linda nodded. "I was out that way a few years ago. It's a great place to live."

"I've never been to New England."

"Full of history. Right now, full of ice and snow, so I prefer this." Linda seemed unfazed by the surge-falter rhythm of the boat as their pace increased toward the island.

"So why the wacky castaways for your bon voyage?"

Linda shrugged. "It's a guilty pleasure. Goofy show."

"Well, the Professor can make a radio, refrigerator and bunk beds out of palm leaves. That why you'd prefer it to *Lost*?"

"Nah." Linda gave her another lopsided smile. "Ginger."

Marissa blinked and wondered what she ought to read into that remark. "Ginger? Over Evangeline Lilly?"

The charming lopsided smile balanced out to a broad grin. "I've always liked a curvy redhead."

"Oh." Marissa took a deep breath and tried for a confident snicker. "I can't disagree with your priorities."

Linda winked conspiratorially and Marissa grinned back.

Dear Mom,

> The impromptu cruise toward an uncharted desert isle has clarified certain of my preferences. For future purposes of arranging blind dates for me, please note that I prefer Ginger, Mary Ann, or even Mrs. Howell, to the Professor or the Skipper and most certainly to Gilligan. Mr. Howell is more your type, don't you think?

Love, Marissa

P.S. Sorry about the Mr. Howell remark. I'm a little bit stressed at the moment.

The life boat lurched on a wave and her thoughts came back to the real world.

"Do you think we're caught in a current?"

Linda shrugged. "Yeah, probably."

They were quiet for a while, listening to the broken English conversations of the rowers. Marissa wanted to ask Linda lots of questions but Linda's attention was on the rower nearest her.

"I can spell you," she said to him when they all paused to take a rest. There were other offers, so a change of shift was implemented. Only when Linda stood up did Marissa realize she had to be only an inch or two short of six feet. From the back, with tanned, wide shoulders and dark hair down her back, she could have been mistaken for any number of tall, well-muscled models or actresses. She had the physique of a cartoon heroine—Batwoman or Wonder Woman. Even Xena.

And, Marissa asked herself, how relevant is this line of thought? Linda had full red lips, tawny brown eyes, yes, but she wasn't exactly gorgeous. Good-looking, okay, but . . . not a movie star. Not quite. Okay, she was gorgeous, but not because Marissa had some sort of crush on Xena, which she didn't. At least not since the show went off the air. Besides, Linda was a real thirty-something woman, not some ageless creation of fantasy.

She watched Linda's muscles ripple and decided the entire situation was freakish enough without hallucinatory ramblings.

Dear Ocky:

I want to thank you for the bon voyage party. It was a lot of fun. As it turns out, watching a movie about a shipwreck wasn't perhaps the highlight of the party, but I know you were trying to give everybody a laugh. So far, this vacation has had adventure! adventure! adventure! just like the brochure promised. There's even a raven-haired warrior princess. I'd introduce you to her but she's busy saving the world, which, for the moment, is this life boat.

Love, Marissa

P.S. There may be some delay before I can enhance the database refresh speeds.

P.P.S. I am thinking over our questionnaire item about "What would you bring to a desert island?" Answer forthcoming.

Their approach to the island was like the ball dropping in Times Square on New Year's Eve. Wait, wait, wait, then suddenly everything seemed to be happening at once. Far to their left they could see a long, inviting beach dotted with palm trees but their boat seemed magnetically drawn toward worn, dark gray cliffs studded with green plants. Marissa had only taken in how sheer the cliff face seemed when she saw that the ocean below it was broken by big rocks. Pointed rocks. Certain Death kinds of rocks.

Linda, who had moved to the bow with Gregorio, gave a shout and pointed. "There's a little beach." Gregorio added a shout of his own and the rowers turned the boat into the current.

> Dear Aunt Rill:
>
> Let me apologize for being such a pain about going to church when we visited with you. I felt silly praying, since I never seemed to get an answer. However, I think had I learned to pray I might be better able to cope with—

Something submerged scraped the side of the boat as it crested a swell then dropped hard. Marissa fully expected sharp teeth of rock to pierce the hull. The rowers made little headway against the current. There were several people talking at once, then Gregorio and Linda joined the two rowers on the left, pulling hard.

> —stressful situations. I'd pray right now if I knew how. In fact, I'm going to forget my lack of expertise and go for it. If I end up in heaven with you, I'll let you know how it turned out.
>
> Love, Marissa.
>
> P.S. I'm a lesbian but you knew that, didn't you?

There was a loud crunch that shocked a scream out of Marissa and she wasn't alone. Fear, like whining, sounded the same, regardless of language. The man in the bow leapt to solid footing on the shallow beach and turned to pull hard on the boat. It nosed firmly into a bit of sand not much wider than it was.

The tide, Marissa wondered, was it high or low? As if in answer, a new swell threatened to lift them off their nano-spit of safety toward yet more rocks on their right.

There wasn't enough room for all of them on that little bit of semi-solid land. Above was a pitted cliff face. Some of them, Marissa thought wildly, could climb that. But there was no way she could.

It seemed she was expected to. Linda, with a muscled agility that had Marissa once again thinking about warrior amazons, scaled the cliff face easily, pausing along the way to mark handholds on the cliff face. Where Linda had found a very large indelible marker, Marissa didn't know. It was the kind of thing a butch could be counted on to have in her pockets but Linda wasn't so much butch as she was outdoorsy survivor warrior gal who probably looked fabulous in silk and diamonds.

Trying to decide how she'd describe Linda kept Marissa from thinking about the obvious fact that everyone expected her to be able to climb that cliff. Had they looked at her butt? Had they realized her arms were good only for moving computer equipment?

Old people were going up the cliff face. Okay, not quickly, except they looked to be octogenarians so any speed was fast. Any speed was faster than she would ever achieve.

From the top of the cliff, where Linda leaned over expectantly, came the decree.

With a smile that seemed intelligent but masked completely unrealistic powers of judgment, Linda said, "Marissa, your turn."

Chapter 3

Marissa didn't say "You must be joking."

Linda read her mind anyway. "You can do this. Take off the life jacket. I'll talk you through it."

The boat shifted under her. The tide seemed to be getting more violent. Still on the boat were a few of the more fit people and they were all waiting for her.

If I refuse, Marissa thought, someone will stay with me. We'll both drown and I'll have that on my conscience for the rest of my life.

Her involuntary laugh at her own idiocy was edged with hysteria.

Again, Linda said, "You can do this."

Marissa unbuckled the life jacket and was out of the boat without consciously making her legs move. After tucking her sneaker-clad foot into the spot Linda had marked "F1," she reached up for the pit in the rock marked "H1." Then she sighted "F2" and "H2." She'd have to pull herself up about two feet to reach either.

"Pretend you're a frog and keep your knees apart."

There were a dozen ribald replies she could have made, she was sure of that, but she couldn't think of any of the right words. Hands and feet braced, she pulled, pushed, lifted, grunted, scraped her cheek, squashed her boobs into the rock and managed to get good grips on the second set of holds. Men, she thought savagely, did not have to deal with boobs.

Looking up, she sighted the next reach.

I can't do this.

"You're right, you can't," her mother said. "There's no point in you taking advanced algebra, Marissa. Girls have different brains. I think home economics is much more sensible."

Great, what a time for a conversation with her mother. She eyed the next handhold, already feeling a suspicious trembling in her arms.

"It's all fine and well to learn to type. You'll always have work, though you won't ever really need to be *serious* about a career as I'm sure you'll get married. But learning this gibberish—"

"It's called hypertext."

"Whatever it's called, it's useless. If you have to learn a second language, try French. You'll know how to order in a fine restaurant."

"I'm twenty-four, wait. I'm thirty-four . . . and I can make my own choices in life, Mother!"

"You can't possibly think that you and that Octavia girl can run a business together. You both should be looking for husbands. I can't tell my friends my daughter runs a dating service. They'll think you're . . . you're . . ."

"A madam? A pimp? But Mother, you told me once you'd rather I was a whore than any kind of sexual deviant, because Jesus forgave whores. That was after dad left, remember? I understand you're bitter about that but it's not an escort service. It's a complicated, intensive program that scores individual likes and dislikes then ranks the comparative intensity against that of other—"

"You should use the service yourself, but look at you! You're

28

overweight, you work eighty hours a week, you have no friends, no social life. You can't live that way!"

"Don't tell me . . ." Marissa took a deep breath and heaved herself up the cliff face to the next handhold. With a frightening scrabble, she got her foot into the right spot. "Don't tell me what I can't do."

"Next time," Linda called down, "set your foot first if you can. You can use both legs to push that way. That was great, though. You've got fantastic upper body strength."

"It's from knocking back Krispy Kremes." She didn't know until Linda laughed that she'd spoken aloud.

"Told you that you could do this."

I can't, Marissa wanted to say. *I really can't.*

"You can't do this to me!" Her mother stood between Marissa and the door, outside which a cab was waiting to take her to the airport.

"He's still my father and I'm going to spend Christmas with him. Him and Phillip."

"What will I tell people? How can you have anything to do with him? He walked out on us—"

"No, he walked out on you!" Marissa glared across the foyer with the echo of a hundred overheard fights in her ears.

"If you'd been anything like a real daughter he could have been proud of, he'd have never left—"

"He walked out on you. He couldn't wait to get away from you. He's gay because of you!"

Marissa dug her fingers into the rock as she thought, "Okay, you knew that was a lie and you can't ever take that back and you never should have said it."

She braced both legs then grunted with the stress of stretching for the next handhold. "But she deserved it."

"Who deserved what?" Linda stared down at her in concern.

"Tell you later."

"Climbing takes glutes," Linda volunteered. "So you've got 'em."

29

Marissa realized everyone below her was looking at her butt. Prime view of the cottage cheese thighs too. It wasn't fair, having to do this. It wasn't fair being stared at, evaluated and always found physically inadequate.

Oh, please, she chided herself. Don't whine about being chosen last for sides in basketball. You can't be a cliché. Besides, when the staring started it wasn't because you were inadequate.

"You got milk in those jugs?"

She'd gazed at Ricky Skilecky without understanding. His snicker, quickly joined by those of his traveling pack of ferret companions, brought a blush nevertheless. It had to be about sex but she didn't get it. She didn't know which was worse, not getting it or how she'd feel when she finally did.

"Milk's good for us, 'Rissa. C'mon, give us a taste."

The pack made smooching-sucking noises and that was when she got it. She turned on her heel, books clutched across her chest. It wasn't her fault. It wasn't fair. She hadn't asked for them to grow. They just did.

Boobs mashed hard against the cliff face, Marissa felt the punch of that old familiar resentment. She didn't hate them any longer, but for the middle and high school years she'd loathed her bust. They'd ruined her slow pitch and left her feeling graceless. Every catcall, lewd gesture and rude remark had been like a slap. She hadn't been able to walk down a hallway without some boy saying something crude, that is, until she was a sophomore in high school and some of the other girls had finally caught up. They finally grew breasts too—those pretty, conventional girls who didn't like math or computers and thought everything boys did was cool.

Her arms were screaming for relief. There were only two more handholds left to go but the light made it hard to see them and gauge the distance. She knew if she fell now she'd break something and die because there was no doctor up there nor some genius who would figure out how to give her blood transfusions with a ballpoint pen.

"That's right," Linda crooned. "You're doing fantastic. Nearly here. One more and I can help. Fabulous, just one more."

"Just one more cookie, Mom, come on." Marissa eyed the perfect oatmeal chocolate chip rounds and reached for the closest.

Her mother slapped her hand back. "Your waistline is bigger than your bust these days. You look sloppy enough. How are you going to get a date for the prom looking like that?"

"Who said I wanted to go?"

"Of course you want to go." Her mother shook the rest of the cookies into the storage jar. "You're not a real girl if you don't."

Marissa wondered if her mother suspected she wasn't a real girl. She didn't like the things other girls liked—the most important of which was boys. She didn't like boys. That didn't make her gay like dad, she told herself.

"I'll get Jean to ask her son. You like Darren, don't you?"

"No, I don't."

"He's a little quiet but he'll be a lawyer some day, just like his father. You're suited to each other, I guess."

"What's that supposed to mean? I'm suited to a nerd?"

"Don't be mean."

"I'm not being mean, Mom. I'm a nerd. I like some nerds."

"You are not a nerd. Don't say that."

"Don't tell me what I can't do, Mom." Marissa gave another hard push with her legs, sobbing for air. She couldn't control the shaking in her arms. Soon she was going to lose her grip and fall anyway. After all this work, that would be a shame.

I am a nerd, Marissa repeated to herself. I like talking to machines and working on my own. I like who I am, even though my mother hates every bit of me. She doesn't even know I'm gay and she doesn't like anything about me. Short of wearing pink and not putting out until some guy gave her a ring, nothing she ever did would make her mother happy.

You just figured out something important, she told herself. You need to remember that. But she had no energy to write a letter to herself at the moment.

She ought to tell her mother that after getting drunk at the prom, Darren hadn't wanted to take no for an answer. She'd known what he was thinking. Fat girls appreciate any kind of attention. He hadn't really believed her until she'd caught his hard penis in the zipper of his pants and then leaned on it with every ounce she could, watching him turn purple.

She was angry about that night, even all these years later. Angry at her mother for making her go and at Darren for touching her, trying to put her hand on his dick and sticking his tongue in her mouth.

"One more, come on," Linda called.

She was angry at Linda but she supposed Linda didn't deserve that.

What she was really angry about was having to climb this cliff while she had to pee, damn it. She didn't know yet who she was angry with about all the Oreos she'd eaten in college but she'd find someone to blame.

"You can't do this," her mother whispered.

"Don't tell me what I can't do, Mom."

"Come on, one more!" Linda looked anxious now.

Marissa realized as hard as she was stretching for it, she couldn't quite reach that last handhold. Her other hand felt numb and suddenly there was air between her and the cliff face.

She looked up at Linda but breathing was more than she could manage. Talking was out of the question. The world went a kind of shivery yellow.

"Don't you dare!" Linda shouted. "Don't you even dare. Get your butt up here!"

She had no breath to say, "I can't." Then she felt a hand brushing up her thigh, then pushing on her butt. She had no breath to scream, "Don't touch me!"

The pounding in her ears was split by a flash of white-hot rage. She lifted herself out of the reach of that terribly personal hand, recalling just in time she was in no position to kick at it too.

Linda suddenly seemed much closer, then her hands closed around Marissa's wrists. Marissa grunted as she tried to find the energy for another surge up the cliff side but nothing responded. She was going up anyway—Linda's face was strained and red with the effort.

More hands reached down from the edge, grabbing her sleeves. With a feeble kick, she got one foot over the lip, then let herself be unceremoniously hauled away from the edge to safety.

Through a haze of red she watched Linda collapse onto her side, panting for breath. The remaining climbers appeared in short order at the spot they had just vacated.

"I'm sorry," Marissa finally managed to gasp. "Sorry for every brownie I ate during all-nighters."

Linda spluttered with laughter. "That wasn't the most picture-perfect climbing demonstration I've ever seen but you're here."

"There goes the boat," someone said, but Marissa didn't have the strength to watch.

Dear Ms. Edwards:

It was not a great surprise to run across your name on a list of famous lesbian entrepreneurs. My business partner, Octavia, still doesn't believe you were my gym teacher. But I'm actually writing to tell you that you were right about chin-ups. I apologize for not listening to your excellent advice.

Sincerely,

Marissa Chabot, Jonas Salk Middle School

Her backpack appeared out of nowhere. "Thank you," she whispered to her unseen benefactor. She wondered which of the Muscle Guys had helped push her up the cliff at the very last and decided against asking. When she had her breath back, she found a discreet screen of tall ferns and took care of her bladder. She was profoundly grateful she had kept control of it during the climb.

Feeling much better, she whispered aloud, "You're going to live," and for once that didn't seem like reassuring hyperbole.

Emerging from behind her ferns, she realized everyone was getting to their feet. With a distinct wobble, she picked up her belongings and looked for Linda. Spotting her with the Muscle Guys, she waited to catch her attention before asking, "What gives?"

"We're going to hike around to the big beach—someone thinks they saw people in the trees. If not, we'll get a signal fire going. Cell phones are still not getting feeds. It's a good plan." Linda slung a trim pack over one shoulder, looking as if she could run a marathon.

Hiking, okay. Marissa nodded and they set out. Watching Linda stride along in front of her wasn't painful. She thought longingly of the M&M's in the depths of her pack. They could still be edible.

Prepared to slog in misery for hours, Marissa was surprised when one of the men gave a hopeful shout only a few minutes later. There was excited babble, then Linda glanced over her shoulder.

"It's a trail, which means we're not the only ones here. There probably will be people at that beach. Looks like we're okay, Gilligan."

Marissa found herself grinning. "Gilligan? Since when am I Gilligan?"

"You could be Ginger."

"My hair's not red." Dishwater mouse about covered it.

"Hair can be dyed." Linda glanced over her shoulder. "You've already got the body."

Just when Marissa thought the day couldn't get any more surreal, Linda was . . . flirting? With her? She did not have a curvaceous, bombshell body. And it was an absurd thing to be thinking about, stumbling along through the jungle after officially being shipwrecked.

When they passed a primitive but clearly man-made distance marker, Marissa laughed to herself. So much for bug buffets and using eyeglasses to light a fire. Heck, there could even be a decent place to sleep and a real toilet by the end of the day. If there was such a thing as the perfect shipwreck, maybe this was it.

On the other hand, this trail could have been blazed by other castaways and they'd find a long-abandoned camp with graves and one last skeleton watching over them. She was certain she'd seen just such a tableau in some old movie. "But your life is not a movie."

"Huh?" Linda glanced over her shoulder.

"Sorry. I have a habit of talking to myself out loud." Marissa stepped over a tangle of roots. "Comes from working by myself a lot."

"What do you do? Computers?"

Marissa nearly said, "No, I do women. I only work with computers," but thought better of it. It wasn't all that true, given how few women she'd actually dated, let alone slept with, in the last decade and a half. "Programming, yeah. How about you? Park ranger?"

Linda laughed. "No, I'm just fortunate enough to spend most of my time exploring. I like rock climbing, hiking, snorkeling, spelunking—name it and I like it."

Marissa wanted to ask what Linda did for money but that seemed too much like she was prying. "Bungee jumping?"

"Oh yeah."

"Then the abandon ship was an adventure to you."

"After the scary part, I guess so. Certainly, it'll be a story to tell many times over drinks. Antonio said he'll get copies of the photos to everybody, so be sure to give him your e-mail address. I wish I had one to give him."

"Antonio? Oh, the guy with the camera. Okay." Marissa decided that pictures—since nothing terribly tragic had happened—would be great mementos of this experience. They'd make for an interesting holiday missive.

"Hey, Linda?"

"Mmm?"

"If I'm Gilligan, who are you?"

"I thought we agreed you were Ginger."

"Okay, if I'm Ginger, who are you?"

It was only a short glance but the unquenchable humor was infectious. "I'm the financier with a yacht, come to take you away from all this."

"Oh." Think of something witty, she told herself. Think of anything. But nothing came to mind, not over the stunned babbling of her inner skeptic, the one that kept shouting, "She is *not* flirting with you!"

The inner skeptic always kept company with the voice of practical truth, which was pointing out, "Nobody that gorgeous is going to look twice at you, especially given the condition you're in right now."

When was the last time anyone had flirted with her? She couldn't remember. Her annual blind dates for the Blackhawk Country Club summer ball never flirted with her. They took one look and that was that. Linda couldn't possibly be flirting with her. "Can you imagine trying to walk this path in a sparkly evening gown and heels?"

The trail widened and Linda dropped back to walk alongside Marissa. "I'm not sure I'd call what Ginger did walking."

"True, she did more slink than walk." Marissa demonstrated, swaying her hips with one shoulder back. "No wait, that's more Nora Desmond at the end of *Sunset Boulevard*."

"No, you were doing great. You're ready for your close-up, Mr. DeMille."

"That hurt." Marissa rubbed her shoulder. "I think I'm going to be sore tomorrow."

"We all are," Linda assured her. "You know, I never realized Ginger and Nora Desmond walked the same way. You've got that whole femme thing down pat."

Marissa threw back her head and laughed. "I wear pantyhose once a year and that's on pain of death."

"So?" Linda gave her a sidelong glance. "There's far more to being femme than wearing pantyhose."

"Like what?" She followed the sweep of Linda's gaze over her body. The intense study left her simultaneously feeling shy and bold—and confused.

"Bet there's a purse in that backpack."

"Okay, sure, most women do carry them. I've never been big on labels."

Linda shrugged. "Me neither, mostly. They're fun and useful

for those who find them fun and useful but they don't change who you are or how other people with other labels might perceive you. Or what a person might find attractive."

Again, Linda's gaze swept over her and Marissa realized that even though she was puzzled by Linda's flirting, it didn't make her feel dissected the way Ricky Skilecky and most men ever since had made her feel. She felt as if Linda was putting her together with her eyes, not taking her apart. Emboldened, she asked, "Are you flirting with me?"

"You noticed?"

"It eventually got through my dampening field, yes."

"Ooo, geek talk. I like that. Talk geek to me more."

"Maybe, if you're a good girl."

"Who's flirting now?"

Who indeed? Marissa fought back a blush by thinking about dead puppies. She immediately felt guilty for visualizing such a gruesome thing and forgot all about blushing. "You noticed?"

"Right away, ma'am."

They walked for a minute in companionable silence and Marissa let her mind wander. With a shock she realized she was picturing herself in that sparkly dress Ginger had worn, slinking along the trail while Linda watched and drooled. With Linda looking at her like that, it wasn't hard to see the entire scene.

Just when she felt the silence had morphed from easy to lame, there were happy shouts and the front of the group surged forward.

"Hotel" sounded the same in several languages, but Marissa didn't let herself hope until she saw for herself that the trail opened to a plaza, at the far end of which sat a sprawling, whitewashed building with a sparkling fountain. Beyond that a curving beach embraced a deep-set lagoon, with thatched bungalows nestled under palm trees. The tableau was completed by an obviously surprised bellman who was rapidly joined by several more equally agog uniformed coworkers.

The babble of languages was overwhelming but in short order

they were all seated in the small lobby, tumblers of fruit juice in one hand and a hunk of fresh, sweet bread in the other. Gregorio immediately went with the manager to use the phone.

"I told you we were on Huahine!" The Brit was extremely pleased with himself, as evidenced by his repeating himself several more times.

Marissa finished the bread—nothing had ever tasted so wonderful—and gratefully accepted a wedge of papaya and a dozen roasted filberts from the tray being circulated by a wide-eyed teen.

If that wasn't unreal enough, Linda sat beside her on the small couch, looking as if she'd just finished a casual stroll.

"It's okay to feel like you're on *Candid Camera*," Linda observed.

"I was thinking more like I'd slipped into an alternate reality. Now I'll never get to be Ginger."

With a fascinating quirk to her lips, Linda said, "You can be Ginger any time you want."

"I'm not sure I want to be that helpless."

"I can see that." Linda finished her papaya slice and licked her long, nimble fingers. Marissa did not stare. Not a lot, anyway. She wondered if near-death experiences caused people to have outrageous fantasies. "Helpless isn't in my comfort zone either. We're both too strong to play that game."

"Strong? If I tried to stand up right now I think my legs would buckle."

"Just reaction." Linda again gave her a cheeky smile. "That or you secretly would like to be Ginger from time to time. Nothing wrong with that."

The conversation was getting as bizarre as the entire trip. Nevertheless, that look in Linda's eyes was mystifying and intriguing. Marissa wasn't sure anyone had ever looked at her like that before. She really didn't know what to make of it. "I'm not sure a Sixties sexpot will stand up as a rigorous analogy."

Linda laughed. "Is there another you'd prefer?"

She went for the obvious. "Xena? Wonder Woman?"

The bright smile dimmed slightly. "Go ahead, say it."

"You do know you look a little bit . . . Okay, a lot like . . . ?"

Linda's smile faded further and for the first time she looked away as if the conversation no longer interested her. "Yeah. Believe me, I know." With an obvious effort at calm, she added, "My eyes are brown so I can't be either."

"You could have your legs shortened and dye your hair gray to avoid any comparisons."

"No thanks. I'm doing my best to stay out of doctor's offices from now on."

Marissa crunched several of the delicious nuts before saying carefully. "Sounds like you've seen too many."

"I needed some fixing up when I was a kid." Linda's face was turned away, her expression as closed as Marissa had seen it thus far.

Marissa didn't want to pry but saying nothing seemed unfeeling. "Better now?"

"Finished now. And have been for some time."

"I'm glad then. I think I have some work to do on me. Not that I aspire to climb up a treacherous cliff on a daily basis, but I wasn't sure . . ." She couldn't quite make herself admit she had been certain she was about to die.

"You were amazing. That was a tough climb. I've had lots of practice so of course it was easier for me but you did it."

"I wouldn't have made it without you all helping and that's the truth."

"I've seen fit grown men balk over walls half that height."

"Were they facing certain death as the alternative? Because let me tell you, that was motivating."

Linda chuckled and the stiffness left her shoulders. "I'll remember that, next time I do a climbing course."

"Do you teach?"

"From time to time."

Marissa nodded. "I can see you being very good at it. You're patient and very positive." In her mind's eye, she could easily visualize the Finders Keepers Personal Inventory Questionnaire complete with check boxes appearing next to attributes for Linda's profile. What kind of mate would be the perfect match? What kind of woman really attracted someone so strong, good-looking and life-loving?

The hotel manager, with a grinning Gregorio to one side, explained in careful French-accented English that the authorities had been notified and they would all stay at the hotel for at least the night, until flights were arranged out of Fare Town.

"If you will all please put your name and city on this list, we can give it to the cruise lines. You are the last group to be found and there was no loss of life."

A ripple of relief went through all of them and Marissa realized while she'd not thought about her cabin-mate since she'd last seen her, she'd been worried, and worried for the people she'd met at dinner. It was such good news.

The manager explained that there was no Internet available on the island and only a few phones, but each of them would get a few minutes soon to call family. Meanwhile, if they could pair off to share rooms and bungalows the hotel could accommodate everyone.

Marissa glanced at Linda, who gave a "Wanna share?" sort of shrug. Marissa nodded and after they both carefully wrote out their names, the manager gave Marissa a key.

"A shower," Marissa breathed. "That is going to be just about orgasmic."

"I feel that way about the swimming pool I can see out the back door. And look at that beach."

Marissa followed Linda's line of sight. "I don't quite see things at the same height as you."

"Step over here."

She sidled to where Linda was standing and her breath caught. The pool sparkled bright blue and beyond that a white sand beach dotted with hammock-draped palms gave way to the deep turquoise of the white-capped ocean. "It's like something off of a postcard."

"My camera's gone," Linda said quietly. "I could have taken a shot of you in paradise."

"I'd ruin the scenery." Marissa turned toward the path that led to their bungalow.

"Not in a silver lamé dress. Or, better yet, a teal green swimsuit that shows off the curves and your eyes."

Marissa could feel herself blushing for the remainder of the short walk, all the way until she unlatched the door to their room. She wasn't used to anyone looking at her with such approval. She felt . . . what was the right word?

Something unfamiliar, but welcome.

Attractive. She felt attractive.

"This is cozy," Linda observed as she set her pack down on the nearest of two narrow beds.

"It's larger than the cabins on the ship, plus there's solid ground outside." She was willing to believe that Linda was perhaps a natural flirt. Some women were. It was certainly fun to be on the receiving end. Alone in a romantic bungalow, though, she'd have to take everything Linda implied with a big grain of salt. It was fun and that was all.

"I like the solid ground thing at the moment." Linda opened one of the French doors and quiet sounds Marissa hadn't noticed before—distant surf, low voices, sleepy insects and birds—flowed into the room.

"I'll just use the facilities." Taking her backpack with her, Marissa slipped into the bathroom.

For a second after she switched on the light, she thought someone else was in the bathroom with her. Startled, she drew back, then realized she was facing a full-length mirror. She didn't know what she had expected to see but it wasn't a grimy, sweat-crusted, tangle-haired woman with a double chin, a button-up shirt that gapped enough to show her bra and pants that cut a round belly in two.

Frozen in place, she stared. There was no slinky sexpot, no paradise beauty.

The woman in the mirror couldn't be her. Nothing she felt deep inside showed.

When did this happen to me?

She didn't want to look at that reflection but couldn't look away either. She studied the only familiar thing, the wide blue eyes.

41

From someplace painful and raw she thought, as Linda had said, that the story of their shipwreck would be worth telling for years. But everyone else would have the amusing anecdote about the fat chick who couldn't climb the cliff by herself. They wouldn't mention the sexy Ginger Linda had planted in Marissa's head nor the attractive woman she'd felt like just a few minutes ago. For the rest of their lives she'd be the helpless fat chick.

I don't want to be a helpless fat chick for the rest of my life.

Feeling numb, she called, "Is it okay if I take a shower?"

"Sure, go ahead. The beds are really soft."

The image of Linda on the bed ought to have sparked something in her hyperactive imagination but something else was churning inside, grinding in a place just behind her heart, too hard to be ignored. The hot spray eased her tight chest and the hotel soap and shampoo washed away the grime and sweat of the night.

What was it that had been in Linda's eyes that had made her think she was in some way . . . desirable? She looked worse than usual and yet Linda seemed to think there was a reason to look at her. She liked herself as Linda saw her. But that wasn't the woman in the mirror. Linda didn't know the real her.

It was harder to look at her body wrapped in an inadequate towel, but this time she made herself take in every bulge and fold. Weren't they accidents of nature, baggage some unseen demon had hung on her, appearing out of thin air?

I don't want to be a helpless fat chick for the rest of my life.

She emptied her backpack and was grateful for the comb but ecstatic that most of the things in it were a little damp but had survived. Her mother had advised her to carry fresh underwear, a T-shirt and socks in her carry-on luggage in case her big suitcase went missing and for once Marissa vowed to tell her mother she'd been right.

She felt human when she left the bathroom. But she did not look in the mirror again.

Chapter 4

"This is the life." Linda's head lolled back on the pool steps as a soft breeze wafted over them both.

Marissa couldn't help but study the half-submerged body—she hadn't thought much about what *sculpted* meant but she was pondering it now. It wasn't just the aesthetic beauty that kept her gaze on Linda, but the way Linda seemed to give herself to the water, as if all the anxiety of the last day was seeping out of her, never to return.

"You got that right." Marissa sat on the edge of the pool, legs dangling in the clear water and wished for some of the calm that Linda seemed to find so easily. Her call home had been distressing and it was taking a little time to shake it off. "I am so glad I bought trip insurance. The lost books alone were worth a fortune."

"A woman who can read," Linda commented. "They're all too rare."

"There's routines I'll set up for the servers to run and while they do that, I read." Marissa shrugged. "Might as well learn something or have a brief escape."

"When I was backpacking through parts of the Alps I read the same book fourteen times."

"Was it a good book?"

"I don't remember. Some straight romance." Linda grinned at Marissa's shout of laughter. "Which probably says a lot about me."

"More likely about the book."

"So your mom was relieved?" Linda pushed away from the steps and Marissa again watched her body sink in the clear water until her feet touched the bottom. Okay, if she was being honest, Linda was more graceful and elegant than most of the models pouting on the covers of magazines.

"She hadn't heard about the shipwreck, so my call was a big surprise." Marissa smoothed the cotton shorts she'd acquired from the hotel gift shop. "I was scolded for waking her up for the first few minutes then she seemed glad to hear I was okay. I had to hang up when we started on topic *du jour*."

"Your mom does that too?" Linda's arms windmilled in the water as she slowly pirouetted in place. "What was today's topic?"

Marissa looked away. "Boring stuff." She wasn't about to unload her mother on Linda. Only Ocky had any clue about how narcissistic her mother was. "But she did want pictures to show her friends of the shipwreck."

"Fodder for the social circle but in a good way?"

Marissa couldn't help but arch her eyebrows. "Yeah, that's about the size of it. How'd you know?"

Linda launched into a slow backstroke. "You're not the only one with a mother." The little smile of pleasure told Marissa how much Linda was enjoying the gentle kiss of the water. The smile, the way Linda let the water flow over her shoulders, the habit of touching surfaces with just the pads of her fingers all spoke of an appreciation for sensation.

I shouldn't be thinking like that, Marissa told herself. She's gorgeous, okay, but this is not real. She tipped her head back to study the incredible sky. Unmarred by clouds and with the sun finally approaching the western horizon, it was a rich, endless blue like nothing she'd ever seen before.

For a moment she heard the Abandon Ship announcement again. She fought off the little shiver that accompanied it. It could have been worse, so much worse, she told herself. They could have been in the lifeboats for days or capsized during the waning hours of the storm. There might have been people who didn't get off the ship in time. She could have been stuck with people not nearly so pleasant as a brave, strong, attractive woman with a great sense of humor and a fantastic laugh. There was no point to wanting even more good to come from the bad.

"Come on in," Linda called to Marissa.

"These are the only clothes I've got—I don't want to get them wet."

Linda's lips twisted in a suggestive smile and Marissa found herself blushing. She was certain she could guess a few topics Linda could bring up at that moment.

"Flirting with you is fun," Linda said, as she waded toward Marissa. Stopping a polite distance away, she added, "You rise to the occasion, even when you're blushing."

Feeling as if her ears were on fire, Marissa could only think that she wouldn't mind being stuck here for several days. Weeks, even.

"Want to walk on the beach?"

Marissa nodded and heaved herself to her feet. "Might not get another chance if transport arrives on time."

"*On Time* means different things to different people. I'm hoping it takes a day or two to arrange the flights back to Papeete."

"I like it here too." Marissa made a little noise of pleasure as her feet sank into the sand at the end of the short walk from the pool. "But the cruise line is paying for the flight back to Papeete, so—"

"Let's stay anyway." Linda scampered past Marissa, then circled behind her again, kicking up a flurry of sand in her wake.

"I couldn't afford this place."

Linda shrugged. "I'll pay."

45

Marissa looked over her shoulder at Linda, eyebrows arched as high as they would go. "Are you independently wealthy?"

"Something like that."

"Well, thank you, but I couldn't."

"Why not? It'll be such fun."

Marissa turned to parallel the shore, close enough for the occasional wave to run up over her feet. She watched the breeze lift Linda's long hair from her back. How would it look worn up, like a princess? How would it look spread out on a pillow? "I couldn't—my mother would have a fit, me accepting that kind of gift from a stranger."

Linda scurried into Marissa's path. "Your mother sounds uptight."

"She is, believe me." Marissa broke their gaze and looked down. Together they watched the surf slowly bury their feet with sand. "But there are social rules, you know."

"Screw that. Stay. You could claim fate led you here and, hell, it might be the truth. I promise I'll have you back in Papeete in time for your journey home. Stay."

Marissa tried not to answer Linda's eager grin with one of her own. "It's not right . . . gifts from strangers . . ."

Linda seized Marissa's shoulders, kissed her soundly, then let her go. "There. Now we're not strangers."

"You're crazy." Breathe, Marissa thought, you have to breathe.

"Something like that. Stay."

With a voice suddenly soft, Marissa heard herself say, "Okay."

"You've really improved in just three days."

Linda's scrutiny as Marissa adjusted her snorkel mask made Marissa feel clumsy. It was hard to get the thing on while treading water. "Yeah, it took four minutes instead of three for me to nearly drown. You'd think I'd be better at floating."

"You saw the baby squid, didn't you?"

"Oh yeah, it was great. And the tiny purple fish in that school.

The angel fish—wow." She grinned. "They were way better than the screen saver."

Linda looked outraged. "I should hope. One more dive?"

"I think I can do one more." Marissa wanted to stay out all day but the sun and rolling water was starting to make her feel light-headed. Thank goodness it was only two hundred feet or so to shore and most of that could be traversed by wading.

"Knew you could," Linda answered before fitting her snorkel into her mouth again. Moments later she had slipped easily beneath the surface.

After inhaling deeply, Marissa executed a less elegant dive but kicked strongly toward the ocean floor. The bright sunlight illuminated the pale sand and volcanic rock formations. A magenta squarespot flitted between tendrils of purple anemones. Her floating hair obscured her view for a moment then a tug on her ankle brought her attention around to Linda, who was pointing out a longfin bannerfish.

They shared broad grins then both kicked toward the surface. Marissa blew her snorkel out and snatched it out of her mouth so she could spit out the sea water.

"I wish I could do this all day but I think I have to stop. I'm so thirsty and my lips feel like they're going to peel off."

Linda, who looked like a sea goddess with wet, red lips and gleaming expressive eyes, said eagerly, "Oh, we can't have that! Sea water is dehydrating. Let's get something to drink."

They were only a few hundred feet from their bungalow, and Marissa waded out of the gentle surf first, her fins dangling from her fingertips. She abandoned them on their porch. "I'm positively craving a Coke."

"Welcome to a retreat from the modern world. I think it's time for a coconut rum with banana, all blended up with ice."

"Sounds heavenly. I just want to towel off." Inside the bunga-low Marissa quickly brushed her hair after slipping out of her swimsuit. A dry T-shirt and pair of shorts was nothing she'd ever take for granted again. The open market in Fare Town had provided all the basics, true, but at a hefty price tag. Worth every penny.

She emerged into the sunshine again saying, "I must be getting old to appreciate clean clothes so much. When I was a kid I could stay gritty and grimy for days and not even think about it."

"If you don't mind me asking, how old are you?"

Marissa arched an eyebrow. "How old do you think?"

Linda rolled her eyes. "Oh please, let's not play that game. I'm thirty-one. I'm thinking you're about that."

"Oh. Thirty-four, just. I thought you were older. Not that you look older, you look about twenty-five. But you're wise and knowledgeable about so many things, and traveled so much. So I was thinking thirty-five at least, to have seen all you've seen."

"I started early on the living thing." Linda had an odd expression on her face but before Marissa could ask further, she said, "The ocean, fresh bread and a blended drink. What more is there to life?"

They ordered their drinks at the thatch-roofed bar, Linda making a few odd comments in French to the bartender along the way.

"I can think of a few things," Marissa answered finally, as she carried her drink to the open-air table under the awning. She took a quick peek for sand fleas—they seemed to like her a lot—and saw none. "Chocolate and sex."

"Yes, to both." Linda winked and Marissa's heart started beating hard again. It wasn't fair that Linda could get such a response, and so easily.

After they had both sighed over the delicious frozen concoction, Linda leaned back in her chair, looking content. "You're not going to want to leave, are you? Really?"

"Ocky is counting on me and eventually, I have to pay my way, so a job helps."

"It's not a job—you're one of the owners."

"True." Marissa sipped from her drink again, enjoying the sharp chill as she swallowed. "Even more reason to go home. I've a lot invested in Finders Keepers." Most of the money she'd inherited from her grandmother, as a matter of fact.

"How exactly does a dating service work? I mean, I guess you use a questionnaire."

"It's nearly seven hundred questions in fifteen categories. Every year we go through it and fine tune, add more, look at the failures and decide which questions aren't giving us the data we need."

"Wow." Linda stirred her drink. "And how successful are the matches you come up with?"

Marissa knew she was flushed with pride. "Nearly all our matches are still dating after three months and of those that date for a year, better than seventy percent are still together two years later. Since the divorce rate is half . . ."

"The idea of finding the perfect mate through a computer is just not something I thought would work. I prefer the old-fashioned method: search, trap and carry back to my cave. What's the secret?"

The brown eyes were dancing with laughter and Marissa realized she would not mind in the least being Linda's prey. She shook herself out of an NC-17 reverie and decided that Linda's smirk meant she could read Marissa's mind.

Fighting a blush, she said, "That's where my stat analysis came in. It's obvious that staying together is the outcome of the right energy and a lot of positive factors. But relationships don't end usually because two people with positive feelings toward each other simply no longer want to be together. They end because two people want to be apart."

"Like my parents? They lived in separate states until my father died six years ago."

"Sounds like mine were equally happy. The divorce was bitter and unhappy." Marissa shrugged. "The biggest reason couples break up is contempt of one person for the other, or mutual contempt. They could be perfectly matched in every other way but if there are traits that would lead to contempt, they won't stay together."

"You lost me." Linda licked a dollop of banana from the end of her straw. "Like what?"

Dragging her gaze from the tip of Linda's tongue, Marissa took refuge in familiar patter about her work. "Say one person has a very high standard for honesty and can't abide even the smallest bending of the truth. And the other person thinks social white lies and the occasional fib to get out of a sticky situation is okay. They could be perfect for each other and yet eventually, the highly truthful person is likely to develop contempt for the other person's ethics, especially if a situation comes along where their different styles come into conflict."

"Okay, I get it." Linda shook back her long, thick hair. "And contempt means it's pretty much over."

Marissa wanted to touch Linda's hair rather a lot. Her drink was very tasty. "I think so. Our questionnaire gets at what a person loves and what they hate but when we run the analysis, we screen out the likely match-ups that would lead to contempt first. Then we connect up the good stuff, like what each person finds amusing and so forth." Marissa paused to sip from her straw.

"In real life, do you think people minimize the things they don't like about someone if there's lots of things they do?"

Marissa wanted to ask what Linda would be willing to overlook as a negative in her but she supposed she didn't have to think about it that hard. Linda was the most active person Marissa had ever known, and she was aware that in all the activities they'd done in the last several days, from hiking to snorkeling, she was holding Linda back. How could someone so . . . energetic, fit, delectable . . . have any erotic thoughts about someone like her?

It was undeniable, how much she wanted Linda to really find her as attractive as all the flirting implied. But she couldn't believe it. The mirror and tape measure didn't lie. "Sure. There are lots of assumptions that the other person will change or the friction point won't come up. But, over time, people are who they are. I guess." Marissa sipped again, more nervously. Why did it seem like every word she said warned Linda off? "I'm not an expert. People don't change easily. And sometimes they can't change at all. My father couldn't be straight."

Linda swallowed after letting a mouthful melt on her tongue. Marissa simply could not stop watching. Linda was getting kind of blurry too. "Was that why your parents broke up?"

"Actually, it was because he moved out to be on his own and eventually moved in with Phillip." Marissa put a hand to her brow. "This is going right to my head. Wow."

"Too much sun." Linda quickly fetched a glass of water from the bar. "Drink up, all that you can. When's the last time you had to pee?"

"That's kinda personal, isn't it?" Marissa dutifully drank from the glass.

"More than two hours? Three?"

Marissa shrugged. "I don't know. After breakfast."

"So five hours. You're dehydrated, you gorgeous idiot."

"I'm not an idiot." Marissa listed to one side. "Not gorgeous either. But I might be drunk."

Linda firmly pulled Marissa upright. "Don't fall over. Stay right there."

Marissa watched Linda stride away and it seemed like only seconds before a plate with several sliced cheeses, glazed almonds and the delicious local bread, toasted, was set in front of Marissa.

Linda's brown eyes were quite commanding. "Eat up."

Commanding in a nice way, Marissa thought. In a way where the only thought a girl would have was *Yes*. "You have some too."

"I will, a little. I ate breakfast, remember?"

"I've never been big on breakfast." Marissa broke off half a slice of strong, dry cheese.

"Skipping meals isn't good for you, you know."

"I know, I know, but I try to watch my calories and giving away four or five hundred first thing in the morning means I won't get an evening snack when I'm really hungry."

"That makes sense, well, on the surface. But you do most of your aging between your last meal and breakfast."

Marissa didn't really want to debate her dietary habits. Everyone always got that look on their face that said "If only you didn't eat so much." Luckily Linda abruptly changed the subject. "How's your head?"

"Better for the food. But I think I'll take a nap." If anything, Linda looked faraway and not necessarily in a pleasant place.

"Okay. I was going to go for a hike. I'll make sure you don't sleep through dinner."

"Probably be good for me—the food here is so delicious."

"You're only here once and you're not going to get fish fresher than this. Low in fat, high in protein—it's all good." Linda lost the haunted look as she talked and by the time Marissa answered, her smile was back.

"You're right. I can't believe I ate raw tuna and I'm looking forward to having more." Marissa found herself grinning at Linda—she felt helpless to do otherwise. "It's good to get away from home, sometimes, because I honestly did not know that goat cheese was the food of the gods."

"I noticed you were fond of it when you licked it off your fingers last night."

Marissa blushed into her drink. "I didn't want to waste it."

"It was quite diverting." Linda arched one eyebrow. "So feel free to do that again with the goat cheese, chocolate sauce . . ."

"You're wicked."

"I certainly try." Linda rose to her feet. "I was thinking of the pounded abalone steak tonight. But I'm going to pass on more breadfruit."

"All ones from me on that." Marissa hiccupped and put a surprised hand to her mouth.

"English? And eat a little more cheese."

"Ones and zeros, binary. *All ones* means total agreement."

"Oh, more geek talk. I like it." Laughing, Linda signaled Marissa to remain sitting. "Finish that up and go nap. See you later."

Marissa watched her walk away, and took the same inventory she'd been taking every day: long legs, slender hips that still gave way to a deeply womanly curve at her waist. Shoulders that created a swimmer's Vee framed a graceful neck. "Unbelievable," Marissa murmured into the last of her drink, glad that Linda couldn't hear her.

"You're going to hurt yourself!" Marissa peered anxiously into the branches of the palm tree Linda had insisted on climbing. The leaves and bark looked sharp. The nap had chased away the dizzy headache and she didn't feel so helplessly besotted either.

"I've almost got it," Linda called. "Hey! Head's up."

A coconut thumped to the ground not far from the hammock Marissa had stretched out in, shortly followed by another, then a third. "That's plenty."

"If you say so." Linda inched her way down the curving trunk.

Marissa couldn't believe Linda's thighs weren't full of scrapes. She wondered if she could suggest checking them out for Linda, but wasn't sure she'd find the nerve. She laughed at herself—so much for not feeling besotted any more. She scolded herself, or tried to. So Linda was incredibly desirable. That didn't give Marissa the right to ogle and lust like some adolescent. "Why are these called the same as the stuff they make chocolate out of?"

"They're not." Linda paused in her delicate shimmy movements, the firm, lean muscles of her arms tensed. "They look a bit like monkey faces, the three holes. See?"

"Oh. I guess. So the natives named them after monkeys?"

"The Portuguese sailors named them after monkeys."

"What do they call cocoa beans in Portugal, then?"

Linda swung around the trunk, and dangled there for a moment. "I have no the hell idea."

Marissa had long enough to admire the curved silhouette before Linda dropped lightly to her feet. "I thought you knew everything."

"I do not—you're the brain here. Like, I have no idea how to open these up."

"Drill?"

"I was thinking big rock."

Marissa grinned. "Well, this should be fun. I'll just be right here in the hammock."

For the next forty-five minutes Marissa rocked and watched Linda try to bash, kick, stomp, hurl and pummel the coconut open. She was nothing if not determined, Marissa had to hand her that. Beyond Linda the surf continued its gentle, endless churning of the sand as tiny, brightly hued birds hopped along the shore.

She didn't want to go home but all good things came to an end. Tomorrow morning they would fly to Papeete. By evening she would be in Hawaii and the following morning at home. Linda would be in New Zealand. She didn't want to think about how far away New Zealand was and the fact that Linda didn't have a cell phone, e-mail or snail mail address.

Maybe they were just friends, just hanging out. But it would have been nice to have kept in touch after spending this time together. Nice was an understatement. She liked being around Linda. Liked looking at her, being looked at. Her earlier scolding wasn't the whole truth—Linda looked at her with desire, Marissa was almost certain of that. What else could it be?

> Dear Dad:
>
> You're the only one I can ask. You're the only person I know who found it and kept it until death did you and Philip part. How did you know? How will I know?
>
> Confused,
>
> Marissa
>
> P.S.   Feel free to send a sign.
>
> P.P.S. I really am going to tell Mom.

But if it was desire, then why had there not been another kiss? Not even holding hands. Just those looks. Sometimes short and quick, between words. Sometimes instead of words.

Marissa tried to talk back with her eyes. It wasn't just Linda's remarkable body she liked but the endless energy to attack each day as a brand new adventure. Linda shimmered with a passion for life that radiated and Marissa sometimes thought she'd get sunburn from standing too close. Burned, yes, maybe I will get burned, she mused. But it'll be the kind of burn that . . . heals, not hurts.

Linda knocked two coconuts together with all her might and bits of husk flew in all directions.

"I think you're getting somewhere." Marissa wanted to dab away the sweat beaded on Linda's brow. "You've been in the sun a while, though."

"Oh." Linda squinted at her. "I didn't realize it had moved." She gathered up her battered coconuts and resettled near the hammock. "My skin won't forgive me for that."

"I don't think you're burned." Marissa leaned out of the hammock so she could press two fingers firmly to Linda's shoulder blade. The white outline of her fingers, when she removed her hand, faded quickly. "You tan wonderfully."

"All in the genes."

"I wish I had genes like yours."

Linda looked up with a little frown but didn't say anything.

The way Linda reacted to anything that seemed like a compliment about her appearance puzzled Marissa. She quickly said, "Well, the genes that gave you so little hair on your legs. I'd like those."

Linda bent her head over the most battered of the three coconuts, lifting one of them between both hands. "That's not genetics. That's electrolysis and laser treatments."

"Really? Maybe I should try it."

"It's painful." Linda slammed the coconuts together, startling Marissa. "Really, really painful."

Marissa wobbled in the hammock, trying to get her balance back. Linda pounded the coconuts together several more times until with a dull crack, the one in her hands split, spewing coconut innards everywhere.

"Bravo!" Unwisely, Marissa leaned forward to see the broken inside. The hammock went out from under her and she flipped to the sand, landing with a surprised *whoof* next to Linda.

"Hey! Are you okay?" Linda dropped the husks, hands coated in coconut milk.

The next few seconds weren't very clear, later, but Marissa finally drew in a breath successfully and was aware then of the aroma of rich coconut and the heat of Linda's hands on her arms.

If anyone in her life had ever made her feel the way Linda did, Marissa didn't remember it. How could she forget a feeling like this?

That look from the very beginning that Marissa hadn't wanted to believe, hadn't wanted to think meant anything, was gleaming, bright and true.

Linda said again, her voice soft with concern, "Are you okay?"

Something got broken, Marissa wanted to say. Something broke that I've kept strong for a long time. Her heart was hammering high against her ears and the warmth of Linda's gaze was making her believe impossible things.

She can't . . . she doesn't . . . she won't . . . the voices inside whispered. And they kept whispering right up until the moment Linda's lips touched hers.

Then the voices went silent and the world was still. Even the surf stopped. All Marissa could hear was the faint sound of their lips brushing softly. Her vision blurred—she closed her eyes.

She could feel the dappled sunlight on her shoulders and it seemed inseparable from the heat of Linda's body next to hers. Whatever had broken was vaporizing to ash as cold places inside her blossomed in the warmth.

Linda's lips brushed hers again, then pressed harder. The still moment ended with a crash of waves as Marissa slipped her arms around Linda's waist. She didn't so much open her mouth to Linda as she yielded to Linda's slow, careful exploration. All of her yielded, including the last vestiges of disbelief.

The moments when Linda had made her feel interesting—

desirable even—had been like rain on her parched ego. The kiss, the deliberate but light movement of Linda's hips against hers, threatened to become a hurricane. And she wanted to be swept away.

Linda raised her head and asked again, "Are you okay?"

"Yes," was all Marissa could manage. She found her reflection in the depths of Linda's eyes and for once it didn't shock her. She wanted to be the woman Linda seemed to see and it was as scary as much as it was welcome.

"I got the coconut open," Linda murmured, and she kissed Marissa again, briefly, but with more fire. But before Marissa could react, she sat up and examined her coconut milk-spattered arms. "Now I'm all wet."

Marissa laughed—what else was there to do? "I think you may be the biggest flirt I've ever met."

Linda paused in the act of dusting sand off her arms. "Takes one to know one."

"I am not a flirt, really. I don't know how."

"That just means you're a natural. I had to go to charm school."

"You graduated *summa cum laude*, didn't you?"

This time it was Linda who laughed as she rose gracefully to her feet. "Shower before dinner?"

"A good idea." There was sand in places that weren't fond of any kind of abrasion. As Marissa followed Linda to their bungalow, carrying one of the mangled coconuts, she relived the kiss, over and over. Something had broken, something had healed.

She wanted more.

The Last Supper, as Linda dubbed it, was as delicious as the others. Marissa had more raw tuna and no breadfruit. The sweet rice with the tuna was perfect when chased by a dab of local mashed root of some kind. She didn't follow the French word for it but her mouth called it horseradish.

"I don't think I should have anything to drink." Marissa dabbed up the last of the rice with her fingertip, aware she was being uncivilized but Linda was doing the same thing and grinning. "My head is still a little dicey."

"Now, how can I appear to be a suave and debonair financier if you're sober?"

Marissa couldn't resist the teasing in Linda's voice. "You'll just have to work harder."

"Give me some pointers." Linda swirled the wine glass in her hand before sipping again from the deep red liquid. "What do you like in a date?"

"Is this a date?" The question was out before Marissa thought better of it.

"Isn't it? You dressed up, after all."

Marissa spluttered with laughter. "Yes, I wore the clean T-shirt."

"So it must be a date."

Marissa wanted to ask why Linda hadn't kissed her until their last day, almost their last evening. The kiss had been worth waiting for but tomorrow was so close now. She wanted something that sealed this vacation in some kind of Hall of Fame. But for what, she asked herself? Terror? Confusion? Crushes on Women Who Looked Like Amazons?

"I like dates that don't end." Marissa grinned but she was serious.

"They all end, eventually." Linda's eyes were in the shadows.

Marissa didn't think Linda meant to send the chill that crept over the table toward her but she couldn't help but shiver. "Some don't. Some people—and I should know—find happy ever after."

"Ah." Linda leaned forward and her face came into the light. Brown eyes soft, she said, "That's not dating anymore. That's living."

"How did you get so wise?"

Linda's eyebrows arched. "There are a lot of things that are easier to talk about than actually do."

Puzzled, Marissa opened her mouth to ask but the waiter

stopped to offer them a sorbet of pineapple and coconut. The cool, creamy blend was refreshing and not too sweet. By the time they were both licking their spoons for the last time and the bottle of red wine was empty, Marissa had forgotten all of her questions. She wanted something other than answers.

"Want to walk on the beach?" Linda paused at the exit that led past the moonlit swimming pool.

"Sure." The moon was incredible, its full splendor streaking the ocean with a path that surely led to magical realms. Don't be foolish, said the voice of practical reality. You're not a fairy princess about to be swept off your feet.

But I want to be, Marissa thought. I want that experience and I never let myself think it could happen to me before.

You're going to get hurt, the little voice persisted, but Marissa shushed it with the memory of Linda's warm lips on hers.

Flip flops dangling from her fingers, Marissa ran to the surf, aware of Linda falling behind. The warm water washed over her ankles as Marissa turned back to look at Linda's dark silhouette. The moonlight illuminated her own footprints not yet washed away by the tide. They were like a path that Linda could walk down if she wanted to join Marissa.

I want her to take that path, Marissa thought. Walk right down here, take me into her arms and kiss me again.

Impossibly, even though the moon seemed to be sprinkling the air with silver dust, Linda fit her feet into the prints that Marissa had left in the crusted sand. Marissa heart stopped when Linda stopped only a foot away.

"I'd like to visit you, sometime," Linda said in a voice barely louder than the gentle surf.

"I'd like that very much," Marissa answered.

She didn't feel bold. She looked into Linda's eyes and didn't feel as if all Linda saw was her breasts. She didn't feel like she was convenient nor that she was supposed to be grateful.

She felt *wonderful*.

Linda kissed her and she felt perfect.

Their lips made the same sound as the lazy surf washing over the soft, yielding sand. Linda made a noise, something Marissa could only define as pleased surprise, and Marissa found herself tipping her head so that Linda could pull her close.

The kiss softened in pressure but increased in sensual abandon. Marissa rubbed her lips against Linda's as their breathing fell into close rhythm. Linda made that noise again and let Marissa go, her lips curving in a full, wide smile.

She said only, "Wow," before she took Marissa's hand and led her along the wet sand.

Marissa kicked the water, letting it rush through her toes. Why she felt so innocent when she was having such carnal thoughts she didn't know but she wasn't going to explore that conflict right now. Right now, she was going to hold Linda's hand and let anything and everything happen.

"I might not be able to visit for a while."

"I still don't know much about you," Marissa pointed out. "You've never said what it is you do."

"I don't have to work." Linda's hand tightened around Marissa's in a rare show of tension.

Marissa wanted to ask more questions but couldn't bear the thought of endangering the fragile connection that finally seemed to be emerging. "I gave you all my contact information. It's unlikely I'll be anywhere else for the next few months."

Linda's hand relaxed and Marissa wondered what the secret was. A mob boss's daughter? Royalty run away from an arranged marriage? You've watched too much cable television, she chided herself.

"I won't lose it," Linda said quietly. She squeezed Marissa's fingers, turning them to face each other.

Marissa felt gathered up and completely enfolded in Linda's arms as she arched into Linda's embrace. Let the moon be the witness, she thought, as Linda's mouth found hers again. I love how she makes me feel and I can handle it if tonight is all there ever is.

She hoped she wasn't lying to herself.

Linda's fingers moved playfully up Marissa's ribs. "You're a good sport, Marissa. Thank you for this week."

"I don't want to be a good sport." A little laugh escaped her. "I want to be Ginger. Just for tonight."

"Helpless?"

Marissa shook her head. "Irresistible."

"I'm having a very hard time resisting you," Linda murmured.

"Why are you even trying?" Up on her tiptoes, Marissa pressed her lips to Linda's, trying not to moan and failing within moments.

Linda made a low, almost growling noise and the playful hands turned forceful, pulling Marissa's hips against her even as she tipped Marissa's head back with the force of her kiss. "I wasn't sure what you wanted."

"I didn't know how to say."

Linda smiled against Marissa's mouth. "You've explained algorithms, statistical sampling and the mysteries of couple dynamics and you're going to stop talking now?"

In the moonlight, Linda's eyes were black but the laughter in them was bright. "It's not a language I'm familiar with. You don't program lovers like computers."

"More's the pity. Want to try?"

Marissa pushed Linda back. "You're incorrigible, you know that?"

"I'm not. Really." Linda's voice dropped and the laughter in her eyes went away. "I'd really like to go to bed with you. I've wanted you since . . . halfway up the cliff."

"You're kidding. Those were the worst moments of my life."

"And you smiled through them. Fought your way through them. I was wondering if you attacked sex the way you attacked that climb." Linda's expression was caught between chagrin and desire. "You were incredibly inspiring."

"I was arguing with my mother."

"Ugh." Linda made a face. "Okay, that ruined the mood."

"Sorry." Marissa could have bitten her tongue off. The fragile moment was gone. Though the sand still felt wonderful between her toes and the moon's mystical path was as bright as ever, the moment was undeniably gone.

Linda padded out of the bathroom with a puff of steam behind her, hair still damp and hanging down her back, leaving a wet trail on her thin T-shirt. Marissa tried to look as if she was reading but she couldn't take her eyes off the tall, lithe figure. Nor could she stop her fantasies from running through her head in full, screaming digital clarity.

"Do you want something?" Linda was looking at Marissa in the mirror over the shared dresser.

Caught staring, Marissa tried for a flirtatious smile. "Yes."

"So do I."

Her heart pounding more and more rapidly, Marissa watched Linda cross the room to the light switch and the last clear vision she had of Linda was the hungry look in her eyes. Then there was moonlight only to illuminate the difference between the dark and Linda's hair.

There was only a hint of sound as Linda sat on the edge of Marissa's bed. One broad hand cupped Marissa's thigh, pushing her gently onto her back.

"Is this what you wanted, Marissa?"

"Yes. Please, yes."

"It's what I want too. Please," Linda whispered in Marissa's ear. "Let me feel how wild, how sensuous you can be."

Soft, scented hair surrounded Marissa's face as she arched to the first tentative touch of Linda's hand between her legs. "I want to be everything I can be for you."

Linda gasped as her fingers slipped into heat and wet. "I've never felt so close . . . stayed so close."

Marissa pulled Linda's mouth to hers and for several minutes kisses were their only conversation. Linda's fingers were playful but indirect. Marissa realized, surfacing from one deeply intimate kiss that they were rocking together like the motion of their lifeboat, and the idea wasn't alarming. Fate lent a hand, she thought, smiling into the next kiss.

"What?" Linda raised her head.

Marissa shook her head. "Sorry, I was just thinking that the lifeboat was fun and it led to this and—oh!"

Linda moved firmly on top of Marissa, her hand pushing Marissa's thighs farther apart. "This is what I want to talk about. What you need right now. How I can give you what you want."

"Touch me." Marissa drew in a sharp breath. Linda's fingers were still not as direct as she wanted and yet she was responding to the light brushes into her wetness. It felt intensely good and she hadn't realized she could get this excited this fast and this way. Yet, what was the surprise? She'd been fantasizing about Linda making love to her for days. Now that it was happening Marissa had never felt so aware of every muscle in her body.

Linda slipped one arm under her and arched Marissa into her. Marissa ran one hand over Linda's back and resented that her T-shirt was in the way of skin.

She tugged the shirt upward. "Oh, please. It's so dark and I want to feel you."

Linda murmured something and sat up. For a brief moment they were no longer touching. Marissa yanked off her own T-shirt and tossed it to the floor, then Linda was there again, and this time they were all skin, yielding and taking.

The breasts Marissa had once upon a time resented finally seemed to make complete sense. Linda's mouth was on them, her tongue and lips bringing tingles to the nerves. Her nipples hardened and they brushed against Linda's in a spasm of awareness.

Linda moaned and this time Marissa could understand the words that followed. "No one has ever felt like you."

"You're making me crazy. Your hand . . . touch me."

The drawl of pleasure in Linda's voice was unmistakable. "I am touching you. You feel amazing. Wet and swollen."

"I've been this way for a couple of days now. I want you so much. I don't know if I'm enough for you—"

"You are. Something about you—I've thought about being wrapped inside you. And this . . ."

Fingers slipped inside Marissa, drawing out a series of shivers. "You're so strong, oh Linda, so strong. I hope I can please—"

Linda shushed her with a kiss. The faint moonlight brought out sparkles in her eyes. "Everything about you pleases me. I love your spirit, that you're willing to try and fail and try again. And I like women."

"I noticed." To her own ears, her voice had gone soft and adoring. It wasn't at all the still-in-control-enough-to-laugh quality that would match the lightness in Linda's voice.

"I like women and you are . . ." Linda made a little noise as her fingers began a tantalizing rhythm against parts of Marissa she'd not realized could be so responsive. "You are *all* woman."

"I'm not—I'm not very—" Very what? Marissa felt as if she ought to confess to something, but she wasn't sure what. She loved the way Linda was touching her and liked the words that she heard with her heart. I'm not very attractive, she wanted to say, and nobody has ever seemed to want to know what you are learning tonight. I'm not very experienced, she could have added, except in my own wild flights of fantasy. "You're so very strong and I'm not."

"Is this what you wanted? Is this okay?" Linda kissed her again with a tenderness that took Marissa's breath away. The flutters became long, sure strokes and abruptly there were no words left in Marissa to answer. She wished the lights were on and she clutched Linda close.

"I'm here," Linda said, her voice rising. "I'm here . . . yes, hold me tight. Hold on to me. I'm here."

Tears were inevitable but they felt like nurturing rain on Marissa's cheeks. Linda's mouth was at her throat then her nipples.

"That's right." Linda made a small cooing sound as she slipped one leg between Marissa's. "That's right. I'm here. You like this, don't you?"

She'd never been touched quite like this, for so long, with such intensity, and she had never felt that the woman touching her was getting more and more excited with every passing moment. She arched, tensing, and worried that she didn't know what to do with all the pleasure that was building. Gasping, she thought she said, "Don't stop, please."

"We're just starting." Linda moaned and twisted her hand, bringing her fingers firmly against muscles deep inside Marissa.

Someone cried out—that's me, Marissa thought incredulously. A ripple of pleasure rolled over her, starting at the places where Linda continued her caresses. She felt something hot and wet on her thigh and realized it was Linda arching against her.

Moaning with release, amazement and joy, with awe, even, Marissa relaxed against Linda for a dozen heartbeats before wriggling out from under her. "I want to taste you. I could feel how wet you are."

Even in the dark it was easy to find what she wanted. She filled her mouth with the sleek, wet folds, then let her tongue swirl and dip. When she felt Linda's tongue dancing on her she moaned, long and hard. It was the most intimate experience she'd ever shared. She luxuriated in Linda's wetness, loving the shudders of response and feeling similar responses in her own body as Linda's mouth explored her completely.

Just as Marissa thought the sensations between her legs would make her forget all about the joys her tongue was experiencing she felt Linda gasp for breath and rest her forehead on Marissa's thighs.

"That feels so good," Linda said, panting between words. "I can't believe how good."

Marissa moaned her pleasure as Linda's hand slipped behind her head, pulling her in even closer and tighter. Marissa slipped two fingers alongside her tongue and then held on as Linda surged to meet the first stroke, then the second, and again, and again.

Words were soft and loving as their arms found ways to wrap tight after Marissa pulled up the sheet to cover them. Against her ear she heard the steadying beat of Linda's heart and it calmed her own.

"You're not even a dream I had," Marissa said softly. "So how can you be real?"

Linda, her breathing slow and even, didn't answer. In the distance the surf quietly rolled onto the beach and Marissa rolled just as easily into sleep.

Chapter 5

Sunrise—it was the first sunrise she'd watched since the one on the lifeboat. Marissa couldn't find names for all the shades of blue and orange, nor for the way the ocean seemed to grow larger and larger until the rim of the sun finally limited the end of the world.

Linda was sleeping, still, and Marissa's gaze traveled from the simple miracle of the sunrise to the beauty of the woman next to her.

In the early light of dawn, she could study Linda at last, memorizing the sweep of her thick, dark eyelashes and the relaxed curve of her full, rose-tinted lips. She slept in a tangle of sheet, one side of her body completely exposed, from the long, tanned, smooth leg, to the deep curve of her hip, to the narrow sweep of her waist. A bare arm wrapped itself around a pillow, which hid breasts Marissa now knew were firm and rounded. The long arm led her gaze to the broad, muscled shoulders, brushed with the orange of the sunrise.

Linda was beautiful. Separately and whole, she was more beautiful than Marissa had realized. Baggy shorts and boxy shirts hadn't hidden her strength and stature but they had disguised an artist's fantasy of the perfect female form. Sand and sweat had masked the smooth clarity of her skin and after showers Linda had always been at least partially dressed when she emerged from the bathroom.

Somehow, Linda's surface to bones-deep beauty had escaped her. Marissa wasn't sure why. If she'd realized she might not have flirted so much, might not have really believed that anything could happen between a goddess-model and an overweight, underfit computer nerd. But something had. Something meaningful, caught between the words and moans, had happened.

The tint of Linda's shoulders lost some of the orange blush as the sunlight steadied into its yellow glory. Marissa resisted the urge to wake Linda with a kiss and soft brush of fingertips where they had been so wanted last night. Yes, Linda was beautiful, but Marissa was missing the laughter in the expressive topaz-brown eyes—the laughter and her own reflection there.

Ten minutes ticked slowly by. The sun gained its foothold in the sky and the ever-changing light illuminated new angles and curves in Linda's face. The moment grew and the feeling that she might never experience anything so peaceful and magical again became painful. There was no such still place in reality. Marissa knew that the moment would end.

She began her journey home today.

She couldn't go wherever Linda was going—she had a life and a company and friends. And she knew that this moment in the sun would not last forever. It lived until Linda stirred, until someone's stomach growled and the need for change, to move forward in the day, arose.

The voice of inner pragmatism reminded her that she could not stop time. She didn't try to argue with that reality. The only thing she could control was how this moment ended.

Leaning forward she lightly touched her lips to Linda's brow, her cheek, then her lips. Her fingers she trailed down the curve of

Linda's hips, grinning with joy as she felt Linda stir against her. The soft noise of waking mixed with wonder was the second most glorious thing Marissa had ever heard—the first, she realized with a shiver of delight, was Linda's voice raised in pleasure. Laughing or climaxing, Marissa understood abruptly that there was little difference. She craved the sound of both.

"Morning," Linda murmured.

"Good morning to you." Marissa continued the light, easy touches of her lips against Linda's face. "I tried hard not to wake you but I didn't know which you'd like less—me waking you early or me watching you sleep."

"I don't mind early." Linda's eyes opened, the brown muted with drowsiness. "I've watched you sleep the last two mornings."

"Oh." Touched, Marissa let her fingers wander more firmly and Linda seemed to melt even closer. "That's sweet, very sweet."

"Make love to me," Linda whispered. "Marissa, please."

Wishing her arms had the endless strength that Linda's did, Marissa slid on top of Linda, using her legs to spread Linda's apart. "You don't have to ask twice, believe me."

Linda's quiet chuckle was stifled by a quick groan as Marissa delved carefully into Linda's slick heat. Her fingertips tingled as Linda melted underneath her. She nuzzled at Linda's ear, listening carefully to the rising pace of Linda's breathing. All that mattered was the awe she felt as she dipped inside Linda, awe that reflected back to her through Linda's moan. Pulling back, she locked her gaze with Linda's and lived each stroke of her fingers through the widening shimmer in the brown depths.

She nearly asked if it was okay, if it felt good but Linda suddenly wrapped her arms tight around Marissa's shoulders and held on as a soft, broken groan escaped her. Marissa thought, for just a moment, that she might cry from the quiet strength of Linda's taut body. Before tears could form, however, they were both melting into the cool sheets.

Linda laughed quietly as she sighed and for the next few minutes Marissa felt caught all over again in a moment of perfect happiness. But after those few minutes there were new needs and Linda, fully awake and eyes gleaming with intent, took care of every one.

"I suppose we should get up." Linda ruffled the sheet on top of them and Marissa wrinkled her nose.

"We smell like sex."

"Yeah," Linda said, with obvious relish. "And I'm hungry now."

"Let's get some breakfast then." Okay, Marissa thought, we won't talk about what we have to do before one o'clock this afternoon.

The talk was light over breakfast and touched on nothing but the fun they'd had snorkeling, walking, swimming, sunbathing, wading and breaking open coconuts. By the time they walked back to their bungalow Marissa was thoroughly concerned that something was wrong but the door wasn't even closed before Linda pulled her firmly into her arms and whispered, "Let's go back to bed."

Giddy with laughter, Marissa grabbed another handful of clothing and shoved it into the cheap duffle bag she'd acquired at the Fare Town market. Linda was likewise engaged and also seemed ready to laugh at nearly anything. They'd done a dozen delicious things to each other and gone back for seconds of their favorites. Marissa blushed to think of how vocal she'd been about what she wanted (more), how (harder) and when (now).

Their shuttle to the tiny island airport left in fifteen minutes and she was dizzy from lovemaking and emotions spent and yet bottled up.

Everything was a blur of smiles and farewells until the tiny plane was airborne over the vivid blue ocean. Marissa thought back over the past few days and remembered how big it had all seemed when the lifeboat was the entire world. There were islands dotting the ocean everywhere, yet they'd seen none but the one they'd landed on.

Linda leaned across to peer out the window. "Seems impossible that anyone would get lost out here, doesn't it?"

"From up here, yes. I was just thinking how easy from down there." I'm lost, she thought. Still lost. I have been since the first moment she flirted with me.

Linda took her hand and they sat quietly for a while. Finally, she murmured, "Last night was amazing. I didn't expect . . . I wasn't sure how you felt."

"I wasn't sure about you either. I mean that we're different. Not just on the outside." With a flash of insight, she added, "Vacation brought out our similarities."

"I'd like to work on finding others." Linda squeezed their fingers as the plane rocked from mild turbulence. "I think there's more."

Marissa could only nod. She wanted there to be more but now she couldn't help but think of all the things she still didn't know about Linda. Like how she could afford not to work and travel all the time. Where she'd gone to school, what her interests were in music. "I'd like that."

"I might not be able to call or write but one day you're going to look up and there I'll be."

Swallowing hard, Marissa nodded. She couldn't think about the next hours, when good-bye was inevitable. She could hear that throaty question, repeating in her mind.

"*Is this what you wanted, Marissa?*"

It had been, all that and more.

The small airplane touched down with a squeal of tires. The rest of the journey seemed inevitable. Home called, there was no denying it. She'd not thought about her mother in several days now and that had been a relief. But work, all her plans and Ocky's too, called. She had a life she really wanted to live—she felt that more strongly than she ever had before. There were more ups than downs, more ones than zeros and it was *her* life, the one she'd chosen.

She wanted Linda, too, loved the feelings Linda brought out in her. Again, she was gripped with knowing she wanted to be the woman Linda saw. But could she be? Every look in the mirror said that Linda was plain nuts to find her attractive. But last night . . . last night.

It seemed impossibly soon that she was standing at her departure gate, watching the first passengers board the flight to Honolulu. Linda was waiting to see her off then had a few more hours until her flight to Auckland. They'd eaten the fruit they'd grabbed at the hotel since none could be taken where they were going. Carefully, with lots of little words, they'd not talked.

They'd not even said good-bye, though Marissa could feel them both shaking slightly as they waited, arms entwined.

Finally, she took the chance. "It wasn't just pity, was it?" The boarding call came again.

"No, of course not." Linda's eyes had darkened but she kept their luminous depths trained on Marissa's expression. "I wanted to love you. Why did you let me?"

"Because . . . I wanted you." She had felt far more but she was too frightened to add, "I loved the way you made me feel, like nobody ever had before. I don't want to go, I don't want to lose the feeling." She might have tried to put some of that into words, but even as she considered it, she realized that she couldn't divide Linda from the emotions Linda brought out in her. Was it Linda who attracted her or the heady, addictive feelings of being desired and wanted? Was it both?

Her feelings were too confusing to risk more when they would be parted in only a few minutes. There would be time to talk, back in the real world.

They called her row and only a few passengers were left. Somehow, Marissa made her hands unclench, made herself walk away, but she couldn't make herself not look back. *Run back now and tell her you think you're in love with her.* But would that be the truth? This is a vacation romance, with a chance to be something more, Marissa told herself firmly. As they advised their clients, be patient.

She looked over her shoulder one more time. Linda's gaze was filled with a soft wonder and a shimmer of tears. *Be patient—and trust what you know you felt.*

Linda stayed there, just the other side of attendant, as Marissa stepped through the door onto the baking asphalt. Crossing quickly to the shade of their plane, Marissa queued with the other passengers then hauled her backpack and herself up the stairs. It was so much harder to climb those stairs than it had been that cliff. At the top, just before she ducked into the aircraft, she looked back and Linda was there, on the other side of the glass.

Long after her plane was airborne, Marissa wondered if that last gesture had been a wave, or if it had been a blown kiss set free on the island breeze to follow Marissa on the long journey home.

Part Two

Chapter 6

Is that what someone would call a limitless sky? The grimy airport window couldn't mask how big the heavens were. In what seemed like only minutes, Marissa's plane was out of sight.

"*Pardonnez moi, mademoiselle.*"

Startled, Linda Bartok abandoned her contemplation of the Tahitian sky, not knowing how long ago Marissa's plane had disappeared into the distance. "*Oui?* What is it?"

"You're behind the secured area," the airline attendant said, with a gesture at the sign.

"*Pardonnez moi.*" She'd not realized she had edged toward the door as she'd watched the plane taxi. Linda picked up her worn day pack and turned toward the boarding area for her Auckland flight.

For a few minutes she could think only of the previous night. There had not been—never, ever—a night like that before in her life. She could still feel Marissa's touch and the depth of her own response. This morning, too, in the full light of day, she'd felt the same intensity and let herself enjoy it to levels she'd never experienced.

The days, too . . . the days with Marissa had been filled with laughter and ease. It had been great fun teaching Marissa to snorkel, to share good food and talk only of topics they felt like exploring. Marissa's hands made curious whorls and sharp slices in the air if whatever the topic was excited her.

Linda grinned to herself. When Marissa was excited she was also quite vocal.

What a week, she thought. What an amazing week. A cruise wasn't her usual style and had been booked last minute on the cheap. How could she have known the challenge and invigoration of their shipwreck and rescue would provide such wonderful diversion? All in all, the vacation had been a blast, a real escape from her life.

She laughed aloud, alarming two elderly women walking toward her. She nodded more sedately and laughed quietly when they had passed her. The week had been an escape—an escape from escaping. How ironic was that?

She'd felt so far away, so perfectly lost. Had the night been so amazing because Marissa knew nothing at all about her? Had it been the brightness of the days and the safety of the dark night that had let her respond that way?

For more days in a row than she could remember she'd had no flashbacks, no nightmares, no waking terrors. The lazy but exhilarating days had freed her from the pain she had never outrun before. All morning she'd felt whole, as if she'd never even been broken.

That is, until a half hour ago, when Marissa had let go and walked away.

Her footsteps slowed as she recalled that painful moment. She didn't know how Marissa had found the strength to let go but when she had, Linda's own hands had unclenched. Harsh reality, assisted by unwanted memory, began to fill her up again like toxic water pumping out the clean from the well of her soul.

Pain was an old friend. Now pain murmured the familiar words: *run away*.

She glanced back to make sure Marissa's plane was indeed still gone. She took a few steps toward the Air New Zealand area then stopped again.

She could still feel Marissa's hands, her mouth, her kisses. She could hear the way Marissa had moaned *yes* over and over. If she closed her eyes she could see Marissa's face red with exertion, beaded with sweat and creased with unyielding determination to climb that damn cliff. She had the heart of a lioness and the strength of a woman. A woman's fragility, passion, sweetness—but Marissa wasn't the only one, Linda reminded herself. There had been other women in her life who were equally remarkable. The sea was full of diverting, intriguing fish. So why, oh why did she long to go after Marissa?

She always moved forward, never back. Going back hurt too much.

Run away, the pain advised. It's always been the safest choice. Let the lawyers track you to the New Zealand bush, to an unoccupied bach not on any map. By then you'll be in Australia.

Why was Marissa different? Like all the others, she'd first noticed the false exterior. As with all the others, Linda had laughed and played, flirted and rambled—it was a mask she had worn comfortably since childhood. Marissa had acted just like the others in response.

Except she hadn't, not when it mattered.

Last night. Last night Marissa had wanted and Linda had gladly given. Last night Marissa had wanted more and in the dark had reached for Linda with hunger and touched the only places Linda felt were really her. She'd whispered sweet and powerful things in the dark, reacting to what she felt, not what she saw.

All the others had stopped listening at some point.

All the others had never failed to whisper the final blow: "You're so beautiful."

She started walking while old pain warred with new, the new pain born when Marissa had disappeared from her sight. Tahiti Faa'a Airport wasn't very big and she had hours until her flight.

Leaving the secured area, she quickly walked to the small market-place just across the street, losing herself in the bright colors and scents of roasting fish and pineapple.

Marissa had never called her beautiful. Instead, she'd called her strong. Instead of going away and watching the rest of the night as if from a high corner in the room, Linda had stayed in the moment. She had felt everything Marissa had done. Felt it and let it feel good. Orgasm had been terrifying but she had stayed, and let it happen.

Just before sleep Marissa had asked, "You're not even a dream I had, so how can you be real?"

She'd had no answer. She hadn't felt real at that moment, not in the least. What had been real was the solidity of Marissa against her.

Wrapped close in Marissa's arms, Linda had been enveloped by a feeling so foreign and so welcome that she'd known, upon waking to Marissa's gentle, sweet kisses, that she had cried in her sleep.

Marissa was gone, and even the memory of the feeling was fading. Abruptly, reliving it was scary. She'd let Marissa close—too close, the pain whispered.

A long coil of cool blue silk reminded her of Marissa's eyes. The crimson next to it was the color of her lips in the early morning light. Marissa was everywhere around her and all Linda could think to do was run away.

You don't have to go to Auckland, she told herself. All you have to do is keep running. Anywhere is far enough from Boston. Keep them guessing, keep them frustrated.

"You've always made up hurtful lies, Linda." At their last meeting, her mother's eyes had matched the onyx beads around her neck. "Money is all you want and you can have it, but you can never repeat these lies again. Sign or get nothing. Sign or we'll see about another competency hearing."

Her pace increased through the swirl of the market. It was always this way, her mother's voice intruding into everything.

Whenever Linda thought she had found quiet at last, she heard her mother.

Memories of her mother had been only shadows in the glow of Marissa's presence. Her laughter, especially—Marissa laughed like sunlight. Marissa had a kind of inner glow that vanquished everything murky and foul.

Marissa was gone now and Linda's mother was back.

Linda remembered joking about being a suave financier, there to whisk Marissa away to safety but that had been a part she'd played, some of the time. Other times she'd been a survivalist, in love with the great outdoors. Still others she'd been tour guide and coach. The only time she'd been herself had been last night and this morning, after Marissa called her strong.

Strong. Do strong women run? Wryly she thought that strong women might not run but smart women did. Her intelligence had never been in question. Dr. Kirkland had even pointed out that a smart woman would always find a way to make denial and avoidance seem like the wise choice.

This smart woman, Linda mused, wanted to go after Marissa. She wanted to reclaim the feeling of that incredible moment when Marissa had seen and touched only the real Linda, the one no one ever saw, the one even she had thought could never be found again.

Marissa had a passion for living and it had shown in the way she'd attacked the cliff. It showed in the way she made love. Even in the way she enjoyed water, sand and new experiences, like raw tuna and goat cheese.

The aroma of roasting pineapple made her stomach growl and Linda turned back to the main marketplace, following the scent with her nose. She bought a plate of rice with a skewer of white fish and pineapple and stood not far from the vendor, nibbling and remembering. She could get lost in the simple pace of the islands. Even here, where tourists passed through constantly, the vendors moved as if they heard music no one else could. The white paper plates were handed to new customers without hurry.

Linda watched a teenager with dark hair accept a laden plate from her mother. They were both smiling while the food in Linda's mouth turned to ash.

Her brain stuck on a vision of her mother, turning in a repeating loop, with a white plate heaped with food in her hand. She held it out to Linda, whose hands were thin and pale but tipped with demure pink, as she accepted it. Nausea rolled up as Linda dropped the rest of her food into the nearby bin, then bent over it with a shudder. She gasped for breath, staring at her strong, broad adult hands clenching her thighs. Don't go there, she warned herself. Don't live it again.

"You can't run forever," Dr. Kirkland had told her. "Memory isn't something you leave behind. Eventually, when you can handle it, you'll remember what hurt you."

Scalpels hurt. Needles hurt. Electrolysis hurt. Throwing up hurt. She remembered it all. So why couldn't she handle it? Why was she still running away when there were such things as magic and love? She'd not touched on that memory in months, years even. It wasn't relevant. It revealed nothing. She already knew what had happened back then. This memory was not new, not a guarded secret and it did not have the power to make her fourteen again. Not after all this time. She wouldn't allow it.

She made herself walk, willing the motion to settle her stomach. She came to the end of the market and knew she had to turn back. But where was she going? Marissa was in California. Her mother was in Massachusetts. The ticket in her wallet said Auckland, but she didn't have to go there. She could go anywhere in the world she wanted.

She wanted to run to Marissa, for the first time wanting to run toward something instead of away.

She wasn't the woman Marissa thought she was, though she wanted to be. What would Marissa think of her when she learned the truth? Marissa had wanted a lie, a mask. Except she hadn't, not last night. Last night, she had wanted the real Linda. Hadn't she?

She bought a bit of the cool blue silk to remind her of Marissa's eyes. Tucking it in her shirt pocket she felt as if she'd found something that would help her remember the way she'd felt last night:

safe. It didn't make sense, but then again the way Marissa had seemed to see all the way inside her, well, that didn't make sense either.

Linda caught herself searching out the window of the Air New Zealand plane for the tenth time since take off. Marissa's plane was long gone and now they were heading in opposite directions. The bond between them was a fragile tether, she told herself, and distance would snap it. The fruitless yearning for impossible things would end.

"You don't live the life other girls do," she could hear her mother say. Yeah, Mom, she thought viciously, you made damn sure of that.

Turning her gaze inside the cabin she caught a glimpse of the blue silk tucked in her pocket. Part of her wanted to stuff it down the seatback pocket and the other to braid it into a bracelet that she never removed. Was last night a lie or truth? What had she seen in Marissa's eyes that she could trust?

If she could sleep she might have answers when she woke but that was out of the question. She never slept in a public place. Instead, she opened the new paperback she'd bought, anticipated boredom and quickly found it. At least the flight wasn't full and there was an empty middle seat, allowing her to stretch out her legs.

"Can I get you a beverage?"

Back to civilization, Linda thought. "Diet Coke?"

The steward asked the same question of the woman in the aisle seat then efficiently decanted both sodas. He leaned over to give Linda hers and the woman in the aisle seat helpfully set the accompanying packet of biscuits on Linda's tray table.

Linda smiled her thanks then braced herself as the woman did the familiar double take.

"You do know that you look like . . ." The woman had a clipped, pronounced Kiwi accent.

"Yes, I know. I'm often told."

"Oh." She brushed long, attractively highlighted blond strands behind her shoulder. "I guess that makes me unoriginal. I'll have to try harder."

Linda knew her smile was stiff and she tried to soften her response. "Sometimes I'm not sure I even look like me."

"I'm always told I look like my Aunt Darea. She's been dead thirty years so I'm never sure it's a compliment."

The mask of interest and flirtation slipped easily into place. "Your Aunt Darea must have been an attractive woman." Even as she spoke, Linda felt herself step back, part of her watching their interchange. She'd done that with Marissa, at first. Then, without even noticing the loss of her detachment, she hadn't been watching herself with Marissa, she'd been experiencing it.

"Oh, my. And they say Americans are rude and boorish."

"We are." Linda stretched slightly in the seat. "Rude, boorish and we suck up more resources per capita than everybody else. But that doesn't mean we don't know a gorgeous woman when we see one."

"Tamryn Messiter."

"Linda Bartok." She shook the proffered hand.

"You're a lesbian."

"And I'm betting you're not." Linda grinned. "Yet."

"Evil! I shall buy you a drink if you keep that up."

"Doesn't that encourage me to suggest you might want to join the Mile High Club?"

The flash of interest in Tamryn's eyes took Linda aback. Then it felt quite normal to take all the discomfort she felt and channel it to the one thing that would create the greatest distance between her and Tamryn. All Tamryn saw was the legs, the body, the perfect nose. Sex could certainly happen but it would be the mask, the shell that touched Tamryn while the rest of Linda went away. That's the way it had always been. It was quick and foolproof.

Until Marissa, her body reminded her. Until Marissa—it didn't matter what Marissa thought or felt or knew or saw. You *stayed*. You let yourself climax in her arms. Dr. Kirkland would call that a major breakthrough.

The war between her inner pains started again, even as she flirted outrageously with Tamryn. Run away or go to Marissa? Stay with what had always been safe or take a chance that she could find that safe place in Marissa's arms again? Escape or finally come back?

Their descent through wispy clouds was lengthy but finally a breathtaking view of green and grey island against deep blue water was spread out below them. Even though Auckland appeared to be much like most port cities, the expanses of clear, untouched land were breathtaking. Out in the bush she could get very lost for a while, Linda told herself. Very lost.

She exited the plane just behind Tamryn and they continued to chat and flirt as they claimed their bags and waited through the customs inspections. Finally, they made their way to the main concourse where Tamryn would catch a domestic flight to Dunedin.

"I should stop at the loo," Tamryn said.

"That's probably a good idea for me too."

"There's a short line."

Linda shrugged. "I'm not desperate."

"You're not?" Tamryn brushed her thick hair over her shoulder. "I've failed utterly then."

"You should be careful, you know. Some women might think you were serious."

Tamryn reached the front of the queue. The next stall available was oversized for wheelchair access. Glancing over her shoulder as she claimed the stall, Tamryn said, "How do you know I'm not?"

"Are you?"

She stood just inside the door, staring at Linda. "I'm not shy. We can share."

Linda wasn't aware of joining Tamryn but the door was now shut between them and the rest of the world.

Tamryn, her cheeks flushed and one hand toying with the top button of her blouse, whispered, "The real question is whether you're serious. Because I am. Call me curious."

"What exactly is it you want?"

"I think you know." The first button was undone then the second, showing an appealing swell of cleavage.

The usual questions welled up in Linda's mind. Is it the full red lips? The perfect breasts? The high cheekbones or the deeply curved waist? What piece of me do you want? You have to pick because you don't get the whole me. There is no whole me anymore.

She asked no questions and the core of her slipped away to watch as her hands reached for the top button of Tamryn's slacks.

Tamryn sighed as she leaned back against the wall. "That's what I want—it's my lucky day, isn't it?"

"You don't have to decide that now." Linda eased the zipper down and noted that Tamryn's skin was warm and her eyes slightly glassy. There were people near, so she would need to keep her voice low. Her mind was alert for any sign that others realized what they were doing and all the other input she could see from her distant watching mind she methodically absorbed and categorized.

Tamryn was thickly wet and obviously excited. Given the place and time, one or two fingers playing with her clit might be best.

Her breathing rapidly escalating, Tamryn whispered firmly, "This is definitely my lucky day, getting fucked by a beautiful woman like you."

Linda watched from somewhere near the ceiling as the beautiful woman fucked Tamryn, even put her hand warningly over Tamryn's mouth when she came with a little cry. The aftershivers and cooing pleasure noises did penetrate Linda's awareness, as did the sensual aroma on her fingers, now coated liberally with sweet, slippery wet.

"That was . . . brilliant." Tamryn ran her hands lightly over Linda's shoulders. "You never said where you were headed. I've got a spare room. Not that I'd want you to sleep there."

"What about that doctor boyfriend of yours? The one you said you were going to marry?"

Tamryn shrugged. "He travels a lot."

Linda's felt her smile dim as her core awareness returned fully to her body. She felt slightly ill and knew she could take no pride in the pink flush spilling across Tamryn's chest. "That's really not my scene. Even if I am bound for the bush. And that's a sentence that in the U.S. would make most laugh."

"Well, that's a real shame." Tamryn once again pushed back her hair, then quickly redid her blouse buttons. "I'm less curious than I was about some things and even more curious than ever about others."

"I'm sure you'll find someone to help you with the rest of your research." Linda's dry tone seemed lost on Tamryn, who nodded seriously.

"I think I will. Meanwhile, thank you. You're really beau—"

"You're welcome. I'll leave you to your research—and the loo."

Tamryn fiddled in her handbag, then handed Linda a business card. "If you get down Dunedin way . . ."

"Sure," Linda said, tucking the card in her pocket. She slipped out of the stall and heard Tamryn click it locked behind her. Backpack slung over one shoulder, she scrubbed her hands clean then departed the restroom. On the way out she flicked Tamryn's business card into the bin.

Her plan had been to walk out the front door of the airport and keep going. She'd find a ride to some place small and keep going. On her left, at the far end of the ticketing area, was a display of local tours. She walked that direction then stared at the brochure with bungalows set on a beautiful lagoon. For the longest time she couldn't breathe in.

She hadn't even wanted to touch Tamryn. And she hadn't touched Tamryn, not with any part of her that was capable of feeling anything. It had been just like all the other times.

Except, of course, Marissa.

Whatever it was she'd found with Marissa, whatever it was that had stayed and felt the pleasure of Marissa's touch, it was gone now. Could she only get it back with Marissa? Well, Dr. Kirkland with all the answers, what kind of breakthrough was that?

Walk out the front door, and keep going—that was the plan. It was the safest thing to do. That was what she'd always done in the past. But you can't get to the future through the past, she told herself. You get to the future by living the present, Dr. Kirkland had said.

She turned to the ticket counters, heart pounding. She wasn't strong, she was scared. She wanted to be safe but suddenly safe didn't seem to be what she'd always thought it was.

Linda knew there was only one route that would take her to a future she suddenly, desperately wanted to have. She put down a credit card, knowing that her mother's lawyers would quickly find out she'd used it. By the time they figured out where she was going it wouldn't matter. She'd be where she needed to be.

The flight was so long she changed her mind thirty-seven times, but on the thirty-eighth she silenced the last of her doubts. This was the only choice she could make. She wanted Marissa, but knew Marissa had no idea what a basket case she had gone to bed with. It would take time, lots of time maybe, to fix that.

Tension kept her from sleeping and the in-flight movies weren't diverting. There was little to do but close her eyes and relive every conversation she'd had with Marissa. She touched the square of blue silk from time to time and wondered what she might see in Marissa's eyes the next time she looked into them.

U.S. Customs let her in the country and this time walking out of the airport, head held high, was exactly the right thing to do. The chilly winter air didn't bother her. The transit system was familiar and she escaped to the suburbs. In no time she was giving a cab driver the address.

This was the right thing to do. In spite of all the other confusion and lack of certainty, she knew this was where she had to be if she was going to ever have a chance to find that place again with Marissa. She couldn't build a future from the Kiwi bush or Ozzie outback.

The elevator whisked her upward and the confined space allowed her to realize she needed a bath. The humid marketplace in Papeete, followed by nearly twenty hours of recirculated air and the lack of sleep left her sinuses dry and eyes scratchy. The elevator door panels reflected back wild hair, a stained rugby shirt and crumpled shorts.

She stepped out into the thick carpet, and took advantage of a man keying in the code to get past the receptionist and into the main office.

"Hey! You can't go in there!"

She sidestepped the startled man, who'd turned at the receptionist's cry. Executives always had the big offices at the far end. Aware of the rising clamor behind her, she picked up her pace. She wasn't watching herself make this journey down the long corridor, she was living it. She was grinning so deeply her jaw hurt. Alarmed glances from everyone she passed said she was acting like a crazy woman, and what better way to go these last few feet, headlong into whatever the future had in store?

She boldly strode past another scurrying assistant.

"You can't go in there!"

"Yes I can," Linda answered as she flung open the door.

For just a moment Linda had the supreme satisfaction of seeing the woman at the desk utterly flummoxed. The onyx eyes widened in shock. Quickly, however, a tiny smile followed but Linda would not let it frighten her again.

Her voice singsong and regardless of the other people obviously in a very important meeting with the president of Price Investments, Linda proclaimed, "Mom! I'm home!"

Chapter 7

"Look how tanned you are! You'd never know you were in a ship-wreck—you look fantastic!" Ocky threw her long arms enthusiasti-cally around Marissa. "Was your flight okay? Tell me everything."

Marissa squeezed Ocky with all the strength she had, then let her go. "The flight was fine. I wish I'd planned a stopover in Honolulu, though. The island looked very inviting."

As they made their way to baggage claim, Marissa chattered about the cabin service and how tired she was while recognizing the old familiar feeling of low-level excitement that meant Ocky was near. She hadn't expected that—Linda was still sharply etched in her mind, but her feelings for Ocky apparently hadn't changed.

In fact, nothing seemed to have changed. The cold winter was the same chilling fog, the traffic just as clogged and Ocky as focused on business as ever. Nothing had changed. *Except me.*

"So I'm thinking this women's network is the best thing we've gotten into so far. I want to try a kind of Tupperware party con-cept—group signups and support."

Normally, Marissa would have eagerly discussed the possibilities but instead she said, "Can we talk about it tomorrow? I'd like my vacation to last just one more day. Well, what's left of it."

"Oh. Okay." Ocky didn't say anything for a few minutes, leaving Marissa to worry she'd pissed her off. Well, if she had, Ocky would get over it.

The clock in Ocky's vintage Rambler didn't work. "What time is it here?"

Ocky glanced at her watch. "Four-seventeen."

"Huh. It's tomorrow in Tahiti, not quite noon. We'd be having fruit soup and a glass of wine."

"We?" Ocky changed lanes to enter the approach to the Bay Bridge. "Damn good thing it's Sunday or you'd be taking BART."

"A friend and I. We stayed on Huahine instead of going back to Papeete with everyone else. I wasn't ready to end my vacation in spite of having only the clothes on my back. Well, I did have clean underthings. I'll have to thank my mom."

"A fate worse than death. Was she attractive, this friend?"

Glad that Ocky's attention was on the traffic, Marissa fought back a blush. "Yes, she was very beautiful. Kind of Xena-esque, or Wonder Woman. The best thing about her was her sense of humor though. We had a really relaxed time together. She taught me how to snorkel."

"You, snorkeling?"

Miffed that Ocky seemed so skeptical, Marissa protested, "Hey, I got good at it. We could walk out of the bungalow, across a hundred feet of white sand and into the lagoon where there was loads of fish and turtles. It changed every tide."

"Wow. That sounds fabulous. Like paradise."

Marissa sighed. "It was. Did you know it takes about two hours to whack open a coconut?"

Glad to have diverted Ocky from the topic of who she'd stayed with, Marissa alternated between animated descriptions of the island and bouts of sleepiness. The familiar landscape whisked by. She wondered, idiotically she told herself, if there'd be a message on her answering machine from Linda.

Ocky helped her with the duffle up to her door and gave her another enthusiastic hug. "Well, it sounds like you had a great time in spite of it all. I'm glad you're back safely, really."

"Oh, me too, believe me." She returned Ocky's hug and caught herself inhaling the scent of Ocky's cologne. "Thanks a lot for the airport pick up. If I'd taken the train I'd have woken up at the end of the line."

"Sleep in tomorrow if you need to," was Ocky's parting advice.

Marissa watched her oldest and dearest friend lightly run down the stairs, firm legs wrapped into snug-fitting leggings topped by an eye-catching sweater that highlighted her slenderness. Yes, the attraction to Ocky was still there but at the moment it felt like a habit she might finally be able to break.

There were three messages on her answering machine, all from her mother. She clicked through the expressions of concern, trying not to be disappointed that Linda hadn't called. Linda was on her way to New Zealand—was there by now. She would hear from her in a couple of days. A postcard, a note, a call—something.

Fighting a sense of dread, she dialed her mother. With relief she heard the voice mail greeting. "Hi, Mom. I'm home safe and sound but totally exhausted. I'm going right to sleep. Talk to you later this week."

She managed to stay awake until seven, heeding advice that the best way to fight jetlag was to get back to the sleep pattern of her time zone as quickly as possible. Hot tomato soup was a far cry from seafood gazpacho and she made a sleepy vow to do better in all of her bad habits.

She showered, brushed her teeth, combed her hair. Was very glad she'd put clean sheets on the bed before leaving. She sank blissfully into her own bed, the familiar smells, light and sounds—sleep came in like a wave, floating her to dreamland.

Blinking in the unwelcome glare of the bathroom light, Marissa stepped off the scale. Stepped back on. Stepped off again and went in search of a new battery for the thing.

She popped open her first Diet Coke of the day on her way back to the bathroom but held off taking a sip until she squared away the scale. She wanted to know what the damage was from the trip so she could add the pounds to her ever-present weight loss goals.

New battery in place, she stepped back on the scale. Stepped off again. Something wasn't right. Stepped on—there was no way she'd *lost* nine pounds. They'd been eating constantly. No hellacious exercise, just the paddling in the lagoon and walks on the beach. Yet the scale didn't change its result.

Even after she'd consumed more than half the Diet Coke, the scale didn't change. Remembering what Linda had said about eating in the morning made her unearth a box of cereal. She ate the rice squares in the car on her way to the office.

"You look fantastic!" Heather greeted Marissa like a long-lost sister. "Octavia said you were tanned and gorgeous and she was right."

Flushing, Marissa had a hard time believing Ocky had said anything of the sort. "Oh, she says that about all the girls."

Pushing her way through the master doors to the bullpen she was greeted by shouts of "Surprise!" and a barrage of camera flashes.

Damien, who could sell computer matchmaking to monks, was using his tape dispenser as a microphone. "Bob Blowhard reporting from the homecoming celebration for local hero Marissa Chabot. So tell us, Miss Chabot, how does it feel to be back from your harrowing adventure?"

"It feels great, Bob, really great." She grinned at the gathered staff, noting the pineapples stuck on the ends of all the cube dividers. "The Professor created huts for us out of palm leaves and then a suave financier whisked me away on her yacht to safety."

There was a lot of hooting, hugging and laughing as she made her way to her office. More than one person commented on her tan and several pointed out her hair had taken on some golden highlights.

"You should keep those," Bianca advised, her perfectly coiffed head tipped to one side. "You look much less serious."

It was a bit of a come down to discover her desk piled deep with paperwork. Ocky was right—the women's business network they'd finally worked their way into was proving a good source of clients. There were concerns from staff about the relative slowness with which clients were getting back their composite profile results. There were numerous concerns about security on the SQL server.

By the middle of the day she was immersed in the job again as if she'd never left. A knock on her doorjamb brought her out of her focus on the last polling reports.

"A bunch of us are going to the Iron Horse Cafe—wanna come along?" Heather brushed a nervous hand through her hair.

Marissa started to say she didn't have time but she knew if she stayed at her desk she'd eat the two candy bars in the drawer and have a headache by three. "Sure. I could use a break."

On the walk to the nearby deli, Marissa answered questions about the shipwreck—yes, it was terrifying, no, they'd not seen any sharks—and found herself enjoying the fresh air. She'd always thought it a bit far to go but today they seemed to arrive in no time.

Just as she was about to order her usual burger and fries she spotted wrapped packages of sushi. A bowl of vegetable beef soup and the sushi was very appealing.

"No way," Heather said. "You're going to eat raw fish?"

"Actually . . ." Marissa peered at the package. "I don't think there's anything raw in this one. Next time I'll get the *nigiri*."

"You are blowing my mind. Where's the Marissa who wouldn't even try California Roll?" Heather bit into her thick chicken salad sandwich.

"Gone, I hope. The seafood was fantastic on the island and I had no idea tuna had a couple of different parts that are different colors and textures. I'm thirty-four and I've discovered raw fish."

"I was thinking you were back on a diet." Bianca pushed her glasses back up her nose. "That's very light fare, overall."

"Actually, I lost weight. Apparently being shipwrecked is a great diet plan. I don't want to blow a trend so . . ." She indicated her meal. "But I don't think I can fit in a couple hours of snorkeling a day, and a long walk."

"I've been thinking about joining a gym." Heather's struggles with her weight paralleled Marissa's own. They probably wore the same size, but Heather was three inches taller.

Before Marissa really thought about it, she heard herself say, "I will if you will."

"Really? I just can't make myself do it alone."

"Sure. I really will do it."

"There's a women's gym on the other side of the freeway," Heather said eagerly. "I checked it out a few weeks ago and it didn't seem at all like a meat market. Lots of ordinary women there. No skinny bitches."

"Hey," Bianca said.

"You're not a skinny bitch," Heather said quickly. "I know how hard you work to stay thin."

"It's not thin I'm after." Bianca chewed another bite of her chopped salad. "Some of us are born cheetahs but I was born a wildebeest. I'm just trying to make sure the cheetahs can't catch me."

"Cheetahs? Like who?" One of the sales reps Marissa didn't know well looked up from her burger.

"Not who—what. My personal cheetahs are heart disease and diabetes. They run in the family." Bianca shrugged. "I want to see my kids graduate high school. I want to be able to chase my grand-kids some day and not have a wheezing fit."

Heather nodded at Bianca over her soda. "I want to wear two sizes smaller by the time of my five-year reunion this summer."

I don't want to be a helpless fat chick for the rest of my life, Marissa nearly said aloud. Given everything that had happened with Linda, she hadn't thought much about that moment in the hotel bathroom when she hadn't recognized herself in the mirror. *I don't want to be helpless. I want to be strong too.*

Someday soon Linda would show up and when she did Marissa wanted to be able to keep up with whatever adventures Linda might propose. She finished her sushi and soup lost in thought. Joining a gym couldn't hurt, that was for sure.

Heather eagerly proposed going to the nearby gym right after work, before they lost their nerve. Marissa thought the club felt comfortable with only women clients.

A perky, size-three trainer named Pinny showed them the basic set up and explained the class schedule for spin and aerobic classes.

Marissa was musing that spin classes sounded more like dance when she realized they were structured stationary cycle workouts. Okay . . . she had some learning to do.

"Let me show you something." Pinny led them to a small table outside the locker room. "This is what five pounds of fat looks like."

Marissa examined the painted Styrofoam model that Pinny was holding in both hands. Lumpy and dun brown, it wasn't pretty to look at and was about the size of a bread box. But she was certain she had five pounds of fat on each thigh alone and Pinny's model was three times the size of either of her thighs.

"And this is what five pounds of muscle looks like." Now the model was a trim coil about the size of Marissa's upper arm. "See the difference? Sleek, and compact—this is what a regular aerobic workout can do for you. Turn this fat into this muscle."

Marissa knew a sales pitch when she heard one and wasn't surprised when Pinny drew up a plan that included three months of intensive training. The price tag was over two thousand dollars and even though she was totally motivated, she balked at the idea of that kind of investment. Heather couldn't possibly afford that either.

"Can't we join up and have someone show us what the machines do and propose a basic, safe workout?"

Pinny looked quite crestfallen but Marissa resisted the urge to make her feel better by getting out a credit card. She wanted to be more healthy—why did she feel like she was buying a used car?

"We do have basic enrollment but your results won't be all they could be."

"Could you show us those figures? And prices for training on an as-needed basis?"

"Sure." Her smile greatly dimmed, Pinny reached for a different binder. Sounding more like Eeyore than Tigger, she added, "It's our most popular plan."

Heather bounced her way to her car after they'd paid their initial fee. "Thank you so much for going with me! I'd have never asked to be shown something else for prices but no way could I afford all those lessons. I'd have made some excuse and left without intending to go back. Thank you *so* much. You are just the best boss ever!"

Startled by the quick hug that accompanied Heather's bouncing, Marissa let herself laugh. "If you hadn't been there I'd have done the same thing. But we're motivated and ready to go. So tomorrow bring a gym bag, baggy sweats and a ripped T-shirt and we'll go after work."

"I am totally with you. No primping for the gym. Not for at least the first twenty-five pounds!"

Marissa opted for the grocery store instead of the drive-thru and ended up having a low-fat frozen dinner. She sorted her laundry while it microwaved and discovered, with a rush of nostalgic tears, that she had Linda's T-shirt, the pale green one with the dog dressed in snorkeling gear. She would look forward to the chance to return it. Meanwhile . . . she wouldn't put it under her pillow or anything like that. At least not until after she'd washed it.

The lean dinner was somewhat satisfying but she only had so much willpower, however, and so chased it with two scoops of her favorite Phish Food frozen yogurt. She enjoyed every bite of her treat and didn't think—at least not often—that it would have all tasted better if there'd been a message from Linda.

Dear Linda:

Real life arrived and it feels weird. I can still feel the sun and you. I miss you and I wish I were there or you were here.

I've decided to join a gym with a coworker because I think next time I'd like to help other people up the cliff instead of being helped myself.

Love,

Marissa, Day 1 without you

P.S.   I think "love" is the right word. I wish I'd had the courage to use it when you could hear me say it.

❧

"I'm so glad you've decided to resume our work. I'm also looking forward to hearing about your travels." Dr. Kirkland quietly shut her door behind Linda, who moved comfortably across the office to the sunny window nook.

"Suddenly it was rather clear that there was more work to do." She set her day pack at her feet as she oozed down into one of the two oversized chairs.

"Do you want to tell me about that?"

Linda grinned. "Yeah. That would be why I made the appointment."

Dr. Kirkland smiled back. "I had to start somewhere, even if it was a silly question. So what happened?"

"Marissa happened."

"You met someone special."

"Yeah. Very. I noticed her right away in the lifeboat. She had this great sense of humor—"

"Lifeboat?" Dr. Kirkland shook her head. "I'm sorry I interrupted you, Linda, but I think you've left out something important."

Laughter bubbled past Linda's lips. "The cruise ship I was on sank in the middle of our first night out."

"That's sounds traumatic."

"It wasn't—see, that's the thing. It wasn't traumatic at all. Marissa and other people were looking to me to help. First, I could translate some of the Italian to English. And I'd read all those survivalist books the last time I was at that place, you know?" Dr. K nodded and Linda continued, "I felt very confident and competent and that was what Marissa seemed to need from me. I don't think she really noticed what I looked like until after . . . she liked me."

Dr. Kirkland nodded with an edge of excitement. "Yes, I can see how that would really feel good to you. That's one of your bigger issues, not being certain why people are attracted to you as either friends or lovers."

"Well, this was obviously not about how I looked, but what I could do. What I did. It was great. I'd never felt better. Marissa's chunky and doesn't work out so there was a cliff everyone had to climb and I didn't think she could do it but I encouraged her and talked to her while she tried and dang!" Linda wanted to laugh just remembering how wonderful it had felt to watch Marissa succeed. "She needed a little push and I did a little pulling at the end but she did it. And laughed when it was over. I think I fell for her right then."

Dr. Kirkland made a note on the left side of her tablet. Linda remembered notes made there would be shared at the end of the session. Notes on the right probably not. "So you spent time together and feelings emerged?"

"Yeah. We spent a few days just hanging out in Tahiti. I wasn't watching myself talk to her. I was *talking* to her. And it went on for all the days we were together. I didn't have any nightmares or sleep problems either."

"You were off your meds?"

"Had been since they ran out—maybe six months?" Linda shrugged. "I started sleeping badly again but it wasn't bad enough to try to get more."

"I'd say you felt safe with Marissa. But not in a purely platonic way?"

"No, I wanted . . . she's really engaging. With this inner humor and zest and I kept thinking about what it would be like to be with her. I was afraid I'd freak her out, though. I didn't want to tell her about my mother and . . . that stuff. And I didn't want to just . . ." Linda frowned.

"Go to bed with her and dissociate?"

"I didn't want to just do her, yeah. The last night I thought well, okay, it would turn out like all the other times I'd tried but at least I could give her something she wanted because she did want me to touch her. At least we could have that memory. I turned off the lights because sometimes I don't go away as quickly."

Dr. Kirkland nodded and Linda relaxed even more. Whether she recalled all the details of Linda's case file from three years ago or not, Dr. Kirkland seemed to be catching up rapidly. "And how was it?"

With a feeling of profound relief, Linda said, "I didn't go away at all. Even when . . . she made love to me. I stayed. I felt connected to my body the whole time."

Dr. Kirkland sat back in her chair with a blinding smile. "That's absolutely fantastic. A major breakthrough. And how did that feel?"

Linda stuck her tongue out. "How do you think it felt?"

"You're supposed to tell me, remember?"

Shifting in her seat so she could tuck one leg under her, Linda answered, "It felt great. I realized what I'd been missing."

After making another note on the left, Dr. Kirkland asked, "So, why are you here?"

"Because she had to go home. I had a ticket to run away more. And on the flight I took there was this woman who flirted with me and I did all the things I've always done."

"One great sexual experience doesn't undo the habits and security behavior of two decades, Linda. Why don't you tell me what happened."

"It was just . . ." She shrugged. "One of those random things. She wasn't even gay—not that she was telling herself anyway. So we were in the airport and starting to get to it. I got clinical— remember? You pointed out how when I don't feel safe I get very clinical as the first step to dissociating?" After the other woman nodded, Linda continued, "I noticed what was going on all around us, if other people would figure out what we were doing, things like that."

"Controlling what you could."

Linda nodded. "And I might not have gone away except . . . she called me beautiful."

One eyebrow went up. "That word has always troubled you."

"But this time it didn't irritate me and so I went away."

When Linda didn't go on, Dr. Kirkland prompted softly with, "What was different this time?"

"It was as if this woman pressed a button. She'd hardly said the word and I was on the ceiling, watching."

"So the word triggered the dissociation, you think? Not the situation, but the word?"

"Yeah. Marissa never said it. She said I was strong." A tiny headache started behind Linda's eyes but she had expected it. Her first two months of therapy had left her with blinding migraines that she felt were a by-product of trying so hard to "see" into her brain, so to speak. "After—in the airport—I felt remote for a long time. I didn't like it. I wanted to feel the way I had with Marissa."

"That's important, you know that, right?"

Linda nodded.

"Important because you know you're capable of feeling more than distant and remote. When we first met you told me being disconnected was the way you were made."

"I didn't want to talk to you."

"Oh, I remember." Dr. Kirkland smiled. "So what did you do about wanting to feel different?"

"I want to have a chance with Marissa. So I came home."

"You didn't go to her? Why do you think you chose to come here instead?"

"Because." Linda rolled her eyes. "Because I knew I needed to talk to you some more. And I could sponge off my mother while I fixed the rest of it."

"So you've seen your mother?"

101

"I went there from the airport. Burst into her office in front of some clients. I made a big stir because someone called security." She chewed on her thumbnail as she recalled the flicker of emotions on her mother's face. "I don't even think she was angry."

"Did you want her to be?"

"No. I don't need anything from her . . ." Linda's voice trailed away. "I mean . . . yes. I guess I did want her to be angry. I wanted to push her buttons for once. She pushes mine every day. But I thought I was past wanting emotion out of her. I didn't get what I wanted, I guess."

Dr. Kirkland made another note on the left before asking, "So how does it feel to be living in your old house?"

"Weird. Familiar, but weird. The rooms are all in the same place of course but she changed all the decorations—probably more than once. Marshall, her long-time escort, is still around, I guess. I still think he's gay. Can I ask you a question?"

"Sure."

"Are you still married?"

Neither eyebrow moved but Linda was certain Dr. Kirkland was dying to arch one of them. "That's a little personal, don't you think? We talked about boundaries."

"I know. I'm not sure why I asked. Do you have a therapist? I mean, it must be hard to hear everybody's problems all the time."

There was humor in Dr. Kirkland's eyes. Linda for the first time realized that, in the three years since she'd seen her therapist, gray had edged into Dr. Kirkland's temples and the divots where her glasses rested on her nose were even deeper.

They had both gotten older. I've gotten older, she thought, I'm not fourteen anymore.

"Yes," Dr. Kirkland said. "There's someone I talk to about how my work affects me and other things in my life. Empathy is very important for me to keep alive but it's useless if I can't also maintain enough distance to notice things my clients might not."

"I get that." Linda straightened up in the chair. "So when are you going to tell me what you've been writing on the left side?"

After her eyes flicked to the clock only she was in a position to see, Dr. Kirkland said, "There's time. I think it might spur some more discussion."

"I'm listening. And I promise not to ask how anything made you feel."

"Thanks so much," Dr. Kirkland said dryly. "When we first started working together it took us a while to get little Linda to talk, remember?"

"Yeah, I remember. She had a lot of feelings she didn't have words for. She was really angry too."

"One of the reasons you gave me when you left a few years ago was that you thought little Linda had nothing more to say. I think you were right. You made wonderful, thoughtful progress. Accepting the things that happened to little Linda and dealing with her hurt and anger has left you capable of dealing with the world in a more healthy way. Some compulsive behavior remains but overall you're well on your way to healing your wounds."

"I can hear the *but* coming."

"You're back here, talking to me. Little Linda isn't the one sitting in the chair. Adult Linda has a few things bothering her, I think, but nothing I think she needs me to listen to."

Linda tipped her head to one side. "Who else is there?"

"I think I've been talking to a teenager for a while. She's angry and confrontational—not with me, but with her mother. Your body language has a touch of defiance. Lots of 'yeah' and 'I mean like.' I've never seen you chew your fingernails before."

Linda swallowed and her headache got worse.

"You're getting a headache, aren't you?"

"Yes. It just got a lot worse."

"I think teenage Linda is ready to talk to adult Linda. You're ready to deal with whatever it was that put you over the edge the first time."

Closing her eyes, Linda flashed on that disturbing, repeating loop of her mother offering her a plate of food. "I don't think so. I'm not ready."

"Don't force it. Do you want to come back day after tomorrow and talk? I can put you at the end of the day."

Her headache eased as she realized she wouldn't have to talk anymore. "Okay, yes."

Dr. Kirkland closed her notebook. "You've made great progress, Linda. There's more work to do but I think we're digging deep."

"My mother is probably going to set up a competency hearing again."

The smile Dr. Kirkland gave her was tinged with an odd kind of pleasure. "Well, your mother can just bring it on."

Linda was halfway through a cheeseburger and chocolate shake before the true import of Dr. Kirkland's final words sank in. Dr. K didn't think she was crazy.

She stood in front of a pay phone for the longest time, looking at the bright piece of blue silk and the paper with Marissa's phone number. But what would she say? Sorry, I won't be visiting soon. Sorry, I'm not where I told you I'd be. Sorry, I'm not who you think I am.

The call could wait. Maybe everything would fix itself quickly and her mother would finally realize, like Dr. K, that she wasn't crazy.

Chapter 8

"Well, don't you look relaxed!"

"Thank you, Mom," Marissa said automatically. She gave her mother the obligatory kiss then sat down at the empty chair at their table for two. Sunday brunch at the club *was* a treat but even after a week of being home, Marissa didn't quite feel adjusted to the time. It had been very, very hard to get up.

"Joanne, is this your daughter who was shipwrecked?" An elegantly coiffed woman paused at their table to examine Marissa with interest.

"Yes, this is my daughter Marissa. She's just back from Tahiti. Marissa, this is my dear friend—I've spoken of her so often . . ."

Marissa made appropriate responses and thought longingly of hot coffee. The hovering waiter wouldn't intrude on the conversation. She didn't mean to be rude but couldn't help but pick up the menu to see what was offered. Like every day since she'd started working out, she was starving.

When she'd made up her mind, she studied her mother, taking in the perfectly turned out white hair, the age-defying makeup and the crisply starched linen blouse. If her mother ever gave her half a chance, she'd tell anyone that she thought her mom was terribly good looking and yes, in her opinion, this apple had fallen a long way from her mother's tree. She could try forever and not achieve that kind of classy elegance.

Then again, she wasn't sure how her mother's carefully constructed world would have fared in a shipwreck. Oh, she'd have climbed that cliff easily, no doubt about that. But without a stylist handy?

Marissa allowed she was likely being unfair to her mother, who was strong-willed and successful. She was just also quite annoying at times.

Her mother's friend took leave of them after a minute of trading gossip that sounded competitive to Marissa's ear. Marissa was relieved her mother didn't seem annoyed that Marissa had stayed out of the conversation for the most part.

"Everything looks wonderful," Marissa said, indicating the menu. "I think I'll have the eggs Benedict."

"Do you really think you should? It's got all that butter, dear."

"I joined a gym this week, so I think I deserve a little treat."

"Oh?" Her mother skepticism was obvious. "Why not come to the one here at the club? I'm sure the equipment is excellent. Your guest privileges are still good."

"I joined with a coworker so we could encourage each other."

"That reminds me of my old sorority. It was always nice to have someone to do things with. If there was no beau around on a Saturday night a group of us would go to the movies."

"I'm not going to the gym because I don't have anything else to do, Mom. I'm trying to get more fit."

"Better late than never. Your father waited too long."

"I know." Marissa hoped her mollifying tone would derail the usual rant.

"He never listened to me—first the heart attack and I'm sure that's what made the cancer move so fast. Even after . . . he moved elsewhere, he could have still used the fitness services here, just like you could."

Sure, Marissa wanted to say, Dad would have been welcome here. Shifting under her mother's piercing gaze, she said instead, "The gym is only five minutes from work. If I had to drive all the way out here I'd not go as often."

"Whatever you think best."

"Thank you for your advice, Mom. I work late sometimes and my gym is twenty-four hours."

"Of course." Her mother's perfectly lipsticked mouth curved in one of the smiles that made Marissa expect a new criticism. "I'm sure you thought it through."

"I did." The waiter arrived with a gleaming silver coffee pot and filled Marissa's cup after she nodded. She ordered the eggs Benedict with sliced melon on the side. She wondered from what ocean her father must have spawned to have given her the genes she had. Her mother ordered the spirulina smoothie, the New York platter—lox, bagel, cream cheese—and a chocolate muffin. None of it would show on her petite figure.

"So how are things at the gallery? Have you made new discoveries?"

The bright smile she received told Marissa she'd asked the right question. "Egyptian themes are back in, just as I thought they'd be, and I already have a small collection of paintings to offer. But I'm really intrigued by a young man from the city who uses light-sensitive plates to create the most interesting forms. He calls them fractal reflections. I love them—won't make much money I suppose. They're a little too arty for way out here in Blackhawk."

"They sound interesting," Marissa said sincerely. She had nothing but respect for her mother's taste in art. Her father had even admitted that he'd first been attracted to Joanne's artistic sense. "Have you ever thought of running a gallery in San Francisco?"

That topic lasted through most of breakfast and part of the time Marissa was aware of her detachment from her mother's hopes and dreams. How much, at this point in her life, was that a self-fulfilling prophecy? She offered only a little bit about her life for review and was generally never disappointed when her mother showed only a little bit of interest.

She realized too late her mother had asked her a question. "I'm sorry, I was thinking about having some strawberries."

"You haven't said a word about your vacation and it was so dramatic."

"It was, Mom, and thank you again for the gift. It was very generous of you. In spite of everything, I had a great time."

"I was hoping you'd meet someone interesting."

"I did," Marissa said before she thought better of it.

"Really?" Her mother's eyes—eerily similar to those that looked back at Marissa from every mirror—glowed with intrigue. "What's his name?"

So there it was, thirty-four years old, Marissa mused, and just a fawn caught in her mother's Mack truck headlights. So she wasn't all that close to her mother but she wasn't prepared to be even more distant. Thirty-four, independent and still afraid of her mother—pathetic.

The waiter warmed up their coffee, allowing Marissa a few more seconds to evaluate her entire life, her father's life, relive the terrifying early hours in the lifeboat and the feel of Linda's hair on her thighs.

"What's his name? Where does he live?"

"Mom." Marissa cleared her throat. "There was this short time while we were abandoning ship that I didn't think I was going to survive. I thought about what really mattered to me. Like I spent all that time trying to choose the perfect books to take with me and that ended up being completely unimportant. Sitting in a lifeboat with no land in sight made me realize that it's not all that important what brand of rum is in my glass or whether my living room is Country French or Nouveau Deco."

Her smile fixed, her mother said, "Please tell me it's not Country French."

"I'm not talking about decorating."

Marissa saw the acceptance in her mother's face before she spoke again. She knows, Marissa realized. She's known all along. "I met a woman. I've always preferred women. And I want this woman to be in my life."

There was a prolonged silence while her mother sat frozen in place. Only the fingers wrapped around the stem of her champagne glass moved slightly.

"I'm sorry if that disappoints you," Marissa said. She had expected to feel relieved to have finally spoken the truth but her mother's reaction mattered. It shouldn't, she thought. You're old enough for it not to matter. But it did. Yes, while hanging off that cliff face she had accepted that nothing but living the exact life her mother desired would ever gain approval. She knew she would never live that life. But that didn't mean more proof of her mother's disdain for the life she did lead wouldn't hurt.

"Well, this is not what I expected to talk about over a nice brunch."

"I just came out to you and all you can say is it's not a good topic for brunch?"

"What do you expect me to say?"

Bitterly, but mindful to keep her voice low, Marissa replied, "How about I love you for who you are? But you never have, so that's a pipe dream."

She picked up her purse and knew that her attempt to accessorize had gone either unnoticed or dismissed as poorly done. Likely the latter; her mother would consider it poor breeding to remark on it negatively.

"You always were more *his*."

"We loved each other, if that matters."

Her exit from the club restaurant was sedate even though Marissa thought there must be steam blasting from both ears.

Dear Dad:

I guess that Mom took my news better than she did

from you. So far, nothing has been thrown at me and she didn't scream that I'd ruined her life. Of course, I told her in a crowded restaurant with friends and rivals nearby. What could she do? The only better place would have been in church, between the Hallelujah and the Amen.

Love, Marissa

P.S.   I don't think I ever realized how much courage it took for you to finally tell her—and me—the truth. I'm proud of us both.

Pinny had promised that working out reduced stress, so Marissa decided a workout was what she needed. The gym was crowded and she had to wait for some of the equipment. Given that she had hated to sweat and exercise her entire life, it was extremely vexing that she *did* feel better when she was done.

◈

Linda wanted to be anywhere but in the chilly conference room provided by her mother's attorney. Her own attorney sat still as the dead. Maybe he was dead.

Three weeks of big headaches and she was no closer to finding out what teenage Linda might want Dr. Kirkland to know. It had to do with her mother but she couldn't make herself describe that recurring image of her mother handing her a plate of food. She couldn't think why it mattered. It was all she remembered. How could it be meaningful? Yet . . . she wouldn't tell Dr. Kirkland about it either. So it had to be important.

The door opposite opened and her mother swept into the room followed by her lawyer in his very expensive suit. Linda didn't look under the table but she guessed his loafers were alligator.

The two attorneys exchanged pleasantries while Linda just looked at her mother, who made a great show of caring about what was being said.

They ran into each other every day at her mother's house and exchanged no words at all. There was no resemblance between them that Linda had ever seen but then the plastic surgeries had begun at six. She would never have that sharp, hawk nose. Looking at her mother in this cold room made her shiver and she heard the echo of her little girl self asking, "What's wrong with my ears? Why is the doctor going to cut them?"

"They ought to lie flat against your head. I don't know why I didn't see it sooner. I think that's why the other girl won last night."

"She was very pretty."

"Pretty is easy. We're not aspiring to be pretty," her mother had said firmly. "We're going to be beautiful."

Linda stared down at her interlaced fingers and saw she was gripping them so tightly they'd gone white. But that memory wasn't new. She had gotten over it, hadn't she?

"So, let's get down to business." Linda hadn't caught the name of her mother's lawyer but in her mind he was Alligator. "A rapidly scheduled competency hearing is in everyone's best interest."

"How so?" Tiny Crawdad, her lawyer, did his best to sound belligerent but it wasn't very effective.

"Because if there's any delay, my client will press charges for the fraudulent use of her credit cards to the tune of thousands of dollars over the last three years."

"I had permission! And if she wasn't holding up my inheritance I wouldn't be living off of her." Her lawyer made a shushing gesture and Linda subsided.

Okay, she thought, that was teenaged Linda. I can't let my mother, or her lawyer, do that to me, make me fourteen again. I don't have to take it.

"What's the basis for the claim my client isn't competent to handle her financial affairs?"

"She's itinerant and has made no attempt to learn any of the facets of its management."

In spite of a warning gesture from her lawyer, Linda said, "I used to ask questions but I never received any answers."

Her lawyer gave her a severe look and Linda subsided. Say nothing, she told herself. Everything they say is a lie and you'll never change their minds.

"Finishing schooling at least through a graduate degree was agreed upon as a sign of competence when she was released from Shady Lawns. She never finished, even after my client paid for two years at Yale."

"The loony bin, you mean. There were no lawns and it is never shady indoors." Dr. Kirkland, Linda wailed to herself, I'm still crazy . . . she still makes me crazy. And she hasn't said a word! Helpless to stop herself from speaking, Linda rushed on, "I didn't finish because I had to have surgery and by the time I recovered the semester had ended and I got deferred but then Mommy Dearest withheld funds and I couldn't afford to finish the degree the following year. Because of her assets and my supposed inheritance I couldn't qualify for any kind of aid. And the surgery I had to have was because the remnant of one of my floating ribs pierced my spleen."

"I don't think this is productive." Linda's lawyer got abruptly to his feet. "Send your motions over and we'll respond."

Still speaking to her mother's lawyer, Linda said fiercely, "If you had a daughter, would you have let someone remove her lower ribs when she was eight?"

Alligator gave her a stone-faced look in return and then held the door for her mother, still silent, to exit ahead of him.

After the door closed, Tiny Crawdad sighed heavily.

"I know, I know. I shouldn't talk." Linda put her head down on her folded hands. "But I'm tired of not talking. Of not being allowed to talk."

Matter-of-factly, he said, "This is what we're going to do. You're going to resume your normal life and I'll delay them. I really don't think they have a case here but it doesn't hurt for you to show that you're well past the trouble you had during and after college. We'll file a motion to force her to relinquish control of your funds."

Linda nodded. "You must hear this a million times a day but the

112

trouble I've had all goes back to my mother. That sounds pathetically clichéd, I know." She turned her head slightly to study him for the first time. He'd been a name on a local bar association list. He was older than she had first thought, perhaps in his late fifties.

"I hear that a lot, you're right. I have two daughters, and no, I'd not have let anyone take out their lower ribs unless their lives depended on it."

"My life didn't depend on it. I think my mother thought hers did, though." She stood abruptly and pulled her sweater up to reveal her midriff. Putting her hands on her waist, she pressed inward, slowly collapsing her waist to its smallest circumference. "It's called a wasp waist. Not only does it create an enviable waistline, muscles in the buttocks are elongated and flattened, see?"

Crawdad—not so tiny in her estimation any longer—looked shocked more than anything else. "How small is your waist as a result?"

"My last pageant it corseted down to about sixteen inches. I stopped cinching it after that. I mean . . . that was when . . . it was a little bit after that when I went to the first institution." She hadn't told him much about the teenage episode with the bottle of pills because he'd said it wasn't admissible in an adult's competency hearing. "Fast forward to my second year at Yale Business School and I got smacked by a soccer ball just right and a point of bone left from the surgery perforated some of my innards. I developed an infection throughout my GI, lost forty pounds and was wasted for four months." Sometimes she wondered if she might have been able to graduate and get her life together had that not happened.

But it had been too big a blow, not to be able to go back to the courses she'd liked and finish them. On top of that, the flashbacks on her childhood surgeries escalated into night terrors. She'd had nothing to build a normal life on. Dr. Kirkland had helped her at least become functional again.

What had she been thinking she could even offer Marissa? Marissa owned a business and was incredibly smart with statistics and computers. Linda had nothing, nothing at all to give.

"I'm really sorry for what you've been through," Crawdad said, then looked surprised at himself. "I don't think you have anything to worry about."

"My therapist thinks I'm not crazy." A new thought occurred to her, something she hadn't told him. "Besides, this isn't about my competence or even the money. It's about me not talking. She offered me the whole deal before I took off last time."

"Why didn't you take it?"

"Because I had to sign an agreement that I'd never tell. Things like I just told you."

"Surely, though bordering on a kind of child abuse, your mother isn't that worried about her reputation."

Linda was quiet for a few moments then said with a quiver in her voice. "You're right, that's not enough for her to go to these lengths. She cares about the Price family reputation a lot, but then again, she had me in pageants, which is not what the blue bloods around here do to score points with each other. She was making me beautiful for reasons of her own. I mean, I'm not the only one who needed therapy. So reputation isn't everything. There must be . . ." Wrinkles creased her forehead as she tried to find the right words. "There must be another reason for her to expend so much effort on me. But I don't know what it is."

It repeated again in her mind: her mother tidied up the counter, then turned to her with the white plate heaped with food. That's all she saw in her memory.

"Are you going to be okay?" Crawdad—Ted Jeffers, she remembered—touched her gently on the back of her hand.

"Yes. If I work on it, yes."

Hours later, after nursing a cup of diner coffee for a long time, she took the bus that got closest to Beacon Hill. Her footsteps crunched on the snow-crusted sidewalk and she wanted to be back on that wonderful beach, far away. Marissa had called her strong. She *had* felt powerful but it was so hard not to believe that it was the place, the time, the woman, the island—and not her—that had been strong.

She made herself climb the stone steps, ignoring the last glint of sunlight off the classic window panes of purple, black and white. The Price family had owned the house for two centuries. The Price family was rooted deep in Boston society but Linda had never felt as if she fit. She fingered her cold ears as she made her way into the chilly foyer. Had they really stuck out? She could hear the surgeon discussing the procedure with her mother—not the words, but the tone of voice, so impersonal, as if it was a steak to be sliced and not a little girl.

"Have you returned for the evening, Miss?"

Linda turned with a startled gasp, not used to the new butler's quiet tread. "Yes. I won't be going out again."

"Perhaps you'd like dinner, then? Madam is also in. It will be served in thirty minutes."

The idea of sharing a meal with the woman who hadn't acknowledged her presence at the meeting earlier and had spoken less than a dozen sentences to her since she'd arrived made Linda want to laugh. Butlers behaved as if everything was normal, no matter what happened. "Something hot on a tray, like soup and some bread, will be sufficient. Thank you," she added belatedly.

The echo of her passage up the curving staircase didn't drown out memories of recovery rooms and summer vacations swathed in bandages. She could easily hear the sadist who had perform most of the electrolysis saying over and over, "Just a little sting. Nothing to cry about."

Abruptly she realized her mother was coming down the stairs. Their eyes met—the only feature they remotely had in common. I hope, Linda thought, my eyes are never that cold, that dead. I don't care what made her hurt so much she had to fix it by turning me into a freak show.

Neither of them spoke. The only reason they were even in the same hemisphere was the past, Linda mused. I wouldn't be here if it weren't for the past. She thinks I'm here for the money, though.

And maybe she was. She knew she could—and would—roll up her sleeves and do any job. She only resorted to her mother's credit card for emergencies. Otherwise she'd washed dishes across

Europe and volunteered to grunt supplies for ecotourism firms. She had tried to fill her life with so many experiences that the past went away and her mother's control of money that was rightfully hers ceased to matter. But her mother keeping the money that had been left to Linda was just that—a form of control, and it kept alive a connection between them that Linda wanted to sever. One way or the other, she would not leave here with the issue unresolved. All ties would be broken because that was what Linda wished, not because it suited her mother.

Looking at herself in the bedroom mirror of one of the many guest rooms, she tried to scold herself out of her mulish expression. "You can't let her turn you into a fourteen-year-old again. You're your own woman now. You aren't so afraid of the past that you have to run from it anymore."

Brave words but recalling her ranting at the alligator lawyer shook her belief that she could maintain her resolve. She needed to get out of this house so she could think but she'd used her mother's money for the last time. She felt as if she was held together with rubber bands of reality that were cracked and stretched so thin that one more thing—like finding a job and a place to live she could afford—would snap her in two. Not right now, she thought. *I will be my own woman*. Right now is just transition.

She went to bed early, exhausted as she had been every day since her arrival. She woke sweating, heart pounding and hands clenched over her stomach several hours later, uncertain of what she'd been dreaming then fell asleep again.

This time she heard the saw and smelled the chemicals and dreamed that she woke to find her arms had been swapped for her legs and everyone told her she looked *beautiful*.

She woke for real with her head throbbing, shaking with terrors of nameless monsters.

I want to name them, she told herself. I want to talk. I want to tell.

⟡

"What's wrong with this picture?" Marissa held up both arms for Heather's examination.

Heather studied Marissa from her seat behind the reception desk. "I'm not sure."

"My sleeves are too tight. And the calves of my slacks are too." As hard as she tried, Marissa couldn't keep a whining note out of her voice.

"But that's one of your favorite blouses. You wear it all the time."

"I think," Marissa said with a frown, "I'm lifting too many weights. I like the muscle but so far none of the fat seems to have gone away."

"Are you overdoing it? You go two more days a week than I do."

"I guess I must be but I'm following their accelerated program," Marissa said uncertainly. She was motivated, she was careful about what she ate and she hadn't been rigorous in meeting her goals—all for nothing. "I know Pinny said muscle weighs more than fat and I've gained five pounds. But when does the fat start burning off?"

In the act of checking for her mail, Bianca said, "I saw an ad for some pills last night. They never said what was in them except it was all natural. Yeah, well, I was thinking that arsenic is all natural too. Anyway, a month's supply was one hundred and seventy dollars. Their whole line was that the results would be worth it. The fat would melt off."

"Snake oil. It's all lies," Heather muttered.

"Shipping and handling for this bottle of pills was another twenty bucks, in the fine print. Also in the fine print was a statement that the pills should be taken after consulting with a doctor *and* in conjunction with a low-fat diet and moderate exercise."

"For heaven's sake!" Marissa put her hands on her hips. "That's like saying a bottle of ointment will give you a golden tan but must be used in conjunction with real sunshine. Why do you watch ads like that?"

Bianca shrugged. "Because I want them to be true, I guess."

Tugging unhappily at the blouse's suddenly tight upper sleeves, Marissa said, "I can see that. I mean I'm working out every other day. I could probably pick up a truck but my clothes don't fit."

Heather said, "I think that I'm undoing all the good by having a treat after. To reward myself for going. Sometimes I have the treat before then I don't go." She sighed. "It's been three weeks and I haven't lost an ounce."

Bianca gave them both a sympathetic smile but Marissa didn't think she could possibly understand their frustration. She and Heather were putting out an effort, certainly more than she ever had before in her life and getting nothing back. Marissa felt as if she was doing something wrong instead of something right. The woman in the mirror still didn't look familiar.

On the way back to her office she wrote her thrice-daily missive in her head.

Dear Linda,

I think about you all the time. I'm trying to be ready for when you get here. Ready to say yes again, I guess. Ready to keep up with you. Ready to try for something I've never thought I could have before.

I know I can achieve a lot on my own and I will. But some things would be easier if I could breathe the same air as you for a while every day.

Are you well? Are you safe? Do you remember what I remember?

Love, Marissa, Day 23 without you

If she actually put them to paper she'd have dozens of such letters by now. If Linda knew how sentimental and corny she was—sleeping with a shirt under her pillow—she'd probably be turned off by it.

There was good news in her office, however, in the form of Ocky who met her at the door with a gleeful smile. "I did it—we're going to offer group parties and discounts. No more stigma and shame about using a mate-finding service. Get your friends involved and all that. There's no end to the number of women who don't have time for bad dates. And where the women start enrolling the men follow." Ocky did a little dance. "Want to go have a burger?"

"No—can't do it today. I eat too much."

"But you're working out."

"I'm gaining weight, not losing it."

"When was the last time you ate a package of Oreos? You've totally changed your habits since we left college."

"Too little, too late. I don't need the Oreos anymore," she added without thinking. "Hey—I came out to my mother."

Ocky collapsed into the only chair that wasn't layered with files. "You're kidding."

"Nope. Just told her. Told her that . . ." Oops, she'd nearly mentioned Linda but she'd not told Ocky about Linda. "I told her that someday I hoped to have a woman in my life. I think she already knew. She was angry because she couldn't ignore it any longer."

"That is so totally cool. Good for you. Feeling better now?"

"Not really. I care about her, I guess. I was hoping she'd prove she cared about me." Why had she stopped eating the Oreos after college? She and Ocky had concocted their Finders Keepers scheme and started it all out of Ocky's garage and with Marissa's dead grandmother's trust fund payouts. For the first four years they'd both had dead end jobs. Marissa's had been doing basic systems maintenance at a women's health clinic.

"You're all she's got. I hope she figures that out finally."

Marissa shrugged. "She will or she won't. I think she'd love to brag about me at the club and compare me to other people's kids—live through me a little. But other than surviving a shipwreck, there's little to brag on."

"Only because she's got whacked priorities."

Marissa had to agree and she finally waved Ocky out of her office, eager to make some headway on several fronts.

But as she spent the next several hours sorting through questionnaire feedback in preparation for their next update, she found herself occasionally musing on the role of Oreos in her life.

⤞⤝

"She didn't say a word, not one word, and I was like you said—like a teenager. Deep down I think that if I talk enough, it'll make her angry and she'll break. She doesn't want me to talk. She didn't like me talking to other contestants and certainly not to my teachers about what it was like to be in a pageant. I wrote a paper in high school about it and she had a fit." Curled in one corner of the large chair, Linda couldn't stop one leg from fidgeting as she talked.

Dr. Kirkland was listening intently and nodding. "What do you think she's afraid you'll say?"

"That's worse than all the stuff she had done to me when I was a kid? I don't know."

"But teenage Linda knows, doesn't she?"

Raking one hand through her hair, Linda said, "I think so. When my mother treats me like I'm not there I think, you know, I don't have to take that from her. I don't have to clean my plate. She can't treat me—"

"Back up. Why did you say that?"

"What?" Linda tried to rewind her last few sentences. "That I don't have to take that from her?"

"No, after that."

"She can't treat me that way."

"No." Dr. Kirkland leaned forward, elbows on her knees. "You said you didn't have to clean your plate."

"I did?" Linda winced at the throb that pulsed right below her left cheekbone. "I mentioned a plate?"

"Yes, you did. Last session you said 'clean plate' when you meant 'clean slate.'"

"Slip of the tongue."

Dr. Kirkland didn't say anything at all, just kept that thoughtful, supportive gaze trained on Linda's face.

"It's just a random memory."

"I've always been surprised that you don't have an eating disorder, given how much your mother pushed you about how you looked."

"She never withheld food."

"Encouraged you to eat, even?"

"She was strict about nutrition but sometimes she'd make me a favorite meal. Especially the one time with the plate I keep remembering. The time that . . . *oh*."

Linda didn't think that Dr. Kirkland was breathing. She wasn't sure she was either. She said again, slowly, "The time that . . . she gave me a plate of food. It wasn't lunch. It wasn't dinner. Just a lot of food. Things I liked. She told me to clean my plate."

In a low voice, Dr. Kirkland prompted her with, "Describe every action, everything you remember. If you don't remember just skip to what you do."

"She tidied up the counter. Threw stuff away, that sort of thing. Then she turned to me with the food. It was on a white plate. She handed it to me and I took it. I don't remember after that."

"How old were you?"

"My hands are . . ." Linda glanced down, visualizing her hands as she saw them in the memory. "They're not so tanned as they are now. My fingernails are manicured and painted. So I must have been fourteen or fifteen."

Slowly, Dr. Kirkland repeated back, "She tidied up the counter. Threw stuff away, that sort of thing."

"Yes, that's right." Linda closed her eyes against the rising pain of the headache. "She tossed out the take-out containers and the yeast packet, then turned—O*h*! God."

She saw it then, the red, blue and yellow packet. Saw her mother tear it open and sprinkle most of the contents over Linda's favorite Chinese take-out.

Pressing both hands over her mouth, Linda relived the bloating, the pressure, the urge to vomit. Sweat prickled in a hot flush all over her body. The next thought, even worse, struck across her mind like a lightning bolt: it hadn't been the first time.

Dr. Kirkland was already on her feet, quickly stuffing the wastebasket between Linda's knees even as she wrapped one arm around Linda's shoulders, saying intensely, "I'm so sorry. So very sorry. It makes me so angry that she did that to you. It's okay. You're not there. It's okay."

Linda gulped for air through her hands and swallowed down the burning of bile. Never again. She remembered now. She remembered *everything* and she wouldn't get sick again.

The light in the office had changed by the time she was able to sip some water and breathe more normally.

"It was the first time I saw her do it but then I realized she'd been doing it for years. Every time I lost a pageant I got sick, really sick. I threw up for days. She'd get all this great food for me to tempt my appetite, she said. She took me to doctors, who were mystified. She told pageant people that I'd obviously had food poisoning the night of the competition or else I'd have never lost."

"So you saw her put the yeast on your food?"

"And she told me to clean my plate." Linda swallowed hard. "I took the plate from her and she said a good meal would make me *beautiful*."

"How long after that time that you saw her did you attempt suicide?"

"Probably a week, maybe a little more. The attacks lasted at least that long and I couldn't keep anything down. I kept the pills down." She'd never been sure whether her failure to lock the bathroom door had been an oversight or if she'd really not meant to be successful. Not that the difference mattered to the fallout.

"And she had you committed."

A white-hot bolt of anger split Linda's head in two. "She threw me away into that place because I was her loser daughter. I couldn't win a tiara and she couldn't present me to the world like a prize pet she'd groomed to champion status."

The migraine blossomed into a full aura of red as she finally broke down into wracking sobs. "That's what she did. She made me sick. I can't tell Marissa. I haven't called her. She'll hate me. She couldn't understand."

She cried into the warm shoulder, frightened and hurt and so far down into the pain that it felt as if she'd never crawl out of it again. She felt fourteen. Fifteen. Twenty-one. Twenty-six when that soccer ball had brought back all the memories of all the surgeries she'd endured. All those times when she had thought the pain of living was too much and tried to end everything.

It hurt so damned much. It hurt . . . and she was all alone to bear it, the way little Linda had been alone and teenage Linda had been alone.

It was a while before she could form any other conscious thoughts beyond the depth of the pain and the intensity of the awareness of how lonely the despair had made her all her life. She wasn't alone, though, there was a thoughtful, supportive and caring woman hugging her, someone who believed what she'd said. She wasn't alone.

"If I can understand, then anyone can, Linda. Anyone who cares about you will be able to listen to your story, hurt for you and understand."

"Yes, but if I told Marissa, it would be like letting my mother hurt her too."

"You don't *have* to tell anyone at all. The only person who needs honesty is you. Your mother hurt you, she hurt you badly. But you survived. You survived and did whatever it took to hold that secret back until now. Now you can handle it."

"No," Linda said between shudders. "No, I can't bear this. It hurts all over again."

"Yes, it does. It hurts just as bad as it did all those other times. The pain you feel is the beginning of healing it. If I gave you a pill right now and told you if you took it you'd die in minutes, what would you do?"

Linda knew right away but it was more than a few seconds before she could work her surprised answer past her lips. "I wouldn't take it."

"No, you wouldn't. You're strong enough for the pain now. That's why you remembered."

Linda slumped in the seat. Her brain felt bruised from the inside and her vision blurred in waves of red. Weakly, she said, "I wish I could sleep."

"I don't do this often, but I have a spare room clients sometimes use. I really think you shouldn't go home."

"Okay," Linda said quietly. "I don't want to go home. It's not home. Just for a little while, then—"

Dr. Kirkland shushed her. "We'll worry about that tomorrow. You've done enough hard work today."

Sometime later as she slipped into sleep, Linda was vaguely aware that she was in a safe place. Dr. Kirkland's husband had a quiet voice. The walls were a soothing, pale blue which reminded her of an ocean sparkling outside a bungalow door. She'd felt safe there too . . . safe with a woman who laughed . . .

Chapter 9

"Well, of course exercise is important. We here at Take It Off have a sensible, modest exercise program that will only further accelerate your weight loss."

Agreeing silently that a plan of four thirty-minute walks a week qualified as "modest," Marissa glanced over the menu program that the perky size-five Emelie had given her. "So the program is two of your TIO shakes a day, two of the special energy and nutrition bars and one of the pre-made meals."

Emelie's smile was blinding. "That's the weight loss program, yes, you've got it perfectly. But when you get to stage three where you want to stop losing weight, there's a different maintenance plan. You could be at your goal weight in a matter of months."

The idea that she would ever not be trying to lose weight seemed outlandish. She remembered Bianca's story about the magic fat burning pills—it was another pipe dream she wanted to believe. She wasn't here thinking the program was an instant cure.

She wanted to be absolutely certain of what she was eating, that was all. "Oh, I don't think so. But it's nice to imagine it."

Emelie leaned forward as if to share a secret she didn't tell just anybody. "You don't have to exercise. It's not crucial."

Marissa knew she'd keep up her work at the gym but she'd do less of it if she was also carefully watching her calories. "I do work out."

"Oh, of course you do. You know, instead of the regular Take It Off shakes, you might want to go with the premium. Extra protein and potassium since you do work out. Working out is good for you, I'm sure."

Marissa wrote a check for her enrollment and the first two weeks of food. Poorer, and not entirely encouraged, she took it all home.

It had been seven weeks since the shipwreck. Six weeks since she'd said good-bye to Linda. There were no messages, no postcards.

Likewise, there was no communication from her mother. She wondered if she should be the one to break the impasse. She'd done nothing wrong—okay, maybe been a little ungracious and abrupt—so why was she supposed to be the one who made nice? It was a bit of a relief not to spend each day dreading a phone call.

Her Saturday night, empty of a beau, loomed long and lonely. Wasn't that the most common reason given by new clients? That they were alone on Saturday night and decided to give Finders Keepers a try? She and Ocky had agreed not to use the FK services for themselves so they wouldn't have to admit they'd failed, should that happen. What if Linda never got in touch? Maybe she should at least profile herself so she could study the profile of her ideal partner? What if it wasn't Linda? What if it wasn't Ocky either? Well, it wouldn't be Ocky—Ocky didn't and wouldn't ever care for her back, not sexually. And, dang it all, after a great night of sex with Linda there was no way she was accepting something less.

Dear Linda,

I didn't tell you about Octavia—not the whole truth anyway. Until you turned around on the lifeboat and talked

126

to me like I had a brain and a body, I was happy enough to have a crush on Ocky. I was alone on Saturday nights because I chose to be. Now I see it wasn't a choice I made, but one made by so many others who saw only a brain in me, and wanted bodies that were anything but like mine. Until you, I didn't know what it was like to be wanted. You made a miracle for me, and I don't know if I will ever see you again. I want to see you again. I want so much more than merely seeing.

Love, Marissa, Day 42 without you

P.S.   Please don't make me survive without you.

She frowned at her dinner. Such depressing thoughts, on a Saturday night all alone, meant there was nothing else for it but to pluck her eyebrows. Staring into the bathroom mirror she realized she didn't flinch as she had for a while after that horrific self-assessment in Tahiti. But the woman on the outside still did not match the woman she now truly believed existed on the inside. The woman who had made it up that cliff was not the helpless fat chick she still saw in the mirror, even after all these weeks of elliptical trainers and core-tightening weight lifting.

In the morning, her eyebrows perhaps a bit too thin, she made herself drink the first shake and tried not to be hungry. She plodded to the gym, even though she felt it was pointless.

Five weeks later, and feeling as if it had been a lifetime, the chill of the conference room was a welcome reminder to Linda that her heart was like ice where her mother was concerned. The week of uncomplicated days and nightly unbroken sleep at Dr. Kirkland's house had brought her more peace than she'd ever thought possible. Only those few minutes after climaxing in Marissa's arms had been better.

From Dr. Kirkland's house, flush with the very small quarterly stipend from the only investment account in her name, she'd found a small studio outside Boston—way outside—and decided she wasn't too proud to flip burgers for food money. The last month had been tiring but, in an odd way, exhilarating.

She did not want to live this way forever, however. She wanted to start over deciding what exactly she proposed to do with her life. Even if she got everything she wanted out of this meeting, she would not go back to being a drifter. Having a driving purpose to prepare for this meeting over the last four weeks had felt wonderful.

She looked over at her lawyer and smiled. Ted Jeffers was a decent human being, as was Dr. Kirkland.

Alligator entered first, just as before, then held the door with an air of ushering in the most delicate woman in the world. Her mother didn't look at her.

There were pleasantries, which Ted Jeffers concluded with, "My client has decided not to delay the competency hearing any further."

Linda had the tiny satisfaction of seeing her mother blink.

Alligator beamed. "That's very good news."

"Of course we believe that a court-ordered enforcement of the full provisions of both my client's grandfather's and father's wills may result in bad publicity for your client."

"We shouldn't argue the case here," Alligator said. "Let's save arguments for the courtroom."

Moving deliberately, Linda set a ream's worth of printed pages on the table. They were neatly bound with a rubber band. "This is exhibit one. Your copy."

Her mother glanced at the stack, but said nothing. Alligator looked at Ted, who nodded. "What should we call this exhibit?"

"My memoir." Linda felt detached but in the right way. She wasn't helplessly angry right now or lost like a little child, she was simply in control and aware of it. She was *conscious*. It would take a couple of years of steady work to break old habits and explore the many, many ways her earlier life had left her damaged.

"It's called *Winning at Any Price: the Story of a Daughter and*

Mother. Catchy title, I think, especially since I'll have my full birth name, Lindsey Vanessa Bartok Price, on it."

"That's blackmail." Her mother leaned forward in spite of a restraining gesture from Alligator. "I'll sue you and the publisher for everything."

"Truth is truth." Linda realized she felt powerful for the first time with her mother, that she had true control over the conversation. "It's not blackmail because regardless of the outcome of the competency hearing, I'm going to publish this. Win or lose, I'm talking. You can't silence me. You have nothing to offer me that I value."

Her mother glared. "You'll never see a penny of my money again and my will is explicit that you get nothing, ever."

Linda said again, "You have nothing to offer me that I value."

"I won't let you ruin our family name." There it was, at long last—a note of panic in her mother's voice.

Linda thought, with surprised clarity, *I'll never look like her, not because of the surgeries, but because inside she's ugly and I'm not.* She would have to share that thought with Dr. Kirkland. Certainly, Dr. K already knew how much the loan of a laptop had meant to Linda.

When Linda said nothing, Ted Jeffers smoothly explained, "There's no way of predicting how publishing a detailed memoir will affect the Price family name. But it might encourage other little girls who were tortured and abused in pursuit of beauty pageant crowns to speak out."

Her mother looked at Alligator, who hurriedly said, "We'll get an injunction."

"What a pity, then, that just this morning I dropped off copies of the manuscript to the *Herald*—both the entertainment and financial editors, as well as posted copies to several publishers."

Her mother went white. "If this isn't blackmail, then what was the purpose of this meeting?"

"To prepare for the hearing," Ted said, with a bland smile. "In the interests of disclosure, Linda is submitting this manuscript as proof that she is more than capable of completing a project while she holds down a job and maintains her own residence. In addition, it explains for the first time the mitigating circumstances on her unfortunate and deeply regretted suicide attempts, something no judge has ever heard. Her therapist—assigned initially by the last facility her mother committed her to—is also willing to speak on Linda's behalf. We're ready for your own psychiatrist's evaluation and this morning—" He handed a paper across the table to Alligator. "This morning we requested the court go ahead and appoint its own evaluator."

Amazed, Linda watched her mother rise to her feet. "How could you do this to me?"

She hadn't thought about what kind of response she'd get from her mother, not really. Was that because she no longer cared? What mattered was how telling her story helped her move on with her life. "My decision is not about you. It's about me finally letting go of what you did to me."

"You've always told hurtful and cruel lies. I gave you beauty—a body that could rival any supermodel's. You repaid me by faltering in every competition!"

Huh, Linda wondered. She'd have to talk that over with Dr. Kirkland. Maybe she had sabotaged her pageant chances subconsciously, trying not to give her mother what she wanted. "I know that it hurts you that you couldn't fill that case you set up in the house for my trophies and tiaras."

"You can claim you hated it all but I saw you. Don't forget I was there." Her mother's eyes narrowed. "You enjoyed the compliments and fawning attention of judges. You enjoyed being the little Lolita. Remember how you used to show your paltry second-place trophies to your grandfather? I knew what you were doing but I only wanted you to be happy."

Linda guessed she couldn't keep the puzzlement out of her face, because her mother quickly added, "Don't look at me like you don't know."

Alligator leaned into the table, holding out one hand. "This meeting isn't going to achieve anything productive. Let's schedule the hearing as soon as possible."

He took her mother by the arm, pulling her toward the door.

"Of course she knows. That's why he left her all that money, because she was his beautiful little darling."

The door closed behind them and Linda realized Ted Jeffers was staring at her.

She closed her eyes and searched her memory. What her mother suggested was ugly, ugly almost beyond words. There was nothing in her mind that she shied away from now. She could think about her mother, her childhood, those horrific teenage years and not hide from any of it. She hadn't known her grandfather very well. True, he'd always asked about her pageants and she'd sometimes shown him the awards. But she felt none of the warning signs—red flags Dr. K called them—that had surrounded her mother, *beautiful* and food.

"I don't know what she's talking about. I don't mean I can't remember. I mean I don't *know*."

"Then," Ted said slowly, "If she repeats it we can counter her libel claims with slander ones on your part. It's a disgusting suggestion. Your mother evidently believes children are responsible for the actions of adults."

"There is a part that's true—sometimes, I did like the attention. I did like being told I was attractive, sometimes. I would forget for a while all about the pain and the torment and it felt good."

Ted gave her a thoughtful look. "I don't know much about this but I don't think just because something good comes out of the something bad you have to be happy the bad things happened. I had a sadist professor in law school and I still remember him and how awful I felt every time I was anywhere near him. I learned a lot, sure, but my passing the bar didn't make him less of a son-of-a-bitch." He shrugged.

"Your daughters are lucky, you know that?" He gave a sheepish nod and Linda had to laugh. It felt as if years of closely wrapped chains fell away. Inside, teenage Linda wanted to dance. "Is Bartok v. Price spelling full-time employment for you?"

He smiled, looking pleased. "With any luck."

❧

Marissa swallowed down the last of her soy meal shake with fake chocolate flavor and surveyed the two envelopes—both junk—that had been in her mailbox. Work was hectic, the food tasted bland and she remained afraid to do so much as sprinkle some salt on the boxed dinners for fear of messing with a magic formula of some kind. Ocky wanted to completely overhaul their questionnaire style, her mother still wasn't speaking to her and Linda could be dead for all she knew.

She was about to throw away both envelopes when she realized that one might not be junk at all. It was from the cruise line—she'd mistaken the splashy logo for an ad. She slit it open and extracted several sheets of paper. A check fluttered onto the floor. After she picked it up she saw it was a refund for a substantial portion of the cruise price. She'd have to forward it to her mother, since her mother had paid for the trip. She mentally dashed off the note.

Dear Mom,

Thank you again for the lovely cruise. Because of the circumstances, the cruise line has refunded some of your money. The check is enclosed. I am still pursuing a settlement from the trip insurance company and hope at least to get the value of the books, camera and clothes back.

Love, Marissa

P.S. Still a lesbian.

The other pages were copies of press releases relevant to the explosion. There was a technical explanation of the decompression and a complete passenger manifest to aid those with trip insurance

132

in filing their claims. Marissa glanced down the list and realized that there were very few passengers whose names she'd even known. She scanned it a second time. She had found one very familiar name—but oughtn't there be two?

Between Cedras, Anthony and Chandler, Susan, was Chabot, Marissa. But Bartok, Linda was not on the list.

Further down was a Price, Lindsey. Lindsey was the only remotely close match to "Linda" on the entire list.

Confused more than anything else, she sat down at her laptop and hit the search engines. "Linda Bartok" brought back hundreds of thousands of pages, the most relevant promising information about classical music. It was exactly the same result as she'd gotten when she'd first thought she might find Linda through the Internet.

Recalling that first exchange of names, she limited the search by adding "Boston." That resulted in still over a thousand hits and the first few were for real estate. She changed "Linda" to "Lindsey," kept "Bartok" and added "Price." To her relief, she got back only three dozen with all the search terms.

Sometimes, when Marissa wasn't paying attention, memories of the beach, coconuts, hot sun and cool breezes would well up inside her and for a few moments she would be right there, with Linda nearby. She'd never known such warmth and ease.

But there had been no mess of real life, she reminded herself. Linda could hate your mother. Linda could hate living in one place. Linda could, upon reacquaintance, decide the everyday Marissa wasn't nearly as interesting as the shipwrecked one. That last thought seemed so likely too. It probably explained why Linda stayed away. *She only made love to you when the lights were out. She only let the fireworks happen when she didn't have to look at you.*

That last thought cut like a knife and the first time she'd considered it she'd been able to shrug it off. But with so many weeks of silence it was harder to ignore. Linda had wanted some sex and Marissa was the only woman in the area who was willing. So very willing and grateful for the attention.

Stomach churning, she made herself read the first of the articles supplied by the search engine. From Boston, there was local financial news. The estate of John Lindsey Price had finally been settled substantially in favor of his granddaughter, Lindsey Vanessa Bartok Price, over the objections of her mother, Lindsey Candace Price, CEO of Price Investments. This settlement, the article explained, came on the heels of rumors about a tell-all memoir penned by the new heiress, who was currently seeking a publisher for the manuscript.

Heiress.

Marissa sat, lost in the memories, long enough for her screen saver to trigger. The slow-moving tropical fish only added to her confusion.

So, Marissa thought with a shaky sigh, Lindsey Price, heiress, was also Linda Bartok, survivalist wonder woman. All of Linda's evasions about her appearance, the reference to having things that doctors needed to "fix"—were those the topics of her "tell-all" manuscript? Marissa could only imagine what kind of surgeries and enhancements money could buy.

There was obviously a lot she didn't know about Linda—well, that was a big surprise. Duh.

The inner voices of presumed rejection and prudent reality combined in asking the million-dollar question. What could an heiress possibly see in her? Had the phone remained silent and the mailbox empty because Linda had moved on with her life?

Why would a wealthy woman, as it seemed Linda was, not have a cell phone? A mailing address? Oh, you're a fool, Marissa, she abruptly thought. A big, fat fool. You believed her when she said you couldn't get in touch with her.

You believed the oldest line in the world after a one-night stand: I'll call you.

She was surprised to feel the keyboard wet under her fingertips. Was she crying? She felt too numb for that to be possible.

Yet, later that night, she tucked her hand under her pillow and felt the soft fabric of the T-shirt. As a moment in time, Linda was the most important thing that had ever happened to her. Knowing

Linda had changed everything. It ought to have been enough comfort for her aching heart.

She hurt. She hurt in places that had long been healed over and there seemed nothing to do but cry.

∾⚮∾

"Beauty queens don't have muscles. The whole point is to make looking beautiful *natural*. Muscles aren't feminine, and they make it appear as if you weren't born with those sleek lines, you had to work for them." Linda paused for breath. "Everybody uses spray-on wax to stick their bikini bottoms to their butts, and the judges know it. But they better not see any traces of it. Because that would mean you weren't born perfect. It's all such a lie."

The two men in their navy blue suits nodded in unison. One—Tom or Dick or Harry, she couldn't remember—said, "There have been a number of exposés on the beauty pageant circuit. We're more interested in your personal story. If we were to accept the manuscript we would need the more complete personal angle."

"I'm not sure I follow," Linda said, even though she did.

"What Harry is trying to say is that what's of interest to us is your personal story."

Linda looked at Tom or Dick—had to be one or the other if his colleague was Harry—and slowly said, "Yes, I believe that's exactly what he said. But I think I need you to be more precise."

"The details of your own preparations for the pageants, for example. Is what you've already written the complete story?"

"Yes, everything is there." Linda knew where they were going—they wanted the same thing the other two publishers she'd met with wanted: more dirt on her mother.

"We could use more, you see."

"This is a memoir, not fiction, though lately the line between the two has been blurred."

Harry gave her a fatherly smile. "What will sell books is the unvarnished truth about how an innocent girl was exploited by her mother all for the sake of a tiara."

"What is there in that manuscript is the unvarnished truth. All of the truth. It's in the context of the rest of my life. This book is not about my mother. It's about me." She doubted they would get the difference.

"We want it to be about you, of course, but it needs a hook."

Linda sighed and gathered her things. "I'm not claiming to be the best writer of all time—in fact, a real writer would probably help. But I've told the truth, the complete truth. There's no more to say. If you change your mind, you have my number."

They made polite noises about considering it and Linda left as quickly as possible. Okay, so much for making the book a priority. She wanted to see it in print if only to prove wrong her mother's accusation that she'd written it purely for blackmail.

Well, wasn't that just another example of her mother pushing her buttons? Okay, she told herself bracingly, if you are going to get this book in print it has to be for your purposes and no other. You want to tell, get it all out, and move on, and that has nothing to do with your mother.

She stopped at the restroom on her way out of the building and found herself, for the third time in as many days, gazing at her reflection with an odd feeling. A feeling of puzzlement, perhaps.

She arrived early for her next appointment with Dr. Kirkland, giving her time to settle the long overdue bill. Finally, the Lindsey Price on the credit card was really her. Part of the court ruling had been that she repay the credit card bills sent to her mother since leaving Yale. Linda had been fine with that—it severed the last claim her mother could make on her.

She now had the eager attention of the trust department of two financial institutions, as well as the lawyers who had probated her father's and grandfather's wills. They were relieved, they said, to finally be able to work with her. Still, it was to Ted Jeffers she turned for advice.

"If you're not foolish, you'll never have to work," he'd explained. "This wasn't an enormous sum of money, in today's world. Your mother is worth many, many times this in her own right."

"So she wanted to control it simply because it let her control me."

He'd nodded and Linda had set about understanding how investments, dividends, fixed income instruments and annuities worked.

"I guess I can self-publish it," Linda told Dr. Kirkland, after she asked how the meetings with publishers over the last several days had gone. "I would like to move on."

"How so?"

"I was thinking of going back to Yale. Just to finish those classes and get my MBA. It can't hurt." She found herself fidgeting in her seat. The sun was setting into a gray horizon. It might technically soon be spring but not in this part of the world.

"That's an excellent idea." Dr. Kirkland smiled her approval. "You've always regretted not finishing."

"It wasn't my fault."

"I know."

Linda gazed out of the window and she saw a woman in the glass looking back at her. She leaned closer. The figure was too vague to see the eyes but the general shape of the other woman's features—the hair, the way she sat—twisted up like a girl who didn't know what to do with her legs—were clear. Linda felt as if she ought to know who that was but she didn't.

"Linda? What are you thinking about?"

Considering her words for a long time, Linda finally said, "That when I look in the mirror I don't know who that is."

Dr. Kirkland nodded slowly. "Adult Linda hasn't really focused much on herself. She spent a lot of energy keeping herself together."

"Yeah, I get that, but that's not what I mean. I'm not talking metaphorically. I mean literally. I don't know who the woman in the mirror is. She's not me."

Dr. Kirkland cocked her head to the left. "What would be different about her, if you wanted to be able to recognize her?"

"I don't know. I don't know what I'm supposed to look like. My ears should stick out, I guess, and I ought to have a hair or two on my chin. My nose ought to hook. My waist should be thicker. But . . . to get back to the woman I would have been if I hadn't had

137

those surgeries I'd have to have more surgeries. And undo . . ." She had an unwelcome thought.

"Undo what was done? To find the real you?"

She nodded.

"Do you want to undo it all somehow?"

"I wish it had never been done."

"But it was. Do you want to go back?"

"I thought I hated it—hated what she made me into."

"Do you, though?"

Slowly, Linda shook her head. Recalling her conversation with Ted Jeffers, she said, "No, I don't. It can feel good to have people admire me."

"That's natural, Linda."

"But I'm not *natural*. I'm a freak show."

"Linda, things that hurt us leave scars. Those scars change us forever—"

"What if that change was for the better? That means she did the right thing, doesn't it?"

Dr. Kirkland sat forward. "No—absolutely not. No, completely and utterly *no*. What she did was wrong. It left you scarred for the rest of your life. You've been struggling for decades to recover from all of it. It was wrong."

Linda realized her hands were shaking. "So how can I like some of it? If it was wrong, how can some of it have turned out good?"

"What turned out good—" Dr. Kirkland left her chair to perch on the little table between them. Taking Linda's hand and warming it between her own, she said in her quiet, certain voice, "Listen carefully, Linda please. This is so important. Anything good that came out of all that pain is what *you* did to heal yourself. If there is good, that is *your* success. She hurt you and you have taken that hurt and transformed it. If you are beautiful, Linda, it's because you have chosen to be so, not because she chose that for you."

"I don't—I don't like it when people stare. When women want only what they see." Linda wanted to press her forehead into Dr. K's hands but instead, she made herself say the rest of the truth. "But I like the power it gives me to control situations."

Dr. Kirkland squeezed her hands, then let go. "We'll talk more about that next time. It's one of the things that I knew sooner or later you'd figure out. That you dislike that your appearance draws people to you but that you then use it to control them as much as you can."

"I'd much rather fuck a woman than talk to her, you mean? It doesn't take a lot of effort to get them to say yes."

"To say yes to the only question you'll let them ask."

"It wasn't that way with Marissa, you know. It was different. I didn't have to control her."

As she rose to her feet, Dr. Kirkland said, "Do you plan to get in touch with her again?"

"Not until I'm not screwed up anymore. Not until I can tell her I know who I am. But I don't even know what I'm supposed to look like. I'm changing so much, all on the inside where she can't see it. I can't ask her to go through this with me. This is my work to do."

"That's an important distinction, Linda. But that still doesn't mean you couldn't have a sympathetic ear to talk to."

"I'm not sure I'll tell her."

"But she could read your book if you go ahead with it. And she'll know."

Linda's jaw dropped. The thought simply had not occurred to her. Did she want Marissa to find out that way? Telling the anonymous "world" was one thing but she remembered so well Marissa's discussion of what contempt did to a relationship. That's an ouch, she thought. I know none of it was my fault, or thought I did. But if I think Marissa could find something contemptible about me because of all that stuff then I really don't believe I wasn't to blame, do I?

She was about to mention her thoughts to Dr. Kirkland, but she realized Dr. K had moved to her desk.

"Our time's up, Linda. I'm sorry. But we'll pick up where we left off at the end of the week."

"It's okay." Linda got to her feet feeling a little dazed. These thoughts weren't as painful as her memories but they mattered far more going forward. If she thought Marissa couldn't see her as blameless for the past, then she was still on some level ashamed of it.

It had been eight weeks since Tahiti. Marissa will have moved on by now, Linda told herself. You should call her, send a note, something. Maybe she'll wait.

But the moment you do, she'll ask questions. You're not ready to answer any of them, she told herself. You still have nothing to offer her. Nothing but a body you don't like very much—and a messed up head.

How can you tell her you want a future when you have no idea what yours is?

Marissa knows who she is, knows what she wants, is making a success of a business and has a great life. So you've inherited a sum of money, Linda told herself, but that doesn't answer the million-dollar question: when she sees the real you, what could Marissa possibly want?

She made her way back to the tiny apartment and got ready for another shift at the burger joint. She'd given notice and planned to work the full two weeks because it was undemanding—somehow liberating to her overtaxed brain.

She knew she sometimes didn't have it quite right in figuring things out but she was working on it. Marissa was so full of life, so kind, so smart and amusing. She deserved to move on if she could. Find someone who would be right for her all the time, not someone who was only right when she was lying about everything from her name to her past.

The nice thing to do would be to let Marissa go and send her a letter that helped her move on. It was selfish not to get in touch and think Marissa would be there when Linda knew what she had to offer.

It was selfish not to write that letter and Linda hoped that the fates and furies—and Marissa—would forgive her for her selfish act of hope.

Chapter 10

Swallowing around a mouthful of Take It Off Premium Energy Bar, Marissa managed to make a garbled response to the intercom. "Mm—yeah?"

Heather said intensely, "The sales staff is in their meeting and we've got a new client in reception with questions about her paperwork."

"What's Octavia doing?"

"She's on the line and not responding."

"I'll see how long she's going to be."

Putting down the remaining half of her lunch bar, Marissa stuck her head around the corner to see what Ocky was up to.

Ocky's back was to the door as she said, "Look, Mr. Patterson, if that is your real name, we have an obligation to all our clients. You've prepared your paperwork under one name and paid the enrollment fee with another. We don't allow aliases of any kind because any relationship that begins with a lie won't succeed. We are about success in the long term. I can only presume that you aren't seriously looking for a romantic relationship and therefore I'm returning your fee."

Marissa ducked back into her office. Ocky would be on that call for a while. This guy Patterson had also failed one of the consistency tests they applied to the profile statistics his questionnaire answers had created. Everything suggested he was creating a false persona to get dates for the purpose of sex only. And that was not what Finders Keepers promised its clients.

Ocky's little speech about starting a relationship with a lie like a false name made her think about Linda. Ocky would say that Linda had never meant to begin a romantic relationship that could endure. If she had, she'd have given her real name and given Marissa the means to contact her. Marissa was so glad she'd not told Ocky about Linda. No point in Ocky knowing what a fool she'd been.

She could almost make herself hate Linda but then she'd remember a hundred good feelings and that incredible night of lovemaking and the most she could feel was regret for a lovely but broken dream.

She checked her reflection, still a little startled by the sleeker haircut and professionally done highlights. Bianca and Heather had mightily approved and she did like it. Fumbling in her desk drawer, she came up with a pair of earrings. At least this sweater was new and looked nice on her. The food deprivation, in its third week, had had some initial results. She hated being hungry all the time and the choices were boring. She also felt weak during her workouts and had had to scale back. This past week her weight loss had stopped altogether again.

She greeted the new client in the reception area and escorted her to a small conference room. "I'm so sorry for the delay. Most of our staff is in a meeting for the rest of the hour. I'm Marissa Chabot, one of the owners of Finders Keepers. I hope I can answer all of your questions."

"I'm Andrea Curel. I signed up last week and I've been filling out the questionnaire but I have some questions."

They settled down with cups of coffee as Marissa said cheerily, "What can I help you with, Andrea?"

After brushing back neatly trimmed shoulder-length black hair, Andrea looked down at her paperwork. "I'm in the process of working with a nutritionist and I've just joined a gym. So I don't know if I should fill out the paperwork as I am now or who I'm going to be in six months."

Wanting to ask what kinds of nutrition and fitness plans Andrea had, Marissa nevertheless made herself stick to business. "You should fill out the questionnaire for exactly who you are now. You can do revisions, and in some cases, those changes will add to our profile and direct you toward slightly different matches. For example, if you lose weight our analysis would be more favorable toward a compatible someone who was also losing weight. A lifestyle focused on exercise and nutrition becomes a common bond and points toward compatibility over food, holidays and leisure time activities. We're always looking for those ninety-eights and sevens."

"I think I see. I just—I had a couple of years that were really stressful and I let myself go. So I'm getting back into shape now. And let's face it, I'm overweight. I don't want to be matched up to a guy because he's overweight too."

"The matching up process is far more complicated than that, I assure you." Yeah, she thought cynically to herself, it'll take into account that you are more concerned with how a potential mate looks than how he thinks or acts. Marissa, she scolded herself, judging a client's personality and preferences was a big no-no. She was just being bitchy because Andrea had perhaps a total of ten pounds to lose. She'd give a lot to be Andrea's version of "overweight."

She assuaged the rest of Andrea's worries and the woman left, saying she'd finish the questionnaire and submit it online.

Isn't it the truth, Marissa thought on the way back to her office, that everybody wants someone attractive as a mate? The segment of the questionnaire about personal attributes that the client found attractive was at the end, but whenever she asked a client what they were looking for in a mate, they invariably started with appearance.

Linda made me laugh and thought I could do impossible things, Marissa considered. That's what I want in a mate—that and general female physical components. They don't have to be sculpted or bodacious.

She had been attracted to Linda because of the confidence, the poise and the sense of humor. That she was also gorgeous had registered after those other impressions.

It was only one side of the coin, too, knowing what she wanted in a mate. She had to know what she wanted to give and how her ultimate dream partner would react to her. I want to make her laugh as much as she does me, and help her believe in herself too.

She had to ask herself what results she would get if she filled out the FK questionnaire for real. Not a test case, but as a real applicant, looking for real matches. Would she be honest? Or would she complete it as the woman she wished she was, not the woman she really was?

She paused to look out at the rapidly greening hills of the Amador valley. In a few weeks it would be so lush with emerald hues that those who knew would say it looked like Ireland. New, fresh and clean—that was how she wanted to feel. She still wanted to be the woman Linda had seen.

The change of seasons was inescapable. Equally unavoidable was the growing certainty that Linda was never going to make contact with her. It had been over and done with the moment they'd left Tahiti.

Dear Linda,

Maybe you didn't know when you left that you wouldn't find me again. Maybe you did and you do this all the time. I don't know what to believe about you. All I know is that being with you changed me. I'd be grateful if it didn't hurt so much. I'd smile if I could stop crying.

Love, Marissa, too many days without you

P.S.   If I knew where to send your T-shirt, I would.

Maybe Linda would show up some day and maybe she'd have an explanation. Marissa would listen, maturely forgive her and then calmly explain that she had moved on. Maybe she'd even say something about remaining friends before she danced away in the arms of some dashing, wonderful woman she'd gotten to know by dating in a normal way.

If that happened she wanted to look like the One That Got Away, the one Linda would regret forever. Now that's a mature thought, she scolded again.

With a weary sigh, she picked up the remaining half of her Premium Energy Bar. Before she could bite into it the phone chirped with an outside call.

"Marissa, honey, I think it's time we talked."

There was nothing else to say besides, "I guess you're right, Mom." Caller ID was an investment that the business definitely needed to make, Marissa told herself.

"Would you like to have dinner this week?" Her mother's tone was as modulated as always—no note of hopefulness or distress, even though Marissa didn't know how she had really expected her mother to sound.

"How about tonight?" Might as well get it over with.

"I'm free tonight. Where would you like?"

It was unusual that her mother offered Marissa a choice. Her mother didn't care for chain restaurants and was hard to please. Marissa always felt responsible if she suggested a place to eat and her mother didn't like it for some reason. Well, maybe some place where there would be no shouting was still a good idea. "Why not the Club? It'll be quiet tonight."

Her mother agreed, they set the time and hung up with little more to say. Marissa chomped viciously into her energy bar, thinking the meal would likely blow her diet and in a single day she'd gain back every ounce she'd lost in two weeks.

She took the time after work to change and tidy her hair. A vest made of stitched together ties—a gift from her mother last birthday—over a white mock turtle was dressy enough. She had a new pair of slacks that were one size smaller than she used to wear and in a pleasing shade of turquoise. The color reminded her of the ocean, the sky . . . her own eyes reflected in Linda's.

Dear Self,

Buy more heart-shaped duct tape.

Love, Marissa.

The drive to the club took her from San Ramon into the far reaches of Blackhawk, past two security gates and up a long, winding drive. She parked her aging Toyota next to her mother's BMW and reminded herself that it was her mother who had made the first overture to resume normal relations. Détente was possible, just not probable.

One empty cocktail glass testified that her mother had been there for a while. But I'm not late, Marissa told herself, I'm right on time. Maybe Mom got here early because she needed a drink. Don't start by feeling guilty for something you didn't do.

"I'm so glad you were free tonight, sweetie."

Marissa blinked at the indulgent tone and wondered if that glass was the first empty or the second. Her mother didn't drink much. Maybe there would be shouting and items thrown after all. "I think we do need to talk, so thank you for calling me."

"Have a drink, if you like."

"No, I'm really watching what I eat, but thank you."

Her mother's nod was understanding. She even looked mildly interested. "In that case, I'm sure chef will be able to prepare something that's right. The Zone? Weight Watchers? Atkins? I've been trying to lose five pounds for the past year."

Marissa bit her tongue so she didn't snarl, "Five? Try fifty-five and then some. Give me a freakin' break here!"

Unsettled by her inner vehemence, she calmed herself by glancing at the day's menu choices before answering. "None of the above. Lots of exercise and those Take It Off meal packs. Right now the fewer choices and thought I have to give to the whole thing, the better. I'm weary of obsessing about every bit of activity and ounce of food."

"The last time we had dinner you said you were exercising more." Her mother's glance was evaluative but not overly judgmental. "You seem . . . a little thinner around your jaw. Are you pleased?"

"It's taking forever to get real results. I'm following every rule, every suggestion. Well, I'm supposed to pull out this Take It Off guide to ordering food when dining out but I have basic common sense. I know the grilled trout and steamed veggies will be just what I need. And more delicious than another frozen dinner, that's for sure."

"I'll have the same." Her mother set down the daily printed menu. "As a show of solidarity. My cholesterol is up, too, so it's best for me."

Marissa glanced at her mother in alarm. "Is it serious? The cholesterol thing?"

"No, not really. I just need, as you say, to use my common sense. I've been a bit depressed lately and chocolate doesn't cure everything."

"I wish it did."

"Amen," her mother said emphatically. "I like what you've done with your hair, by the way."

Surprised at the praise, Marissa could only say, "Thank you."

"On the way here I was remembering you in high school. For some reason that horrific fight we had when you went to spend the holidays with your father has been on my mind. I shouldn't have tried to make you choose."

"Oh." Marissa replayed the most vivid parts of their worst war of words. "I didn't like that you wanted me to choose. But I shouldn't have said what I said, about it being your fault he was gay. I knew at the time it was wrong for me to say that."

"You were angry and I was being a bitch." Her mother now

seemed a little nervous. "The way we parted last time we had dinner made me think about how little we seem to say anymore. Looking back, I realize that I was so hurt, so wounded by your father that I couldn't feel much else. I'm not sure you could understand."

For a moment, Marissa thought it was another of her mother's attempts to claim all of her experiences as unique. "I know what heartbreak is, Mom." She took a deep breath, accepting that there were worse things to lie about than your name. "But you're right. I've never been lied to quite that way."

With a sigh, her mother peered into her empty glass. "This is certainly Dutch courage. I'm not even sure I should tell you this but you're a grown woman and we're finally being honest."

Her mother started to say something else but broke it off to engage their server. "Yes, I think we're ready."

Marissa turned down the waiter's offer of an appetizer and placed her order before returning her attention to her mother. Her mother asked for the same meal but added a dinner salad. "So what did you want to tell me?"

"Your father didn't lie about having been with men before we married. He was honest about that."

"Then why—"

"He lied when he said he didn't want men anymore. And so I married him. I had to marry him. It's what one did in those days. Even in the liberated Seventies." Marissa could hardly take in the wry smile in her mother's eyes. "It was the liberated Seventies that got me in that situation. We were both high and he said he wanted to give a woman a go and I said he'd never go back to men after a night with me. We were stupid and young and it was a lot of fun."

Conquering a squeak in her voice, Marissa asked, "How many drinks have you had?"

"Enough. I'm not going to pretend that I'm not extremely conscious of social position and how important appearances are. I married a gay man so our child would be legitimate. I live in a takes-five-million-just-to-walk-through-the-gate community. I know you think my life is vapid and self-centered."

Part of her numb with disbelief and part of her reluctantly drawn to the ironic humor in her mother's tone, Marissa said, "You've summed it up pretty well."

Her mother nodded. "I thought so, thank you. You might not like me much but I am your mother. The important thing is that I like myself. I do enjoy my life and what I do. If I have been a bitch to you about yours, it's because you don't seem to be able to say the same thing."

"I like my work. I truly do." Marissa found herself reflecting her mother's wryness. "If you and Dad had gone to Finders Keepers before you married we'd have told you there was little chance of your staying together. His preference for men and your insistence on monogamy were guaranteed points of conflict."

"That was the problem. It wasn't that he was gay, it was that he'd told me he could live without men. I thought he loved me enough. I thought—" Her mother swirled the empty glass. "I really did love him and it all hurt. He lied because I wouldn't marry him if he told me the truth. He may have even been afraid I wouldn't let him see the baby. And he loved being a father. You know that, don't you?"

Marissa blinked back tears. "Yeah. I know he loved me. I feel it all the time."

"But you wonder about me. If I love you."

Marissa frowned at the basket of rolls and crackers the waiter set down between them. Two rolls each and several packets of saltines now tempted her. Hell, she really wanted a drink now. Several drinks and a hot fudge sundae. "You spent a lot of time telling me I was unattractive. That I wasn't a real girl. That all I needed was a man to take care of me—I didn't need dreams and ambitions of my own. Here was my mother, who has endless alphabet soup after her name and a respected reputation as an art appraiser, telling me not to follow in her footsteps. How was I supposed to interpret that?"

"That maybe I didn't want you to make my mistakes?"

"But *mother* . . . All your advice seemed to be about changing me into *you*. Clothes and food and college courses—you never stopped pushing me toward all the things that you had done. Like if I joined your sorority I'd wear a size eight and have all the social graces instead of being fat and better talking to machines than people."

Deep inside, she was still thinking about the idea that her conception had been an inebriated *oops*. Right now a frothy margarita on the rocks alongside baked brie with honey and almonds on fresh sourdough would be really tasty. How many calories did a saltine have, anyway?

She was losing her mind, this much was clear. Starvation madness, something like that.

Her mother stared at her for the longest time, even when her salad was delivered. The server, perhaps interpreting their silence as ominous, scurried away more quickly than usual.

"You know, Mom, I already didn't like a lot about myself by the time I was a teenager. You made it abundantly clear you didn't like me either. So I did the one thing I knew where I could excel—I learned programming. I learned reasoning and statistics and logic-based quantification strategies. I liked that part of me. But I always felt a failure because I couldn't make you happy. I won't wear pink with white gloves in the summer for church. That's just not who I am."

Finally, her mother shifted in her seat. "Your father always said you and I were oil and water. I thought if I said something enough you'd hear me. I thought if I told you how I became so unhappy you would learn from my mistakes."

"I didn't think you believed you'd ever made any mistakes." Marissa shook her head. "But oil and water, that makes sense. Maybe . . . maybe because I'm a blend of both of you."

"You are like him in so many ways. And like me, and goodness knows I'm stubborn."

Marissa rolled her eyes. "That's the understatement of the year."

Her mother sat up straight in her chair. "Just because we're having this little heart-to-heart doesn't mean you can be rude." Then she burst out laughing.

150

At some point the evening had turned into an Altman film, Marissa decided. Or Fellini—any minute a juggling dwarf would walk through the room singing the Notre Dame fight song. "You're stubborn and I inherited it from you. Deal with it."

"You inherited being gay from your father."

"Maybe." Marissa shrugged. "If you don't eat your salad right now I'll eat it for you. And how long did you know I was gay?"

"Years." Her mother finally poured some dressing on her greens and took a bite.

"So what the heck was with the dates every year for the summer ball? The annual fussing about what dress I wore and if my date and I will take a good photo? Geez, I hate all that."

"It's your own fault. Well, partly." Her mother speared a chunk of feta cheese. "What else was I supposed to do? I asked about your romantic relationships. I hinted broadly that you were free to bring anyone you wanted home. You wouldn't tell me you were gay. I thought if I pushed men at you that you'd tell me the truth."

Dang it, that sort of made sense. It really *sucked* that her mother might have had reasons for some of the ways she acted. "But you were so totally homophobic about Dad. I thought you'd act just the same way toward me. And when I told you, you did get angry. You had that disappointed face you get, which I hate, by the way. You said I should have picked a better time and place."

"I meant . . . maybe I lost my temper a bit. I'm human. So sue me." Her mother lifted one shoulder in an expressive gesture that simultaneously dismissed her own flaws and suggested Marissa would do well to dismiss them as well. "What I meant was maybe you could have told me a long time ago. You kept so many secrets about yourself from me, and it did hurt. It felt . . ." She took a quick sip of water. "Goodness. I never thought of this before. It felt like your father's lies. It hurt and I blamed you and him and myself for not being able to show you that I could be trusted. I had to find out about you and Octavia starting that business from a friend."

"Is that why you told me we'd never be a success?"

"I was angry." She chewed thoughtfully on a crouton. "I get childish when I'm hurt. I own it and I'm sorry."

Marissa had to swallow hard before she could speak. "I didn't know you were hurt like that. I thought it was just . . . disappointment in me. That it was always me not meeting your standards. From my waistline to my friends to my career."

"Do you blame me for some of my reservations about what you were doing with your life? You gave up that good, meaningful job at the women's clinic for what looked like a pipe dream with Octavia. You work nonstop and never seem to sleep or spend any time on yourself. You never seemed happy to me."

Her mother, tears swimming in her eyes, waited until her salad plate was taken away before she finished. "I thought you and Octavia were a couple and you weren't telling me that either."

"We're not a couple." Now was not the time to divulge her senseless crush, especially if it was finally waning. It was hard enough not to sob openly into her napkin. "You were successful and brilliant and elegant. I never felt as if you thought I could be any of those things. Don't you think I'm strong enough to be successful in life?"

"Oh, 'Rissa . . . I didn't realize."

They both wiped away tears over their trout and steamed veggies. "Lemon juice is gross," Marissa pronounced, after sniffling.

"What brought that on?"

"Diet books are full of lies and I think the biggest is that vegetables with just lemon juice and a bit of pepper are delicious and satisfying."

"But lemon juice and pepper are delicious," her mother protested. "Just what we need." She signaled the waiter, who was promptly solicitous.

"My daughter and I require hollandaise sauce. Is there any available?"

"Of course," he said. His pace was decorous as usual as he departed on his quest.

"Mom, I can't eat hollandaise."

"Of course you can. It's lemon juice and pepper."

"With butter and egg yolk."

"And those vegetables will be delicious tossed in one or two tea-spoons. How much damage is that to your diet?"

"I've been so careful. I don't want to mess it up." Marissa stub-bornly ate a piece of unvarnished broccoli. Oh, yummy, she thought. I am so loving the flavor of this. "I am a grown woman. And I'm sitting here obsessing about whether I can have a freakin' saltine. You're *thin*. This is the thing that hurts me that you can't possibly understand."

Fresh tears sprang to her eyes. She felt very vulnerable all of a sudden. Her mother was not behaving in the ways Marissa expected and the difference was deeply unsettling, even if it was for the better. How could she tell her mother, of all people, how frus-trated she was that her hard work at the gym and faithful adher-ence to near starvation wasn't doing much for her waistline? Her mother would only say she wasn't doing something right.

She remembered, abruptly, hanging to the side of that cliff and thinking she'd find someone to blame for all the junk food she'd eaten in college. But she had eaten all that food all by herself and not done any exercise. There was no one to blame but herself. She'd even known she shouldn't eat like that but she had anyway.

"You're right, I don't understand, sweetie. One day I noticed you were putting on some pounds and I couldn't figure out what had changed. You had always been reasonable about food, even as a little girl. You never had much of a sweet tooth."

Marissa made herself start on the trout, though she didn't feel hungry. Her mother did likewise. When a small gravy boat of hol-landaise was presented with a flourish, she poured what she hoped was just two teaspoons worth onto her vegetables. It smelled won-derful. There was very little, she decided, that butter didn't improve. "Okay, this was a good idea. You're right, in small quan-tities, butter is a beautiful thing."

"I'm sure if you keep up your hard work you'll be successful. And sooner or later I know you'll find the right person to make you happy."

"I don't want someone who notices me just because I'm thin."

153

If I lose weight and suddenly Ocky wants to date me, well, that sucks, Marissa decided. I don't want that, she thought. Yet, I want someone who thinks I look good.

Hell, self-image was confusing. She didn't want to be loved just for the way she looked and not just for who she was inside. She wanted someone to love her for the whole package, three-hundred sixty degrees.

She nearly brought up Linda then caught herself in time. Instead she said, half-smiling, "Mom, are you actually urging me to date women? Really? You're sure it's okay with you?"

"Oh, for heaven's sake."

To Marissa's utter shock, her mother rose to her feet, then stepped into her chair. With a grin at Marissa, she planted one Mephisto pump next to the bread basket and the other alongside the salt and pepper. Standing on the table, she looked down at Marissa as the dining room fell silent.

"Marissa, dear, I want you to be happy. If that means you date fifty women, I don't care. That's right!" She gestured at the rest of the room. "My daughter, my brilliant analyst entrepreneur daughter, is a lesbian and I am her very proud mother."

Her speech ended, she took the waiter's hand and he helped her down from the table as if he was assisting a queen from her carriage.

Conversations resumed. Anyone who walked into the room now would never believe that only moments before the elegant woman dining with her daughter had been standing on the table.

Finally, Marissa said, not smiling at all, "That's not the first time you've stood on the table, is it?"

"I don't know what you mean, Marissa, dear. Eat your vegetables."

It was like eating dinner with a stranger after that, but not in a bad way. It felt like starting over. After the table incident it wasn't that hard to believe she'd been conceived during a night of inebriated, giddy passion.

After a discussion of everything but the Standing on the Table

Incident, Marissa said, "Thank you for dinner. It's just what I needed—fresh but reasonable."

"You're welcome, sweetie. I know that the science has changed in the last twenty years but when I was trying to lose weight after you were born I did realize how easy it was to put two hundred or three hundred extra calories into any meal. Thinking two tablespoons of oil was only one. Salad dressing—I absolutely have to have it or I get hungry right away. But it's so easy to think you're only having half of what you actually poured. And I know the first time I saw how little four ounces of steak was I was shocked."

Marissa nodded vigorously. "I figured out I don't miss beef in my diet, that's for sure, not when I can have twice the fish or chicken and still have eaten half the calories and fat, most of the time."

"Goat cheese."

"What about it? I love it—just discovered it on vacation."

"It's full of air and water so you can have a great big dollop on nearly anything."

Marissa perked up. Finally, some good news. "I've been trying to accept that I'm one of those people who has to look at the oils and the cheeses and the dressings all the time. Not just one meal a day. Every meal. Forever. It's . . . depressing. And I feel a bit stupid for having waited this long to figure it out. Like if I ate a dozen Oreos every day eventually they would stop being fattening."

Her mother chuckled. "They say if you do the same thing over and over expecting different results it's a sign of mental illness."

"Guilty as charged, I guess." Though she was joking, inside Marissa could feel herself sobering. There was something to think over in what her mother had just said.

Later, after a stroll around the exterior of the golf course, Marissa headed home in a confused state of mind. A light drizzle had ended another spate of clear, cool weather and the scrape of the wipers was annoying.

She knew part of her was reeling from the idea that her parents had gotten high and she'd been conceived as a result but she sup-

155

posed it wasn't that uncommon of a story. Added to her mother's explanations of some of her hurtful behavior and general acceptance of Marissa as a lesbian, it was enough to feel as if she'd landed in the Twilight Zone.

But that wasn't what left her feeling distracted and deeply puzzled. She kept turning over and over the idea that as a teen and young woman she'd been overeating, willfully. She had needed the food more than feeling good about herself. She knew she'd started wearing big clothes to hide her breasts. After a year of snacks, sweets and second helpings at the school cafeteria, the big clothes had fit.

Stopped at a long light with valley lights twinkling through the drizzle, she said aloud, "All those boys you pushed at me, Mom, I never got along with any of them. And more than one was a perv. They had their hands all over me no matter what I said. You sent me on dates with boys and only you thought they were gentlemen. I think . . . I think . . . because you got a friend to get their son to ask me out, they thought I was desperate and I'd let them do anything they wanted. I was the fat girl who was supposed to be *grateful*."

The light flicked to green and she turned in the direction of the boulevard that would take her by the office. "Maybe I didn't eat because I was unhappy. Not entirely, at least. I ate to be bigger than they were, so they'd stop grabbing me. When my waist was bigger than my bust, it worked. It worked like a charm."

The Oreos, the donuts, the rice and gravy, she thought. I ate because college computer classes were mostly boys and they were all around me. I didn't want college to be like high school. I wanted to be darned sure my work was what people knew about me. As soon as I went to work for that women's clinic I stopped eating so much.

Oh, holy shit, how clichéd was that? She pulled up to the curb in front of the office building. The security guard glanced up from his desk and she sketched a wave as she got out of the car.

Once in the elevator she continued her monologue. "You know,

Mom, I think I ate because I wanted the boys to stop thinking I was attractive. I was scared I was going to get raped. I mean, lots of people think lesbians are lesbians because they hate or can't deal with men. Here I am overweight and obsessing about every little thing I do and eat because I let *boys* scare me into putting on twenty, thirty, fifty, seventy pounds? I thought I was smarter than that."

Hell, her plan to get the boys off of her *was* smart. It had worked, hadn't it? Jeez.

"Finally, Mom, I meet someone who actually finds me attractive for the me inside and she doesn't scare me at all. In fact, because she likes the me inside, I'm trying to work on the me outside. I think it's what I should do, even if she dumped me. Because I think she dumped me. Typical of me, I don't even know if I've been dumped. Pathetic."

She let herself into the Finders Keepers suite. She didn't even need to go to her office. From Heather's desk she took a set of ten bound pages and a sharp number two pencil. She was done being pathetic. She wondered how bad it would be to call that new client and ask for a nutritionist referral. Who cared? She'd do it first thing tomorrow.

Later, when she undressed for bed, Marissa eyed the flab and extra rolls that still hung from her body and muttered, "Boys. No way, no how, are *boys* going to win."

She sat down at the table with a hot cup of peppermint tea. "If money was no object," she read aloud, "which of the following three activities would you do?" Discarding attending Wimbledon and dining at a five-star Parisian restaurant, she carefully filled in the bubble for taking a flight on the space shuttle.

Chapter 11

"You're kidding, right?" Linda peered up at the gigantic structure. "This is 'the cabin?'"

Matt gave a little grunt before saying, "Yes ma'am. Hard to believe you never visited when Mr. Bartok was alive."

"It wasn't something my mother was keen on." Matt—no last name offered—had worked for her father for years as caretaker, mechanic and driver. "I know that may sound odd. Does it help explain a few things if I point out that when I was born my given last name was my mother's, not my father's?"

"Sounds like she's a strong woman then."

"If anyone could get that river down there to run backward, it would be her. Continental Divide be damned." She gazed up at the sprawling house. The only real property she had inherited was this place and its contents, including the vehicles. She had been thinking "rustic" but the word simply didn't apply.

They came to a halt in a large garage where a second car, an

Outback, was housed on the far right. In between the spot where the Range Rover evidently belonged on the far left were stacks of bottled water and bagged wood pellets.

"This is just the handy emergency storage, ma'am. There's more in the shed."

"The shed—is that the building I saw behind the house that could sleep six?"

Matt cracked a smile. "We do things large here in Montana, ma'am."

As Matt showed her the six bedrooms, kitchen and large study where her father had spent his days cataloging local flora, Linda was aware of the new shine of her boots squeaking on the hardwood compared to the worn softness of Matt's as he moved quietly and quickly from room to room.

"I really didn't know him," Linda said as she looked over the stack of bound volumes where he'd fastened dried leaves and blossoms then labeled them with their Latin and common names. "But because of him I tried to learn about the same things. Limited success."

"Well, he was good people. He has a few scrapbooks about you in here. Was real proud of you being so beautiful."

Not wanting Matt to see how that idea hurt rather than pleased, Linda made herself smile. It stung, the thought that her father had only known her from photographs. Nobody ever expected how backward "normal" had been in her life. "I wish my mother hadn't been keeping us apart. I'm glad to be here now. You've kept the place so well."

"Thank you. You're provisioned for two months of fuel at maximum consumption and as you saw a lot of drinking water should the well pumps fail. Solar panels will keep the backup batteries full, though. We get sun most every day." Linda followed him back to the garage where he pointed out skis, boots and snowshoes neatly arranged in cupboards, fuse boxes and reset switches plainly labeled, then helped her carry up her suitcases and most of the boxes until Linda insisted she could carry the rest herself and waved him home to his "missus" and his supper.

159

The picture window at the north end of the great room framed the still white-capped Gallatin Mountains. Stark white gave way to deep greens in patches and the peaks stood bare in shadowy blues as the day waned. The sun would be lost behind Lone Mountain in a few more minutes. She'd seen beauty like this before but never with a choice of six comfortable bedrooms and a fully-stocked kitchen and pantry at hand. In some ways she missed the tents and bedrolls.

Turning back to the room she said aloud, however, "Oh, who are you kidding?"

She made her way down to the garage for the last box, which contained the course books for the classes she would be taking at Yale this summer and fall, as well as the required readings for the prerequisite classes she'd taken years ago. She was frankly surprised that the admissions committee had agreed to accept her somewhat outdated previous work and had willingly agreed to three additional classes to bridge the time gap. That meant two classes during the accelerated summer "semester" and the remaining five during the fall semester. By the end of the year at least one of her life goals would be complete.

Not that she knew what she would do with an MBA. She wanted to finish what she'd begun, that was all. It was obvious she might be far happier spending her life immersed in her father's botany and biology pursuits. Small wonder her mother had insisted that the natural sciences weren't in the realm of possibilities. Lindsey Vanessa was a Price, not a Bartok, and the Prices went into business.

Perhaps by year's end she'd know what she intended to do with her life, something that didn't involve living through and for someone else. She wanted to get in touch with Marissa but was wary now that Marissa could be another kind of running away from the emptiness in her own life. Besides, it had been nearly three months and Marissa no doubt hated her and had moved on.

One idea that tickled was combining her hands-on cultural experiences and ecotouring with her MBA and looking for an environmental group she could work with. She would finish up the loose ends of the past and then look around at what the world might need that she could give.

She explored the cabin thoroughly, finding more traces of her father. Her parents' estrangement had been decades in duration. She frowned at the painting of her father that hung in the study. Though she'd not hinted anything to Matt, she was mad at her father sometimes. Just because he hadn't gotten along with his wife didn't mean he had a right to abandon his daughter. His absentee parenting had left her vulnerable to her mother's twisted plans and he, better than anyone maybe, should have known what her mother was capable of. It was sad that he, like so many others, had only seen her as *beautiful*. He never knew she inherited a love of nature from him. They never had a chance to do any of the things they might have loved exploring together, and that was his choice.

She took down the painting, angry and hurt, but not confused. She might as well acknowledge it, feel it. She'd put it behind her in due time. Meanwhile, the painting went into the closet. The bound volumes of his carefully preserved plant samples she would treasure.

Nightfall brought a beautiful vista of scattered sparkling lights down the mountain, then sprawling across the wide valley basin. Above her was a dazzling array of stars. She hadn't seen a night sky quite like it since the Alps. A glass of hot cider in hand she picked out familiar constellations and counted falling stars. She was not the same woman who had gazed at night skies from all over the world.

The icy wind threatened to freeze the tears in her eyes but she endured the cold a little longer. Only the weather was chilled. Inside her heart, down the length of her spine, Linda felt hot and alive, the way she had during the most intense moments of the shipwreck. Except now she had the feeling most of the time—and she loved it.

Living in the present, thinking about the future—that was why she was here. The past would need occasional attention but it no longer controlled her choices. She would make mistakes. She'd talk to Dr. Kirkland again and no doubt at length. But she and no one else would be responsible for her life from now on.

The fire was reassuringly crackling as she lifted the first of three boxes onto the long library table in the middle of the study. Not the course books, not yet. She upended the box and watched as hundreds and hundreds of photographs spilled across the dark surface.

There had been a time when she couldn't bear to look at herself in these pictures. Revulsion and dread fascination had warred until she had convinced herself the girl in the photos was a stranger. But teenage Linda was part of her.

She lifted one eight-by-ten to study the expressive face. Teenage Linda's disconnection from the pain in her life was complete as none of it showed in the glowing dark eyes or the elegant curve of full crimson lips.

"I'm sorry," she whispered to the girl she had been. "You survived and now we're here, in our future." She tenderly touched an image of hair burnished to a shimmer. "Thank you for being strong enough to endure."

She spent the next two days snowshoeing in the mornings and picking over photographs in the afternoons. She had every intention of publishing the book even if she paid for it herself and printed only a dozen copies. It was a record. The remainder of the photographs needed to be put in some kind of order and then she would find some place to store them where, if she wanted to, she could look at the past. There could be a time in her life when she wanted to do so again.

With the weather predicted to bring in a late March four-foot snowfall, she decided it was time to see the little town of Big Sky and get some fresh food. The Range Rover handled the steep inclines going down as easily as it had coming up. The town was packed with snow enthusiasts and showed signs of recent and extensive growth. She found the grocery Matt had directed her to—one of two available—and was mostly pleased with the choices.

"Are you sure you want that cheese?" The checker's question was directed at a nondescript lump of mild cheddar.

"Yes," Linda said hesitantly. "Why wouldn't I?"

"Well, I see greens, kalamata olives, red onion and no feta. You can't have Greek salad without feta." Linda was regarded with a motherly gaze.

"I couldn't find feta."

"Over there," the woman said, pointing over her shoulder. "I'll finish ringing you up while you grab some."

Aware of the waiting line, Linda scurried to what had been a hidden corner of the store. Feta, goat and pepper cheeses and deli-sliced mortadella were all welcome sights. First, "the cabin" turned out to be a luxury home and now the small grocery offered a few urban delights. She grabbed what she wanted and got back to the register just as the woman finished up with the rest. "Thank you so much."

"Just good retailin'. Cash or credit?"

Linda handed over her credit card. "I'm new and was thinking I'd get a bite to eat—"

"Bugaboo, down to the highway, go left, make another quick left. Good people."

"Thanks." She carried her bags to the Rover and easily found the restaurant, which was steamy warm and crowded with skiers of all ages clomping around in snow gear. She fit right in, she decided, even if her boots were suspiciously new. A chair quickly opened up at the bar and she studied the menu as she sipped a Fat Tire beer quickly provided by the bartender.

"Need help with the description of anything?" The bartender wiped the counter again, then stood poised with her order book.

"Everything looks good," Linda said, and it was the truth. Stuffed crabmeat rolls and pulled BBQ pork both tempted. "I don't have a big appetite is the thing."

"I can do you a half of anything, plus a side of mixed greens. Our orange pepper balsamic dressing is really good."

Linda found herself smiling at the thirty-something bartender, whose second earring on the left sported rainbow colors. "The pork then. Thanks."

"Don't mention it." She tapped something into the screen at the end of the bar, then returned to say, "I don't think I've seen you around here before."

"First time. The lady at the grocery store sent me. I gather 'good people' is high praise."

"Oh sure." Firm shoulders shrugged under a grey-green ribbed sweater. "Around here anyone who can get through winter without needing a jump, hauled out of a ditch or who will give someone a jump or haul someone out of a ditch is good people. You pull your own weight, lend the occasional hand and this is a very tolerant place, you know?"

"Not a bad system." Linda found herself keeping prolonged eye contact, then let her gaze flick to the rainbow earring and back.

"Where you staying?"

"I have a place on Osprey Ridge." It came out as a question because she didn't know if the name would mean anything.

Apparently it did, because the bartender whistled. "That is some high rent."

"I inherited the place. It doesn't . . . suck."

A rich, amused chuckle drew the attention of people nearby. "I'll bet. Just you? Those places are huge." Blue eyes softened in speculation. "You must feel all alone."

Linda nearly said, "I'm sure you could think of a way to end my loneliness." Then she thought of, "There are lots of spare bedrooms. It would be a while before we'd have to do laundry."

She said none of her thoughts aloud, however, and felt the beginnings of an unusual, awkward blush. She was spared by someone calling "Chrissy! Phone for you."

After a hurried sip from her beer, Linda realized she'd never felt like that before. She wasn't sure she liked butterflies in her stomach and feeling functionally mute. Did she have to give up being a consummate flirt as part of healing?

She had no answer for that but what she did know was that while she thought Chrissy was attractive and nice, she didn't want to have sex with her. She didn't *have* to have sex with her to control their interaction. And if at some point in the future she did want to have sex with Chrissy, she wanted Chrissy to want her back, the way Marissa had wanted her. For the person she was, not the body on the outside.

Hell, how egotistical was she being? She had no reason to think Chrissy was doing more than being nice and she had Chrissy on her back and moaning already. Okay, there were definitely a few habits she had that she didn't much like. Time to outgrow them.

Chrissy, with the phone cradled between shoulder and ear, delivered her half sandwich and salad with a wink. "Uh-huh. I think that's a good idea, Mom. Uh-huh."

The sandwich was lean and delicious, the dressing as tasty as promised. Chrissy, kept busy by the increasingly crowded bar, didn't linger again. When Linda was ready to go she waved and held up a twenty with an enquiring look. Chrissy nodded distractedly and Linda headed for the door after securing the bill under her empty beer bottle.

"Hey, big spender!"

Turning back, Linda found herself the center of attention from the customers at the bar. "It's enough, isn't it?"

Chrissy laughed. "Yeah, and if you tip me that much people will talk. Here."

Linda took the proffered five. "You were busy and I didn't want—"

"Just be sure you stop in again. You talk nice and you're way more easy on the eyes than the rest of these ugly bastards."

There was good-natured rumbling from the crowd as Linda made her escape. Her ears were burning. She felt as if she'd just passed a test of some kind and she didn't know what it all meant.

But she knew it felt okay to be found pleasing, even if it was just a fleeting encounter. She would endeavor not to need a jump or require rescuing from a ditch. Being "good people" was not a bad place to start life over.

જન્ય

Glancing around the room, Marissa was pleased to see it was mostly women and a variety of sizes and shapes. Like her, most appeared to have arrived directly from work and all had the unmistakable harried air of not having time for this. But they were all here.

Feeling too self-conscious to engage anyone, Marissa studied the small notebook she'd brought for taking notes and reminded herself why she was here. Yes, she could read nutrition books, diet books, watch fitness videos and the latest in health news. It was just the same with anything else. She studied up on hardware and software advances, didn't she? And when she got into a situation at work she couldn't figure out for herself, she called a consultant.

In this case, the consultant was Helena Boxer, the nutritionist that their client had recommended. She looked as nondescript and unassuming as Andrea Curel had described, that is, until she started speaking. Helena Boxer wasn't thin and she wasn't bulging muscles. If anything, she had a bit of a tummy, but it looked womanly. As she spoke, she glowed with vitality and Marissa was taken in by the directness of her gaze.

"Basically, I'm about to tell you all a bunch of really depressing facts. They are all things you don't want to hear and don't want to believe. If you decide you don't want to go ahead, then you've lost nothing but some time. That's why I don't take sign-ups until after the first session."

Well, that was fair, Marissa thought, considering how many checks she'd already written to the gym and Take It Off.

"So I'm going to start at the top. I'm not going to tell you what diet to follow. There is no best, one-size-fits all nutrition plan that leads to weight loss and fitness. Everyone is different. Our bodies change constantly. What works this year might need tweaking next year. Our evolution is based on adaptability and flexibility—success in weight control requires both."

So okay, Marissa thought, if there's no plan to follow . . . then what? She felt a tickle of confusion and more than a little frustration. She was so tired of working so hard for so little.

"I can tell you, though, how to spot a bad plan. One simple rule will eliminate ninety percent of what's being hawked out there. If the book or guru or infomercial says you do not have to exercise to succeed it's a fraud."

Marissa blinked.

"I know, I know, that seems harsh and I'm not given to blanket statements. But this is one I feel strongly about. It's just my opinion. Exercise, physical activity, like walking, swimming, hiking, tennis, dancing—it's vital to your health and well-being. You can't maintain a healthy weight without it, especially as you get older. Our bodies are designed to move."

Helena turned back the first sheet of her obviously well-used flip chart. "Here's the list of the big lies. One—you don't have to exercise. Two—you don't have to watch what you eat. Three—you don't have to wait for results. Four—you don't have to change. I am telling you the more these statements are used in any so-called weight control program the bigger the lie and, curiously, the more they charge for their advice and products."

Remembering the price tag on Bianca's late night infomercial miracle pills, Marissa found herself nodding as she scribbled notes.

"You want to believe it—I want to believe it too. I've struggled all my life to control my weight. I want a magic bullet. It wasn't until I accepted that fitness and meal planning were a reasonable use of my time—not just reasonable but justifiable and vital—that I had success. So think about that for a moment. We can train ourselves to plug in our cell phones, take the car in for oil changes, moisturize our skin, brush our teeth every day, absorb the news important to our lives and jobs. These things take time but they're necessary to maintaining our lives. So when is the last time you allowed time to maintain your body?"

Marissa frowned. Actually, she was spending five hours a week maintaining her muscles. She was here because it wasn't getting her anywhere with losing the fat.

"Everywhere you go you're looking at advertising that says it's okay to spend time at the coffee bar or shopping or talking to our friends or whipping up a weekly home facial. But there's no money for anyone in telling you that an hour's walk five times a week is not just okay, it's great for you." She turned another page on the flip chart.

"And women. Oh we women are multitaskers. We take care of everyone else and the time to take care of us is always at the end of the day. Who can take a walk at ten p.m. when the kids are finally asleep? Who feels selfish for letting the kids make their own breakfasts so you can get some exercise?"

There were nods all around Marissa.

"Here's the last thing I'm going to tell you that you don't want to hear. You're going to have to change. Not just what you eat and how you get exercise. You are going to have to change how you look at yourself. If you don't think that is true then I simply can't help you."

"Okay," the woman next to Marissa said. "I can really use something I want to hear now."

Helena grinned. "Fair enough. How about this? Unless you are one of the rare people with a bona fide physical problem, you *can* control your weight. You can lose the fat, you can eat the foods you like. It's up to you."

"That's better," the woman muttered.

"Here's the bad news." Helena paused to laugh as many in the room groaned. "You have to do all the work by yourself. I can only guide. Your friends can only encourage. Gyms can only provide equipment. The work is yours."

"I'm already working hard." Marissa couldn't contain herself any longer. "I exercise five hours a week and I'm eating like a bird. I should have lost twenty-three pounds according to the math but I've only lost nine."

"I understand and it sounds like some analysis of what you're doing might help you find something that works smarter. But that does bring me to an important point about reasonable expectations. How long did it take you to gain the weight you want to lose now?"

"Ten, fifteen years."

"Some of the diet gurus will tell you that it'll all come back off in three months."

"I get that they're being unrealistic." Abruptly, Marissa had tears in her eyes. "I know it's going to take time. I'm willing to invest the time. I just don't want it to take ten years to get it back off. I don't want to spend the rest of my life working this hard just to stay even."

"What about two years?"

Marissa found a half-smile. "I don't want it to take that long, either."

"But you'd spend two years getting a degree that might be a lifetime investment in your career, wouldn't you?" Helena spread her hands in appeal.

"True," Marissa admitted.

"I'm not saying it'll be two years. I'm saying it's an investment of time to get a result you think is important. Like taking a night class to get a better job. This is about scheduling your life to get a better physical machine through consistent exercise and good nutrition. If you don't think that you are worth this investment then you will never succeed. You have to like who you are, right now, enough to want to spend time on yourself for the payoff of a body that will carry you healthily into middle and old age."

Off to Marissa's right, someone asked, "Are you going to cover diet plans and approaches at some point?"

"I will. My program is this series of five classes. Next week we're going to do metabolic math and talk about hunger hormones and the recent suggestion by some researchers that fat is an organ, like the pancreas, and it acts and reacts on a very complicated level. In addition, you'll each get two hours of consultation, scheduled any ol' way you like. If you want more, we can talk about private consulting."

The woman next to Marissa raised a hand laden with chunky rings. "You're not going to tell me I need to stop having caffeine and diet soda and eat seaweed pills, are you?"

Helena laughed. "I believe that there are herbals that can help some people and if I think that's the case with you I have the names of a few homeopaths. Caffeine—no one can decide if it's good or bad, in excess or moderation or what. Some people eliminate caffeine and feel great. But the last thing I want to do is tell you to take all the joy out of your life. What's the point in that?"

"Damn right. There's no point in me doing something that just makes me want to die."

Nodding with understanding, Helena paused to look carefully around the room. "I want to be clear—I'm a licensed nutritionist and a veteran of the weight loss wars. I'm not a doctor, a homeopath, a fitness trainer and I'm certainly not a therapist. I will tell you if I think you need any of those things—"

"Oh, please," the woman next to Marissa scoffed. "I just like food too much. I wasn't abused as a girl and now I stuff myself because of the trauma, boohoo poor me."

Marissa, feeling as if her eyebrows had hit her hairline, said, "Maybe not, but some of us here were." Reflecting on her epiphany that wanting to be unattractive to boys had led her to put on extra pounds, she added, "Some of us probably haven't figured out that one's got to do with the other."

Helena took back control of the session with a quiet, "As I said, we're all unique. Our issues and histories are all different. What we need to do for ourselves will vary."

The session went on for another twenty minutes of question and answer. When it was over, Marissa got out her checkbook to enroll in the full series of classes. She wished she'd been able to convince Heather to come as well. Though she still went to the gym, she too was dejected that she'd not really had any results either.

The woman next to her leaned close and said, "I'm really

sorry—that sounded incredibly insensitive. I have this problem with my mouth. Too much food goes in and too many words come out."

Marissa found a smile. "It's fine. Are you going to sign up?"

"Yeah." The woman smoothed her already tidy blond curls and Marissa admired the perfect manicure. "She made a lot of sense, especially that one size doesn't fit all. I don't want to exercise. I hate it, in fact. But I can't hide from the fifty pounds on my ass anymore. I went to the theme park this weekend with my kids and there were two rides they wouldn't let me on because the belts wouldn't go around me. And I thought, well damn. I like roller coasters more than Egg McMuffins."

Marissa laughed. "Sounds like you got quite a jolt. I had to climb a cliff or probably drown and I nearly didn't make it because of the weight and my total lack of fitness. So here I am."

One beringed hand swept through a mass of black curls. "It's also true that my ever-lovin' husband said this was a waste of time. What he meant was he didn't want to be making his own dinner once a week."

A tall, broad-shouldered woman who looked as if she could play football turned from the sign-up table. "Oh, you got resistance too? It was my boss who didn't want me to leave 'early' which was actually not quite as late as usual. You'd think a woman would be more understanding."

Rising, the woman next to Marissa added, "My husband thinks it's a good idea for me to lose weight. He just doesn't want it to take any special effort away from him. But the time has to come from somewhere, unfortunately. Just writing a check to the gym isn't going to work. I have to actually *go*."

Marissa sighed. "I get up earlier than I used to. I'm not dating anyone right now so I do have time to myself but otherwise I work long hours. And this isn't a weekends-only effort. Some of the time has to come from the work day. I guess I need to remind myself I'm lucky I have some control over my work schedule. A lot of women are not so lucky."

After paying her fee and scheduling a thirty-minute consultation with Helena for the following week, Marissa strolled out of the community center building to her car. Ocky, when Marissa had let her know she had to leave before six, had groused a bit, saying, "You'd think they make classes like that at a convenient time."

"I work most Saturdays so it's not like any time is convenient," Marissa had answered. Now she was wondering why it was that Ocky, her oldest and dearest friend, hadn't applauded madly when she'd said she was going to try out a weight control consultant recommended by one of their clients. Didn't Ocky want her to be healthier?

She was still mulling over Ocky's attitude and even entertaining the idea that just maybe she was over her crush on Ocky as she settled in at home in front of her computer. The unfinished Finders Keepers questionnaire seemed to wink at her. What was she waiting for? Other women were lamenting time away from their loved ones to exercise. She only had work as an obstacle.

She stubbed her toe on the way back to the kitchen for a second bottle of cold water. It wasn't the first time she'd nearly tripped over the boxes of *Finders Keepers: the Early Years* records. Feeling grumpy, she surveyed the crowded living room. She knew Ocky's garage was full to the hilt, but honestly, this was ridiculous. Something had to change.

"I swear," she told her computer monitor as she opened her e-mail, "I will not turn forty and still have significant pieces of furnishing supported by cinder blocks."

She checked her messages, telling herself she wasn't hoping to see something from Linda. There wasn't and she told herself it didn't matter.

There was, however, a message from the man who had taken all the photos of their adventure. He apologized for the delay in sending them out to everybody. Marissa quickly sent back an effusive thank you and downloaded the zip file.

She was smiling when she opened the first one—there it was,

their doomed ship looking so bright and unsinkable. The next photo was the lifeboat. It looked so small. She spotted herself in the last row. She didn't remember being that far back. She'd gotten the second-to-last seat on the boat, it appeared. Had she been any slower getting to the emergency station she'd have been in a different one.

Just in front of her, of course, looking alive and lovely and tall and strong and all good things there could be in a woman, was Linda.

She zoomed in on Linda's face and realized she'd forgotten Linda's precise features as a whole. The mouth she remembered perfectly as she did Linda's eyes. Her hands remembered the texture of Linda's hair even if she'd forgotten how richly dark it was. Her fingertips tingled with the memory of Linda's skin even if she'd not remembered the perfect olive tone.

What had happened? Why hadn't Linda been in touch? May was just around the corner.

Clicking forward she found the photo of Linda, body stretched and taut as she made her way up the cliff. Her legs were impossibly long, her arms impossibly powerful but Marissa knew they were real. She'd felt both around her.

Her stomach growled and she wanted to have a second dinner. She was so tired of being hungry. Trying to do something with her hands that didn't involve opening the marcona almonds, she decided she'd weigh herself, which was always a mistake at the end of the day.

Predictably, the scale said she'd gained a pound in the course of her starvation. Something inside her broke and she stomped hard on the stupid thing before smacking both fists equally painfully onto the wall. The little print of wildflowers slipped off the nail and she cut her big toe on a shard of glass.

Sitting in the middle of the mess she cried, cried like she hadn't before and called Linda a lot of names. Then she spent a sniveling hour finishing the questionnaire.

She gazed one last time at the clearest photo of Linda's face.

Dear Linda,

Maybe I loved the way you made me feel and not really you. But I felt something for you and it was real. It didn't deserve to be ignored and forgotten. Even though the time with you was arguably the best thing to ever happen to me, I'm angry and hurt. You better not be dead, because someday I will make sure you know that you broke my heart.

Marissa, moving on

P.S. Please don't be dead.

At bedtime, her body feeling like lead, she looked at the pale green T-shirt peeking out from under her pillow. She used it to dry new tears, then folded it into the back of her sock drawer.

⚬ᘓᕷᘓ⚬

"Marissa, you sound so motivated." Helena Boxer glanced down at the printouts Marissa had made from her nutrition and exercise tracking program. "You are working incredibly hard."

"And getting nowhere fast."

"Plateaus are inevitable but I actually don't think that's what's going on. You're exercising too often and not long enough. Plus while the weights, stationary cycling and elliptical are good cardio training, they're only helping you keep and build the substantial muscle you've got, not burning fat."

"But I didn't have muscle before."

"Actually," Helena said with a smile, "you did. You had muscles sufficient to pull your entire body up a flight a stairs. Your muscles were finely toned to do short bursts of heavy effort. Your training at the gym is more of the same. Some of it is even less of the same because only the elliptical isn't sitting down. So the muscles in your legs and butt that used to carry your entire body around are working a weight machine but only having to move your legs. What you're doing isn't challenging enough in the right ways. Tell them to get you off cardio and onto aerobic—slower, longer. You need endurance."

174

Marissa made a note. "I spent a lot of money at Take It Off and that feels like a waste too."

"Actually, programs like Take if Off and other weekly meeting groups are valuable, at least initially. Some people love the support group atmosphere and find it motivating too. But the big benefit is retraining yourself on portion size. I doubt, though, that you're getting enough protein to sustain your muscle mass. You're not going there anymore?"

Rolling her eyes, Marissa said, "A couple of weeks ago I figured I could buy a piece of fish, cook it badly and steam some broccoli all by myself."

"Good for you. You have great snacks, too. Nuts, lean cheeses, reduced fat lunch meats. Don't be afraid of carbs—"

"They suck up so much of the calories, and so quickly. It's hard to eat a half a bagel."

"A good-sized handful of pretzels is satisfying crunching. Look for the fat-free variety. You know, your diet is excellent, but low in protein and I'd say low in treats." Helena gave her a toothy grin. "That's right, you need more treats. You've learned a habit of moderation. If you can apply it to things you really enjoy, there's no reason why you can't treat yourself a couple times a week to whatever tempts you."

"Cookies." Marissa realized she sounded like she was praying. "I love cookies."

"Then get some of the individually-wrapped snack packs of your favorites. Portion controlled that way, but still a reward. As for the protein, you can add powder to nonfat milk for a shake or increase the portion size of the fish and lean chicken. You need about ten grams more a day, preferably without a lot of fat. Without enough protein, your body will cannibalize your muscles to allow you to exercise."

"And that's completely self-defeating."

"Right. The more muscle you have the more calories your body will need to keep going—the more you can eat. At some point the amount of lean body mass to fat will hit equilibrium and that's where you'll be for the rest of your life if you continue the exercise. Does that make sense?"

"Sure." Marissa could easily picture the intersection of weight and lean body mass on a chart. Getting to that point was what she wanted. "I can follow that. I was reading about how a lot of information about body mass index and body fat percentage is too simplified. You can have a body fat of twenty percent and still be unhealthy."

"That's my goal—I want you to find the healthy spot for you. That could be twenty-five percent body fat. Technically, that's overweight. But if you are carrying solid lean body mass and able to do all the activities you want and eating a nutritious diet, then what's the percentage matter? And it's depressing but true, it's easier to get from thirty-five to thirty percent body fat than it is to get from twenty-five to twenty-four. Your body is smart. It has perfected a lifetime of saving fat in case you need it."

"I've never thought about food that way. That eating badly and sitting on my hinder was a kind of training. Anti-training, even."

They chatted for a few minutes about gaps in public education and resource materials with scientifically-grounded information.

"It is frustrating," Helena acknowledged. "If I really want to depress myself I go web surfing for diet advice. There is downright dangerous stuff out there that somehow sounds reasonable on the surface. Urban myths, especially, with ridiculous celebrity diets."

Thinking of Heather, Marissa said, "I have a friend who's really frustrated and she wants to try one of those five-day shock loss low-calorie diets. She says she wants to 'jump start' her system."

"Talk her out of it," Helena said immediately. "Let's say she eats two thousand calories a day. Not unreasonable but for her, it's too much. So one day she eats five hundred. The hormone leptin stops producing—it's the hormone that tells you to stop eating and it also tells your body it's okay to burn energy. She spends the night too tired to move and feeling quite hungry."

"In college there was this so-called Dolly Parton diet and I didn't make it two days." She could still recall the smell of onion and cabbage soup.

Helena shuddered. "That's because on the second day the hormone ghrelin—I called it gremlin—kicks in. And it screams at your stomach to growl, cramp and will even send out messages to shake and pump less blood to your brain so you're dizzy and feeling sick."

"That's when I gave up." Marissa didn't admit she'd tried it a half-dozen times, with the same result every time. Doing the same thing over and over thinking the outcome would change. Huh, she thought—when the outcome of a stupid plan didn't change no matter how often I did it, who did I blame? Not the plan. I blamed myself.

Enough of that, she told herself.

"Good, you listened. The gremlin's entire purpose is to get you to eat. After all, you are starving to death—what else is your body to make of your low-calorie intake? Then!" Helena paused meaningfully. "You suck up all the willpower you've got and make it day three. You are now technically starving. The diet says you're losing water and fat. But you're not."

Trying not to recall how many times she'd tried similar diets during her early twenties and always ended them with a bag of Oreos or pepperoni pizza, Marissa asked, "What is happening?"

"Your clever body, the product of tens of thousands of years of evolution, burns what you don't need—muscle. You're starving, you don't need to run a marathon. So it burns muscle. The scariest bit is that your heart is a muscle like any other. So its capacity is being reduced along with your glutes and deltoids and so on."

"Wow." Marissa tried to take that in. "So a diet like that you don't lose fat and when you give it up you feel like crap both psychically *and* physically. That's a complete downward cascade."

"And after losing muscle you're even less likely to exercise and your body desperately hoards fat because of the starvation trauma you just put it through. The entire experience trained your body to keep the fat."

"So there you are—every pound comes back, double." Marissa sighed heavily. She had been there so many times.

"So talk your friend out of it. A diet that restricts choices, prompts moderate and wise eating is what we all need."

"Thank you. I'll talk to her tomorrow. Um, so, about my exercise. Too often and not long enough?" A quick trip to the gym fit so easily into her schedule. She felt good about making herself go almost every day.

"Yeah. You need more variety and the good news is there are things you can do that are almost free. Your time is a valuable enough investment. They involve getting out of the gym. When you make some progress, the gym can help you hone specific areas. In bad weather those machines are great. But right now, given that you seriously want to lose fat and build some endurance, walking with hand or ankle weights for no less than an hour, three times a week, will give you slow and steady progress toward your goals. Change your gym focus from cardio like I said, and go no more than three times a week."

"Walking is so boring, though."

"I know. Music, books on CD, they pass the time. Oh, do you know how to skate?"

"No, never learned."

"Well, if you're feeling adventurous, go to the rink and rent pads and blades and give it a try. It's good aerobic exercise and does fantastic things for your butt. A variety of exercises, just like a variety of foods, is what your body needs. In the long run, having choices will keep you motivated and enthused."

"You've given me so much to think about. Thank you. I feel a little overwhelmed, but really, this has been great," Marissa said.

Her head spinning with too much new information, Marissa resisted the urge to go to the gym as she'd just been yesterday. It felt weird, fighting the urge to work out.

Instead she went shopping. Wandering in the department store she looked at expensive walking shoes and socks that must have had gold thread given the price tag. Perhaps she should treat herself to some gear. Did she want red shoes or blue ones? They would make a nice reward for starting a new program.

Oh no way, she told herself sternly. Giving yourself treats and rewards before you actually *do* anything is the wrong kind of training. She made a note about the red walking shoes. If she found the time and commitment to stick with Helena's suggestions for three weeks, she'd get them then.

Instead, she marched over to the accessories and plunked down eight dollars for handheld weights, then set out on the Iron Horse Trail that ran along the back of their office building. Her ordinary gym shoes would be fine for now.

The first half-hour felt great. The second half-hour, to her surprise, took more effort than she had anticipated. Her hips hurt, her knees hurt, her shoulders hurt. So her gym workouts hadn't improved her ability to do something as simple as walk for an hour. That was mind-boggling. It wasn't supposed to be that way, she wanted to whine. She nipped the impulse in the bud and instead told herself firmly that it was proof she was unique. Dang it all.

She got home later than usual and missed one of her few favorite television programs. But I'm worth it, she told herself in the shower. I like myself more than TV, more than Oreos, more than a hot fudge sundae.

Her reflection wasn't the woman who had frightened her in Tahiti. She wasn't yet the woman she knew was inside her either. But there was a change, a definite change, one she wanted to pursue. One of these days she was going to look on the outside the way she felt on the inside.

The next morning she tucked the finished Finders Keepers questionnaire into her satchel. It was time.

Part Three

Chapter 12

Of all the ways that Marissa had imagined finally confronting Linda again, eyes stinging with sweat and smelling like a locker room was not one of them. Linda, of course, looked as if she'd just left a day spa, immaculate, relaxed and gorgeous. The hurt and pain Marissa had worked so hard to put away were immediately at the surface, combining in an inner cry of, "This is *so* not fair."

She gave herself a moment to think by fumbling for the iPod shut-off. She couldn't have felt more unattractive, in spite of the running shorts Heather said made her bootylicious. She finally made herself look at Linda again. This conversation was not supposed to happen standing in her parking lot before the sun was completely up.

"What do you mean you want me?" Marissa tried to face Linda square on, fighting off all the memories of her skin, her laughter and the soft, welcome words that had made Marissa feel attractive and wanted. "You wait a year?"

"I know. And I know you've reason to be mad."

"I got over being angry a while ago. I don't feel anything but regret now." Okay, given the way her heart was pounding, that was a boldfaced lie. But a pounding heart didn't mean good feelings, only strong ones.

The dark eyes shimmered with emotion—oh, how does she make her eyes do that, Marissa wailed inside. It wasn't fair. "I have a lot of regrets too," Linda said quietly. "I know I must have hurt you. If you'll let me explain, at least you'll know why."

"Does it matter? I'm past it."

A new set of lines around Linda's mouth creased as she smiled, but not happily. "I was hoping it would still matter to you."

"It would have nine months ago. You broke my heart, do you know that?"

"I'm sorry."

"Are you just here because you want me to forgive you so you can move on? Fine." Marissa wiped sweat off her brow and, dang it all, wished she didn't look like a drowned rat and smell worse. "You're forgiven."

"Can we maybe get together tonight and talk?"

"I have a date." That, at least, was true. She didn't have to explain it was a first date in a short series of first dates as she worked up the courage to call the women her own program reported were 98% highly compatible with Chabot, Marissa.

"Then you pick a time. I was going to call tonight and let you know I was in town but I couldn't wait. I thought I'd at least see where you lived."

"I don't see what there is to be gained in all of this."

Linda took a deep breath and it was not fair that somehow, though her face had new lines, she looked even more embraceable than before. It's just physical, Marissa told herself angrily. She's the last woman you went to bed with. Well, Eve tonight might get lucky, because she wasn't going to let Linda hurt her again just because she wanted Linda bad. Oh hell.

"Okay, well, let me give you this and maybe if I call after a while we'll be able to talk. Because I've missed you. And I'm here for the right reasons finally. I know that doesn't make sense. But if I'd shown up earlier it would have been for the wrong reasons."

Linda held out a wrapped package she'd drawn out of a shopping bag. It was about the size of a box of chocolates, but when Marissa reluctantly took it she decided it felt like a book.

"I'm not going to tell you to call. I'm not going to tell you I want to talk over old times. That's just not the way it is."

"I am so sorry I hurt you, Marissa. I knew that I probably was hurting you but—" The brown gaze flicked to the package in Marissa's hands. "There were reasons. But no excuses. I behaved badly and I'm sorry."

Her breath catching, Marissa hated that she was blinking back tears. "I won't let you break my heart again."

"That's not going to happen, no."

What did that mean? Wasn't Linda here to try to rekindle their Tahitian flame? "So forgiveness is all you want?"

The flash of light might have been a car moving in the parking lot or it might have been Linda's smile. "I'm not saying that either."

"I have to go to work."

"I have an appointment to get to as well."

"Fine."

"Okay."

Even as Marissa was biting her tongue not to ask questions, Linda strode toward a nondescript sedan that screamed "rental." And just like that, she was gone.

Dazzled, befuddled, bemused—Marissa couldn't find the right word to describe how she felt. She would not spend the rest of the day, as she had spent so many days, wishing for Linda to call. She would not go back in time.

"Hey, girlfriend. You've got some mail and here's your very own newly minted Finders Keepers Questionnaire." Heather handed Marissa the bundle of envelopes with the questionnaire on top.

"The printer finally came through. Halle-Berry-lujah."

"I'll get the waiting list out to the prospective clients today and Ocky is looking for you."

"I love the hair clips." Marissa peered at the glitzy blue and white barrettes holding back Heather's hair.

"Tar-jay, Le Chic."

"Oh." Marissa leaned close and said in a whisper, "I'm buying a condo."

"Oh—you talked to Octavia? That's very cool. Wait until you tell your mom."

"She'll be picking out carpets." The prospect of sparring with her mother over decorating was actually quite pleasant. "Little does she know how much crap I have."

Marissa tried to settle into her work day but the morning encounter with Linda had been deeply unsettling. She had been certain she was over Linda. She no longer thought of her every day and when she did it wasn't with, well, anguish or anything. Regret was a good word. Nothing more than a vague, wistful regret. Right.

"Is that another new shirt?"

Marissa glanced up to smile at Ocky. "You noticed."

"You're becoming quite the clothes horse."

Her smile dimmed. "You say that like it's a bad thing."

"Not a bad thing. I mean, I should talk." Ocky settled into the only clear chair in Marissa's office. "So when were you going to tell me you'd signed up as a client?"

Uh-oh. "When I was actually dating someone. I mean, I signed up months and months ago. I just didn't . . . make any calls until recently. I wasn't ready."

"Still getting over that vacation fling? Oh, please," Ocky said, in response to Marissa's raised eyebrows. "I have eyes. You were walking ten feet off the ground when you got back. And then one day you weren't."

"Okay, fine. But I don't see how this is really your business." Whatever you do, don't tell her that the other woman showed up on your doorstep this morning.

186

Ocky blinked. "I thought we were friends enough that we shared stuff. You didn't share."

"I felt I'd been a fool. And as for sharing, well, you had all the girlfriends. I had my mother."

"But your mom's a lot better, huh?"

"Yeah."

"Nice job of sidetracking me." Ocky frowned, but she was clearly not that upset. "You're a client now. If you don't find someone we might have to say as much if asked."

"I know we both agreed that would be bad but I'm not so sure it would be. And who knows, I could be in the three out of four." A thought occurred to her. "Is that what's really bothering you?"

"Yeah," Ocky said with a lopsided grin. "If you get the happy love thing I am going to be the most pathetic person I know."

Marissa wasn't sure she was smiling as she laughed. "So until now I've been the most pathetic person you know?"

"I didn't mean it that way. You know that."

You didn't mean it, Marissa thought after Ocky went back to her office but it doesn't mean it's not how you felt. Well, that was a sure-all cure for a crush, finding out she was the person Ocky kept around so she could feel better about herself. That cleared up a lot of things just dandy.

Normally, she'd let Ocky know she was taking a longer lunch break but Ocky was not her boss and she was going to stop acting as if she was. She was in an agitated frame of mind when she got to Helena Boxer's office for her once-a-month check-in, but the moment she walked into the quiet space with pale blue walls and the faint smell of sandalwood she felt better. This little office was full of good feelings and positive energy.

"The running hurts my knees, even though it feels good at the same time," she told Helena after they reviewed her current progress. "I'll be glad actually not to do it when the time comes. I'd rather walk with more weights. I still haven't tried skating—that might be next."

"It's low impact, that's true." Helena glanced up from the printouts Marissa had brought. "Until you fall down, that is. Please get all the safety gear, okay?"

"I'll start at the rink with full body padding, promise. So anyway, you can see it. Adding a minute of running after every two minutes of walking worked well. I lost some more fat but now I'm at another plateau. I don't want to waste two months doing something that's not helping."

"Everybody brings their own skills to this process." Helena looked up with a grin. "You have a gift for data analysis. I adore your charts and graphs, and you are spotting trouble earlier than most people would. That's a great asset you've got in maintaining your lifelong health."

"Oh." Marissa blushed. "I hadn't thought of it that way."

"You're one of a kind, absolutely. And the data says it's time to tweak again."

"It feels like I'm tweaking all the time."

"And this is bad why?" Helena tipped her head to one side.

"Shouldn't something that works for me, work all the time?"

"Well." Helena tapped the graph that showed Marissa's slowly falling weight line. "Since you began we've tweaked every six to eight weeks. You've lost sixteen pounds on the Tweak It program."

Marissa chortled. "Okay, so my plan is to have no plan?"

"Your program is to be flexible. Mixing things up, varying your exercise—that is succeeding steadily for you. You work with computers. When you set them up does that solution last forever?"

"No. You're right, it doesn't. I'm lucky to get two to three weeks on a configuration sometimes. Then it needs, well, tweaking."

Helena leaned companionably on her desk, her eyes gentle with compassion. "Your body, my body, all of us, we are the most complex and diverse systems in the universe. We are as complex as this planet, as the stars, because that's what we're made up of. No computer could ever be as complicated."

"Okay, all ones from me on that."

"Some people," Helena said, "eliminate butter from their diet and never struggle with their weight again."

"Bitches."

Helena shared Marissa's laughter. "I love it when you make an appointment because I know I'm going to laugh."

"My work is done, then."

"Mine isn't." Helena put the last month's worth of nutritional breakdowns on the top of the stack. "I think it's time for you to ease up on protein in favor of low fat carbs. I'd recommend the extra carbs be eaten after your workouts—a moderate complex carb."

"Then not fruit. Candy bar?"

"A small one, with nuts if possible. And there are some sports nuritionals that would do the trick—energy shots and the like."

A hundred possibilities of a modest treat clamored in her mind, "Pick me, pick me." Deciding would be almost as much fun as licking her fingers after she ate whatever morsel she chose.

They chatted a little bit more and Marissa left feeling motivated and reassured that she was doing sensible, rational things and her expectation to continue losing fat and gaining endurance was reasonable and achievable. She was proud of herself.

Back at the office, she wasn't proud of the fact that she checked for messages on her answering machine at home, on her cell and on her private e-mail. She wasn't going down this road again. Annoyed with herself, she went in search of her belated lunch.

Heather was taking her lean frozen entrée out of the microwave. "I'm starting up again, boss."

"I know you can do it, Heather. If I can, you can."

"You're amazing."

"So—" Marissa fixed Heather with a steady gaze. "So are you."

"I know I can do it but I don't do it. I went to see your Helena."

"You did? That's great! I was just there. What did you think?" Marissa grinned at Heather.

Heather was abruptly very quiet. In a low voice, she said, "Helena thinks I should see a therapist. She gave me some names."

"Oh?"

"Just . . . some stuff I never told anybody and I didn't think mattered. But maybe that's why I sabotage myself. I don't want to succeed. Apparently, the Man of My Dreams scares me."

Marissa put a hand on Heather's arm. "You have incredible willpower, Heather. And if there's something you need to work out so you can get on, then go for it. If you need a regular hour off or something, you know we can work that out."

"Thanks, boss. I think I'm going to make some calls on my break. I'm tired of feeling like a failure."

"You're not a failure, Heather. Look at you."

"I *am* looking at me, Marissa." Her eyes brimmed with tears. "I look at me every day. I see a fat girl."

Vividly recalling how her mirror had made her feel nothing more than a helpless fat chick, Marissa folded her arms as she regarded the woman in front of her. "I see someone with the stamina and self-esteem to put herself through night school while she sends money home to help her younger sisters. I see someone with wit and fashion sense and hair and skin I'd kill for."

Heather frowned. "Don't say I have a pretty face."

Marissa swallowed hard. "Believe me, I know how that one stings. Even when it's true. You have style I can't carry off. And sometimes you're so smart about process development that it makes me moist and excited as only a true computer geek can be." She winked.

"Are you hitting on me?" Heather's frown melted into a grin.

"Only your mind—you have that whole straight thing going for you. I can't wait until you finish up that computer science certificate. It's good-bye receptionist desk the moment you do."

"That will be such a huge deal. Thank you. You're so encouraging, especially when I'm so down on myself sometimes."

"Heather, girlfriend, you are incredible Play-Doh, full of potential to be anything. You've let life shape you but I think you're ready to shape yourself now."

"And lose some of the dough."

"Like I said, if I can, you can."

Heather glanced at the wall clock. "I might be able to make a few calls now."

Marissa grinned into the refrigerator as she retrieved the components of her lunch. If she'd had a younger sister she would have liked someone like Heather. "Oh, hush," she told the gremlin in her stomach. "Food will be here shortly."

She smeared about two tablespoons of herbed goat cheese on a paper plate, then began counting out slices of pepperoni.

"That's quite a pile." Ocky scooted around Marissa to retrieve a soda from the refrigerator.

Marissa finished counting her eighteen slices before looking up. "Fifty calories, six grams of protein and a half-gram of fat. With the goat cheese, a mere hundred calories of tasty goodness. Later, I get an organic energy bar with soy protein and twenty essential nutrients for active women."

"I was rude this morning," Ocky said abruptly. "I'm just unsettled by how much you've changed. I don't like feeling that I don't know you."

The apology felt genuine and something in Marissa eased. She was certain she no longer had a crush on Ocky, and maybe that would let them be more balanced friends. "Sometimes, Ocky, I don't know me. But I'm learning more every day."

When she got back to her desk she discovered a single truffle, her favorite dark mocha, resting on a piece of note paper which read, "You're not just a great boss, you're a nice person."

The truffle tasted wonderful with her afternoon tea during the sales staff meeting. She savored every last nuance of robust coffee and hints of pepper and cinnamon. She had earned it, she told herself. She also told herself that her heart had not leapt, not even for a moment, thinking before she read the note that it might have been signed by Linda.

Linda turned from her study of the plaques adorning the reception area walls as a man paused near her and said, "Ms. Bartok?"

"Yes." She shook his hand. "You must be Jim Manchuik."

"Welcome to the Sierra Club. If you'll come with me, I'll introduce you to the California Senior Chapter Director."

Tom Jawed had a firm handshake and the three of them sat around a worn desk barely visible under stacks of paperwork.

"I had to say," Tom began, "that when I read your résumé I thought that you would be completely wasted as a Volunteer Coordinator. We don't get a lot of Ivy Leaguers in that job."

"I know it seems a little odd but you'll notice that there is no paid employment on my résumé beyond what I'm supposed to call being a Food Services Industry Technician. I flipped burgers."

The two men laughed, then Jim said, "You volunteered all over the world—that counts to us. I don't think you'd have a Yale MBA if you were a flake."

Linda felt a coil of tension in her spine unwind. She hadn't been at all certain she'd be taken seriously and she was grateful to have gotten this interview. A job of any kind, related to something she really enjoyed, would help her settle and look around—and she'd be near Marissa. The last six months had been exhausting. Breaking old habits was hard. "I won't lie and say I didn't have some family issues that slowed down my progress at Yale but they are completely resolved now. I am very interested in this job and would be willing to make at least a year's commitment to it. Why don't you tell me where you would like to see the management of volunteers. You must have hundreds—"

"Thousands," Jim corrected.

"Thousands, then. What would an ideal volunteer organization look like?"

The two men laughed again and Linda relaxed into the interview, feeling more and more confident. If not this job she would find another but the interview process was feeling more and more comfortable by the minute.

She left the Berkeley offices around noon and strolled through the Telegraph Avenue district. World-famous among college students, it struck her as familiar—street vendors, musicians, pizza-by-the-slice, organic restaurants and many, many earnest young faces. Her stomach growled near the falafel cart and she carried the fragrant pita up the steps of the landmark bell tower as it chimed twelve and found a comfortable spot to sit down.

With a very welcome winter sun caressing her face, she finally let herself think about Marissa.

How incredibly alive she had looked . . . her skin flushed from exercise, her brow beaded with sweat, her hair back in that cute ball cap. The confidence, the willingness to strive was as present as ever, including, Linda thought with chagrin, the self-will to push Linda away to avoid getting hurt again.

She had anticipated the anger but not taken into account Marissa's strength of mind. It would take more than an apology to start a conversation. And if they didn't talk, well, there was no hope at all.

She'd written dozens of letters in her head to Marissa while she'd been in Montana, then at Yale. Apologies, explanations, some whining. One desperate night, overloaded with coursework and dealing with a professor who seemed to delight in underscoring her rustiness in some areas, she'd packed her bags and nearly left. She might not have gone through with it but it was also true that one of the things that slowed her was thinking about how she'd explain to Marissa that she'd run away, one more time, when life got emotionally tough.

She dabbed tahini sauce from her chin and smiled into the sun. It was twelve degrees in Boston. She could use some sunshine in her life for a while.

With her suit jacket neatly hung on the hanger hooked on the passenger seat of the rental car, she made her way through the congested traffic, only missing her turn twice. Driving was still a new skill. The rental car had no trouble with a steep climb to the tunnel that would take her from Berkeley to the inner valley where Marissa lived and worked. It was also where her motel was.

She glanced in the mirror, meeting her own gaze. "That's right, you're not going to act like a stalker. Give her a few days to maybe look at the book."

She'd written all the letters in her mind but the book was real. Congressional members could request any title be added to the Library of Congress, so, in time, the story she had so needed to tell would be permanently stored. She could let it all go now and hope for the side benefit of it making up for the words she'd never sent to Marissa.

She treated herself to some side trips off the freeway, finding rolling hills and little towns that surprised her so close to such an intensely urban area. She enjoyed a hot coffee overlooking a sparkling reservoir, counting clouds scudding across the vivid blue sky. It wasn't Tahiti or the Alps or the golden plains of high country Spain. This is the world that made Marissa, she thought. I could like it here.

The winter sun had set by the time she returned to her motel. She was getting addicted to high-speed Internet and was glad to find a few messages from some of her classmates and even a newsy one from Ted Jeffers. She sent back a note congratulating him for his daughter's placement at a regional track meet, then stared at the empty screen.

She carefully typed out just a few sentences. No mushy stuff. Just the bare facts. This time, unlike any time in the past year, she clicked send.

Chapter 13

"You're Marissa, right?"

Marissa smiled nervously at the bright-eyed woman who paused hesitantly next to the little table where Marissa's coffee sat cooling. "You're Eve."

She scooched her chair to the left to make room for Eve's knees in the small space. A chair leg tipped her purse and some of the contents spilled across the floor. "Oh, heck!"

Eve helped her collect things, including a lipstick that had rolled near someone's foot. "Here you go."

"Thanks. Okay, I think we can safely say when I admitted to being a bit clumsy I was being honest."

"I'm a total butterfingers too. Is that a Nano?"

"Yeah." Marissa handed the slim music player to Eve.

"Wow. That's so sleek. I love gadgets, very cool. I've been thinking about getting one."

Marissa studied the dark-fringed brown eyes, liking the humor evident in them. They were a lively feature in a round, pleasant face surrounded by straight black hair typical of Asian heritage. "It was my twenty-five pound reward."

"Oh, I should think of skipping my daily muffin and save up the cash. That would be a complete win-win. Very slick." She handed back the iPod and a little silence fell. Luckily, Eve's name was called at the coffee counter and by the time she returned, Marissa had found her tongue.

"So, I know this isn't original, but what made you decide to use Finders Keepers?"

"A couple of friends did. One's dating a nice guy now. The other wouldn't call anybody. I'm pretty shy so I'm glad you called me."

"Well, I don't want to sound like the questionnaire, but what's your favorite thing to do on a date?"

Eve gave a nervous laugh that wasn't unpleasant. "Talk. I know that sounds terribly cliché, women like to talk, but I'm a kindergarten teacher and I spend all day with sentences of four words or less. Some days I get in the car and say words like 'multi-syllabic' just to prove I am."

Marissa chuckled. "I can see that. I'm not a great talker unless, I've been told, I get all worked up about something." Linda had commented on that, and the way she used her hands to talk. Self-conscious, she shoved one hand under her thigh and let the other toy with the stir stick in her coffee. "I should confess that I'm a computer geek and I don't talk to real people. Well, actually, in the last six months or so I've been talking to a lot of real people. It's been a change."

"You know, you look familiar, but I can't place you."

"Might have been one of the photos at the back of the Finders Keepers brochure. I'm one of the owners."

"Oh!" Eve sipped her coffee. "I would have thought you had the perfect match already."

"No time to look. Then I realized if I let work take all the time,

I'd be forty and single and no telling how many perfect matches would have passed me by."

"You think there's more than one?"

Marissa shrugged. "Maybe for some people. I think that those who are fairly easygoing can be very content with a number of people. I mean solidly, happily content. Not to be confused with settling."

"But shouldn't there be more than that? I mean, I can't imagine living with someone without a strong sense of contentment." Eve frowned slightly as she chose her words. "But what about that certain zing? The passion?"

"I know what you mean." She was liking Eve more by the minute, just as she'd liked Cicely and Wyndy when they'd had coffee. The computer had been right about a high-degree of compatibility—all had been in the 96 to 98 percent range. Conversation was easy. She had thought all three attractive in their own way and each had had an engaged intellect she found she could relate with. But her pulse had never risen, not the way a single look from Linda could make it race. If not for Linda, she might easily have found Eve a perfect, comfortable companion. Because of Linda she knew she wouldn't be happy with that. She didn't know if that knowledge was a gift or a curse. "Passion matters to me."

"So," Eve asked, after another little pause, "another question. What's your favorite place to go on vacation?"

"Anywhere but work." Marissa smiled into her cup then added more seriously, "I was in Tahiti last year and I'd love to go again. Preferably without the shipwreck."

"You were shipwrecked? How thrilling!"

Marissa found herself telling the tale, leaving out the part about Linda, Linda's hands and mouth all over her and the resulting broken heart. She even chided herself for being on a date with a very nice woman only to think about Linda. "I finally did get the trip insurance money and I bought the books again, all prepared for that next trip."

"That sounds like the adventure of a lifetime. One I could do without, probably. I want to see Alaska." Eve shook back her hair, looking as if she was truly enjoying their conversation.

The coffee was long gone when they both gathered their things and walked out of the coffeehouse together.

Summoning her courage, even though she was certain of the answer, she asked Eve, "So, are you feeling any of that zing?"

"I like you," Eve said immediately. "I'd like to see you again. But if there's a zing, it's going to take a while, I think."

Relieved, Marissa said, "That's about where I was. I can always use more friends and someone who has read all the Darkover books, more than once, that's a real treat."

"There's a Xena convention in the city in a couple of weeks. They're fun and zany. What do you think?"

Marissa made a show of biting her lip. "I have to confess I never watched the show." The mention of Xena made her think of Linda. What didn't? "I never gave it a chance. The history thing bothered me."

Eve laughed and it was full-throated and utterly charming. I could like her a lot, Marissa realized. I bet making love with her is easy and fun. There's just no room in me right now for something so simple. Which is a completely messed up way to be.

"I have so many friends who feel the same way. Okay, so not your speed. Can I make a confession?" Eve's expression turned serious as they sidestepped out of the way of more people exiting the coffeehouse.

"Sure."

"I really did sign up because a friend did and filling out the questionnaire was really interesting. It was like a mini-therapy session. I had to think about a lot of things to be really honest. But I've been out of a relationship for about six months. It was a really *bad* relationship and I like you. Enough that I'm thinking hey, I could date you. And then this little voice asks me if I'm really ready to subject someone I like to some of the leftover stuff. I'm totally over her but some of the things that happened I'm not."

"Oh. Thank you for being honest about where you are, really." Marissa briefly touched Eve's sleeve. "I'm, well maybe I'm a little bit in the same place. I got hurt, well, let's say I let myself think something was more than it was and when it was clear it meant nothing to her it took me a while to get over it. I'm not sure that I am. The hurt, I mean." Plus, she knew she could have added, the woman in question just showed up again and now I don't know what I'm feeling.

"Well," Eve said, her eyes taking on her easy smile again, "I think what all that means is for now, let's not presume we're going anywhere with this."

Marissa had to grin. "I think that's a total violation of the Finders Keepers recommendations. We signed something, didn't we, that we felt ready and able to enter into a new relationship?"

"Yeah." Eve flushed. "But doesn't everybody think that in the abstract? But when faced with taking that next step, everything feels a little different."

They turned toward the parking lot as Marissa said, "You and I are going to bring down the Finders Keepers statistics."

"I am hungry now, though." Eve had an engaging grin, and Marissa had no trouble imagining a room full of five-year-olds thinking their teacher was a total rock star.

"Me too. Think we should have dinner in the same place and share a table? For expedience, not because it's a date?"

Eve chuckled and pointed at a burger place across from the movie theaters. "They do a turkey burger with mashed avocado and a lime sauce that's pretty good. We could skip the fries."

"I'm loving it already."

Okay, Marissa thought, as they companionably consumed their meals, there will be no meaningless getting-over-Linda sex for me tonight. Not that she had seriously thought there would be. She'd had very little meaningful sex in her life but what there had been she'd downright enjoyed. She wanted what she'd felt with Linda— but not with Linda she thought hastily. Maybe she wasn't as over Linda as she had thought and maybe she had no business dating

Eve or anyone else. Was that why she'd never followed up with Cicely and Wyndy? Had they also sensed that Chabot, Marissa wasn't ready-for-prime-time dating?

"Hey, Mom."

"Don't tell me you're calling to cancel the salon appointment on Saturday morning."

"Okay, I won't tell you that, because that's not why I called. Do you think I have some kind of relationship death wish?" Marissa veered around a speed bump then turned out of the megaplex parking lot.

Her mother laughed into the phone. "Are you asking me how to stop hanging onto a bad thing so you can take advantage of a good thing that comes along?"

"I suppose I could ask someone else but you're the only person I've told about the Tahiti situation, though I'm not sure at all why I told you."

"It was Christmas and you'd had that extra glass of red wine. Besides, I'm your mother and you tell me everything."

They snorted in stereo at that idea. "Yeah right. Anyway, this woman tonight seemed very nice. But as soon as I started thinking about U-Hauls the flashing neon lights went off."

"Then you're not ready. I'm not so sure it's pathological though."

Marissa turned onto the freeway ramp and accelerated toward home. "Oh, I don't know. I had a crush on Octavia for years. It was a good shield against having to even try to date anyone. Besides— hang on, I need to merge."

After a lane change, Marissa continued, "Besides, Linda turned up this morning. Alive and well and she said she wanted me."

"Oh, *please*. After a year?"

"Yeah, I know. I know."

"The nerve."

"She looked *really* good. Every time I see her or a photograph I realize I've forgotten how drop-dead gorgeous she is. It's like I never see that. I see something else, but I don't know what."

"Please be careful."

"I'm not going to see her again."

"Oh, of course you are. If nothing else you're curious."

"My heart's still got duct tape marks."

"Just be careful."

"You can bet on that."

The words rang in her head as she climbed the stairs to her apartment. The sunshine earlier in the day had given way to a chillier front that threatened rain. There were no flowers on the doorstep, no letters in the mailbox, no messages blinking on the answering machine. She ignored the brown-wrapped package Linda had given her that morning—it already seemed ages ago—as she made herself some green tea and sat down to check her e-mail.

She scanned the sender addresses on the new messages and her heart stopped. She closed her eyes briefly but when she looked again it was still there, a message from Linda. Her throat tightened as she relived all the months she had wanted to see that name. The subject line was "Up to You."

Dear Marissa,

I'm not perfect, but I'm not a bad person, either. If you do look at the book I gave you I am hoping you can understand why I let go of you until now.

I will be in the area for at least another week, perhaps as long as a year if I am fortunate enough to get the job I interviewed for. I'm only telling you that because I won't be in touch again. It's up to you."

Yours, Linda

The bottom of the message gave a cell phone number.

"It would serve you right if I never got in touch," Marissa said to the screen. The stinging tears of hurt were a surprise. Hadn't she cried enough? Hadn't she changed enough? Why was Linda so far under her skin?

She glanced over at the package on the counter then resolutely went to bed.

The package was still there in the morning. After communing with the scale, opening her first Diet Coke, munching an energy bar and packing up a few things from the fridge, Marissa could ignore it no longer.

"I'll glance through it at lunch," she told herself. Running through the rain she got to the car in record time. She tossed her daypack on the passenger seat and the package on top of that.

It was a very long red light to get onto the main boulevard toward work, so it made sense to pick the package open at least. After all, the paper was wet. She didn't want to ruin the book. It would save time doing it later.

"Damn," Marissa swore, when the light turned green. She set it aside, paper half torn, and dang it all, the lights were green all the way to the office.

It wasn't until after an all-staff meeting followed by a sales staff meeting followed by a management meeting where she and Ocky drank too much coffee and fussed about loan interest rates that Marissa found any time alone in her office where she could finish unwrapping the book.

She didn't know what she had expected, but it wasn't a trade paperback with a blue cover and simple white lettering reading *Winning at any Price: the Story of a Daughter and Mother.* At the bottom the author was given as Lindsey Vanessa Bartok Price. So Linda had written a book?

She flipped the pages to find an About the Author or Foreword but instead the book opened to a substantial middle portion of photographs. The first literally took her breath away.

She would know those eyes anywhere, the curving smile equally so. They belonged to a teenager with incredibly long legs, a waist that seemed nonexistent and long, dark hair that shone as if with its own light. Clad in a glittering one-piece swimsuit and strappy sandals, she posed with one leg back, one hand resting lightly on her hip.

The caption read, "Junior Miss Massachusetts was the height of my pageant career with a first runner-up finish. The winner was able to complete all of her duties and fulfill all of her obligations and so I remained a non-winner."

Intrigued, she turned to the next photo. Linda looked perhaps a year or two older and was clad in a long silky sheath dress and a sash that proclaimed her "Miss Suffolk County." Linda's allusion to time in doctor's offices, to needing "fixing"—had that been to be a beauty queen?

The caption was so bizarre she had to read it twice. "Though I was again crowned Miss Suffolk County, the state pageant was a complete rout when I didn't even qualify for the finals. The next day I realized that my mother was tainting my food and had been for some time."

Stunned, Marissa turned to the next page. Linda, at nineteen, looking gaunt and foreign with her hair shorn, had no smile. "My mother took this photo when I was being transferred from the emergency room that treated my cough syrup, wine and valium cocktail to the mental hospital where I would be treated for anorexia, a condition I did not have."

Marissa's heart seemed to be missing beats. She flipped through the remaining photographs and they were all the Linda she knew. Whether a too-grown-up little girl's body, a waiflike anguished young woman or the stronger, more familiar form of a Yale coed, Linda was there. Marissa looked back at the second photo and made herself reread the words, " . . . My mother was tainting my food and had been for some time."

She wanted not to believe it, the way she hadn't wanted to believe a mother would drown all of her children or a father shoot his entire family. Monsters wore white sheets and hid in the shadows. Monsters weren't real, she wanted to believe with all her heart.

Except they were. Sometimes they wore a religious smock or a banker's suit. Sometimes they looked like the best father in the world and walked around free in the sunshine. Linda had been raised by a monster.

Her heart was breaking again, in a different way. She looked at the little girl one last time and turned to the front pages to confront the opening words.

"There was a night, not long ago, when I experienced moments of complete happiness. When every instinct in my body told me to run away from this happiness I knew there was something wrong, deep within me. I did run away from happiness because I wanted it for all the wrong reasons."

"Marissa, whatever is it?"

She gasped and realized she was still at work and that tears were running down her face. "Sorry, Heather. A sad book. Silly, huh?" She whisked a tissue out of the box and dabbed the corners of her eyes. "I'm going to make a ruin of my makeup."

"Must be some book."

"Yeah, it is. So you caught me, reading on the job."

"I just stopped in to tell you that I'll need to be gone for an extra hour at lunch on Thursdays. If that's okay."

Marissa managed a shaky breath. "It's definitely okay. I think we can get Ruthann to agree to another hour on the desk—besides, she sort of hinted if you move into the tech side, she'd like the chance to prove she can do reception."

"Well," Heather said seriously, "she's young but let's give her a chance."

"She's the same age you were when I hired you."

"True." She grinned and Marissa wondered how it was Heather knew that shade of lipstick would make her mouth look wide and appealing. Guys were idiots—Heather was a doll. "I thought I could make up the hour by coming in thirty minutes early and leaving thirty minutes late?"

"It's a plan. I'll let Ocky know. I'll call it cross-training and administrative staff development opportunities."

"You," Heather said cheekily, "are so full of shit sometimes."

"You say that like it's a bad thing."

Heather laughed as she headed back to the front office. Marissa could feel the book warm under her hand. She didn't want to look down. She'd only start crying again. She closed it without another glance and pushed it gently into her daypack. Then, before she could rationalize away her impulse, she turned to her computer.

Dear Linda,

There's a beautiful rose garden not far from my office. Could I meet you there Saturday afternoon at three for a walk?

Marissa

P.S. If yes, click this URL for directions.

She held her breath for several moments before she clicked the send button. Then she found herself holding it again, waiting for a reply, which was a silly waste of time. Linda could be anywhere, of course.

She wasn't disappointed. The chime had barely finished playing before she opened Linda's answer.

Dear Marissa,

I'd love a walk on Saturday. Thank you.

Yours, Linda

❧

"How much is this going to hurt?" Marissa thought the warm goop felt kind of good as it was spread on her knees.

Her mother, being similarly painted with wax, said, "Not as much as electrolysis."

"Huh. If you had wanted me to be prettier when I was little, would you have taken me to electrolysis?"

"Of course not—well, how little are we talking?"

"Twelve. The moment my hair went from fine and blond to wiry and dark."

"No, not then. If you had had some kind of problem where you were getting teased in school or something, we might have talked about it. But twelve is hard enough. Brace yourself."

The wax specialist who was in charge of Marissa's legs smiled. "It's not that bad. Just take a deep breath and flex your calf muscles for me."

Marissa did as she was told and for a frozen moment of time she didn't feel any pain. Then a rectangular patch of skin on her calf seared with fire and she gasped. "Holy ma-loy! What are we doing this for?"

"To have legs that feel smooth as a baby's bottom for three days."

"But I had to endure not shaving for nearly two weeks."

"Ideally, we'd be going to the Oscars tonight."

"Now I know how Jack Lemmon felt preparing for *Some Like it Hot*." Marissa braced herself for the next strip removal. She hissed after it was done. "Tell me that mud soak thing we do next isn't painful."

"It's not. So why were you asking about electrolysis?"

"I know someone who was taken in at twelve and everything that a skimpy bikini wouldn't cover was removed."

"Ouch. What for?"

"Beauty pageants."

"Well, someone had some skewed priorities."

Marissa swallowed back tears, thinking about the chapters of Linda's life she'd absorbed during two nearly sleepless nights. "Plastic surgery. Nose. Eyelids. That started when she was nine. Her ears were pinned when she was six." She hissed again and heard a similar sound from her mother as her specialist began removal.

"Goodness, what were her parents thinking?"

"Dad wasn't around. Mom was crazy. That's why she didn't get in touch with me, Mom. Linda. She went home to confront her mother."

"Oh. Okay, well, that took a day. What did she do with the other three-hundred and sixty-four days?"

Marissa's rueful smile was wiped off by the next wax strip, this time from over her knee. "Sshhhh-sugar that hurts. Well, it took more like two months. Lawyers were involved."

Her mother nodded understandingly. "And after that?"

"She got a job, figured out how to keep her head straight then went to Montana for a while. She wrote a memoir so there would be a record somewhere that her mother was bonkers. Then she went back to Yale to finish a degree she'd given up when she had emergency surgery."

Marissa found herself telling her mother everything, from the rib removal to the suicide attempts. Hot wax hurt coming off but it was nothing to the pain Linda had endured and as a reward Linda's mother had called her a failure and tried to throw her away.

She was so wrapped up in the telling that she didn't initially realize what the wax specialist wanted when she moved from her legs to her midsection. "What—Oh no. No way. I am not getting waxed there. It's winter. I won't be in a swimsuit for months."

"Some women think it feels cathartic," her mother said.

"Are you doing it?"

"Are you crazy?"

"Me neither." Marissa found a smile for the spa worker, who looked understanding. "Thanks, but no thanks. Honestly, I don't think I'll be doing any of this again." Sure, she was eager to look better and feel good but masochism just didn't work for her.

"Your friend," the small Asian woman said. "The one you were talking about. Is she okay now?"

Marissa wasn't about to explain that Linda's healing had begun the night they had gone to bed in Tahiti. It awed her, in a very deep place that believed in miracles, that her arms had been safe enough for Linda to stay. She'd relived that night and now when she heard Linda's whispered, "I'm here," she knew it hadn't been for Marissa's benefit, but for both of them.

The year of remaking herself ended with Linda's unsparing honesty of her own lapses into despair and defeat and the difficulties she had had trying to stay in one place, to finish what she had begun and not respond to emotional distress by running away.

She finally answered the woman's question. "You know, I think so."

"Are you sure, sweetie?" Her mother had slid off the table and stood wrapped in a thick towel, all of which was at odds with the look of concern on her face.

"Yeah, I do. I'm going to have a walk with her this afternoon."

"Well," her mother said briskly. "We'll talk about that in the mud bath."

In spite of her mother's well-voiced concerns, Marissa stood at the entrance to the Osage Rose Garden a little before three. Rain was threatening and she hoped she didn't regret her vain disdain for a raincoat and waterproof shoes in favor of a clingy sweater that made her eyes turquoise and slender, foot-flattering slingbacks. Her freshly painted toenails were Pretty Boy Pink to match her fingernails. The wind threatened to destroy the complicated hairdo the spa stylist had urged her to try.

She didn't feel quite like herself but she forgot all about that as she watched the nondescript rental car turn into the parking lot.

She had always seen the tall body as strong and the woman within even more so. But now she knew that there was vulnerability and steel mixed together. Linda wasn't a fantasy made up by vacation endorphins, she was a flesh-and-bone woman, as complicated as any.

Linda paused for a moment, looking across a small patch of grass toward Marissa. The wind that presaged the storm front lifted her hair from her face and Marissa knew now not to say what pierced to her core, that Linda was beautiful, beautiful beyond Marissa's ability to describe. If she said it Linda might never believe that Marissa wasn't looking at her face or her body, but the whole of her.

She found a smile. She couldn't believe she was thinking about trusting again, not when the hurt was still there from the last time.

"Hi," Linda said softly when she finally reached the spot where Marissa stood waiting.

"Hi. I read the book." Then, to her surprise, Marissa started to sob.

"Oh, honey," Linda murmured and she pulled Marissa into her arms. "Don't cry about it. Please. That's not why I gave it to you."

"I know, I know," Marissa said when she was able. The firmness of Linda's embrace was intensely comforting. "I didn't realize I was this upset."

"I almost didn't give it to you because you're so tenderhearted. I never want to make you cry again."

"It's not you that's making me cry. It's what happened to you. I so much wish I could have been there and helped you somehow."

"I'm here now, that's what matters."

The shaking in her arms eased and Marissa relaxed into Linda's embrace.

It could end here, Marissa thought. Monsters and inner demons slain, the two lovers could find peace together, forever. It had happened time and again in all those movies she'd watched with her father. But it wasn't that simple. Softly, she said, "You can let go of me now."

When Linda's arms eased from around her, Marissa stepped back. "I don't know why I even picked here, of all places. The roses aren't in bloom."

"I did wonder, but California is full of wonders." Linda smiled that cocky grin that Marissa remembered far too well.

"We can walk around the park, though."

"It's all ice at home. White and grey slush. The hills here are all green. That alone amazes me."

"This is only the start." Marissa led Linda along the footpath, trying not to imagine Linda's hands exploring her. Her body was very different from the last time Linda had held it. "By spring the green will hurt your eyes."

"I hope to see it. You look wonderful. You're shaped all differently, but you still . . ."

"Still what?" Marissa didn't risk a look at Linda's face.

"You still fit. Your head under my chin and my arms around you."

"Oh." Marissa had forgotten how hard she had to crane her neck to look into Linda's face. "What would have to happen for you to be here in the spring?"

Linda's eyes said one thing while her mouth said, "A job, I hope. A kind of a tryout sort of thing, at the Sierra Club."

Ignoring the melting message in Linda's gaze, Marissa asked, "Putting all that ecotouring to use?"

"Yeah, actually. Herding groups of people, understanding habitats, cultural variations, all of that. I think, ultimately, I'd like to work on global eco-issues, and there are a number of foundations and funds where I could be truly useful but this will be a start."

"I hope it works out." Linda just gazed at her and Marissa could no longer pretend she didn't understand. "I need time. I still have feelings for you—"

Linda made a small sound but Marissa held up her hand.

"I do have feelings for you but it's a big jumble in my head right now. I understand why you did what you did. But it hurt."

"I know."

"I forgive you, I really do, Linda. Can we just leave it at that for now?" She wiped away an errant tear, then felt a drop on her face.

Linda peered up at the sky. "It seems we're going to have some rain."

Marissa turned back toward the parking lot. Within a few steps the drops turned into a proper downpour and she quickened her pace. "My car is closer," she yelled, and broke into a flat out run.

She paid for her vanity halfway to the car, losing her footing in a bit of mud. The impractical shoes found no purchase and she sprawled, face down, across the path.

"Ah, hell," she said, after she spit out a mouthful of mud.

Linda was down on one knee in the mud. "Marissa, honey, are you okay? That was quite a fall."

"I think I'm oh . . . oh . . . no no *no*." She rolled over and her left ankle protested. "Dang it, I think I've twisted something."

Linda gingerly touched the rapidly swelling skin. "You've definitely done something. Let's get you into my car."

"Mine's closer."

"Mine's a rental and you're covered with mud."

"Good point."

Linda lifted her easily onto one foot, then before Marissa could protest, all the way into her arms.

She sniffed. "Just don't go thinking this is how it is. You Financier, me Ginger needing rescuing."

Linda was making good time along the path. "Fair enough. I'll rescue you just this once, then."

"Well, there was the cliff."

"You did that yourself."

"You helped. This isn't what I had planned."

There was a rumble in Linda's chest that Marissa knew full well was a laugh. "I can't say the same."

"I hope I can walk by tonight."

"Do you have a date or something?"

"Yes, I do. A very important one. Reservations made months ago."

"Well, milady." Linda set Marissa down next to the sedan as if she was a porcelain doll. She wasn't even breathing hard, not that Marissa could tell.

Marissa wiped rain out of her eyes and her hand came away covered in muck. She had to hop to keep her balance as Linda found her keys. "Yes, good sir knight?"

"If necessary, I will carry you on a pillow to your assignation."

"It's not an assignation." Linda got the door open and Marissa gratefully sank into the passenger seat. "It's Philip's sixtieth birthday."

Leaning out into the rain to examine her ankle in the somewhat better light outside the car, Marissa prodded and winced.

Linda opined, "Just a sprain. If you ice it now and wrap it, you might be able to hobble. Shall I take you home?"

"My car."

"Can someone come and get it?"

Marissa reached into her sodden handbag. With some careful adjustments she was able to swing her legs inside and allow Linda to shut the door. Her cell phone chirped that it had found the signal. "Mom? Where are you? I've twisted my ankle."

"I was just running an errand in Danville. What do you need?"

"I'm at the Osage Rose Garden. Maybe you could drive my car home and Linda could bring you back for yours?"

"Oh, you're with Linda."

"Yeah. I slipped in some mud."

"I'll be right there."

Too late Marissa realized this was perhaps not the best of plans. "If it's too big a bother—"

"Oh, I assure you, it's no bother at all." Her mother hung up before Marissa could say another word.

"Sorry," she said as Linda eased into the driver's seat.

"What for?"

"Mud all over that gorgeous blouse and my mother is on the way."

"Oh. Huh. Your mom."

"She's changed a bit. We're getting along better. It helps that we listen more. She's, um, eager to meet you."

"Hell."

"Yeah, well, like I said, sorry."

Linda turned in the seat to look at her. "So, here we are."

"Tell me about the job you interviewed for." Don't hold my hand, Marissa wanted to say. Don't sit so close. Don't lean toward me and kiss me, please, don't do anything like that, because right now I couldn't care less about the pain in my leg. Right now all I can smell is your cologne and all I can feel is the warmth of you. Right now I couldn't find a no to save my life.

Linda dutifully launched into a detailed explanation, and that passed the time until Marissa saw her mother's BMW streaking across the lot toward them. She rolled down the window and waved, then dug in her purse for her keys as her mother pulled into the next space.

"Shall I follow you? I'm not sure I could find your place on my own."

"Sure." She passed the keys over and her mother backed out again to re-park next to Marissa's car. "Okay," Marissa said to Linda. "Go out to the street and bear right."

"If you get me onto Raven Canyon, I can find it from there."

"Oh."

"I had a lot of time to look at maps."

"Right then. At the stop sign turn left." She rubbed her arms and could feel nothing but cold and muddy.

"How about some heat?" Linda played with the controls at Marissa's nod. "Poor thing, you're shivering."

"Just reaction." Sure, it had nothing to do with the mud and icy water she could feel running into her underwear. "At the light turn left. Then you're on the freeway."

"I know where I am now, thanks. Just close your eyes, okay?"

Well this was a mess, Marissa thought. She wasn't sure she wanted Linda in her life, and whoopee, she got carried up her own stairs by Linda and now Linda was surveying the wreck of her living room and the dozen years of Marissa finding new and interesting ways to fit more crap into the same space.

Plus, her mother was watching. Truth be told, her mother

looked a little bit faint—she hadn't seen the inside of Marissa's place in years now.

Her mother recovered from the shock enough to say, "Carry my daughter into the bedroom and I'll take it from there. Then you can drive me back to my car."

"Bathroom, take me to the bathroom. I want a hot shower." Marissa could feel that Linda's heart was beating hard. She pointed.

Linda set her down in front of the sink. The room was quickly crowded when her mother joined them.

"I don't need an audience to my shower, thank you. It was just an accident, a mistake, just like I was an accident." She rolled her eyes at her mother.

"Marissa, sweetie." Her mother looked at her in shock. "You might have been an accident but never, ever were you a mistake!"

"I'll just leave now." Linda quickly stepped into the little hallway.

Marissa shut the bathroom door, only to snatch it open again. "Call me, okay?"

"I intended to bring you breakfast tomorrow morning."

"Oh." Marissa nodded. "Okay. We'll try for something a little more normal than you heap big strong, me weak fall down."

Her mother firmly shut the door between Linda and Marissa again. "You didn't say she was *that* beautiful."

"Oh, Mom, I mean, what's to say? Look in any magazine and they're describing electric dog polishers as beautiful. I don't have words to describe her adequately."

"How does she make you feel?"

"Like a blithering fool. And I actually don't like the feeling very much. I've worked really hard not to go to pieces just because she looks at me like she can't wait to get me into bed, like I'm the one who's beautiful. Oh hell, Mom. I can't talk to you about sex and my ankle really hurts."

"I asked how she made you feel and that's talking about sex?

Think that over, sweetie." Her mother had turned on the shower. "I'll be back with some pills. Will you be okay?"

"Sure, yeah."

Fifteen minutes later, already feeling a little better for some Advil and an ice pack, she listened to Linda and her mother leave. She didn't really care what her mother thought of the place but Linda got the emergency tour to the world of someone who still lived like a student though college was ten years behind her.

She did not want to know what they talked about. She did not want to even speculate. She threw a pillow at the wall and didn't feel much better.

Yes, Mom, I think about Linda and I think about sex. I have never wanted a woman this way. This was the *zing* that Eve had been talking about.

But instead of the cool and dignified conversation where Marissa allowed that perhaps they could carefully date and get to know one another in a more seemly fashion, she'd become Ginger. And she had a sneaking suspicion that Linda had enjoyed every minute. And she wasn't sure that she had minded much either. And that couldn't be a good thing. Could it?

A little voice of reason told her to be careful. Ankles mended— hearts possibly did not. Breakfast in the morning and nurturing were all fine and good but leaving without a word and not coming back for a year was not.

Oh, you're a fool, Marissa Chabot. She knew she would give a million dollars to know what her mother and Linda were talking about.

Chapter 14

"So, what are your intentions toward my daughter?"

Linda put the key in the ignition and turned it before answering. "I'd like to date her for a while, see if she likes who I really am. Can I ask a question?"

"Yes, you may." Well, Linda could clearly see where Marissa got her expressive face. It was plain as day that Linda was a slime bug two seconds away from being stepped on.

"What should I call you? We haven't been properly introduced."

"Joyce will do fine."

"Thank you. I'm Linda.".

"I know."

"The woman who broke your daughter's heart."

"I know that too."

Outside, the day looked balmy by comparison. "I know I'm on probation."

"Good." Joyce crossed her arms then abruptly said, "I think your mother is guilty of felony child abuse, by the way. Where did she find a plastic surgeon who would operate on a child for cosmetic purposes?"

"Swiss doctors did the ears and first nose job. After I hit puberty, New York doctors did the second nose and the eyelids. The rib guy was in Buenos Aires."

"I'm sorry," Joyce said. "I'm being morbid but you're obviously a strong, resilient woman."

"And you love your daughter, even though sometimes she is a big puzzle to you."

"What makes you say that? Turn right here."

"I . . ." To her embarrassment Linda felt her eyes fill with tears. "What you said about her not being a mistake."

"Well, it's true, though apparently I spent her entire teen years convincing her she was."

Linda was very aware of the sharp, observant intelligence behind Joyce's gaze. There was no doubt in her mind where Marissa got her brains. Before she could think of anything to say, Joyce cleared her throat.

"Why do you care about my daughter?"

Meetings with lawyers and publishers were starting to look like play dates. She opened her mouth, only to be interrupted again.

"Don't tell me she makes you laugh."

"Okay, I won't. What about how she's fantastic in bed?"

Joyce gaped. "Now you're being crude."

"You and she sound alike, did you know that?"

"Yes, but you can't tell her that."

"I don't plan to. And it was a joke. Marissa makes me laugh, yes. You know how we met, right?"

"Yes, the shipwreck. You made her climb a cliff."

"I didn't make her. She did it herself." Linda thought of all the things she wanted to tell Marissa and decided many of them were not going to be said to Joyce.

But there were things she was willing to tell anyone who would

217

listen. "I feel as if I got to see a side of her she didn't know she had. We discovered it together. She's strong and vibrant and smart. I love making her laugh. I love watching her face light up with new thoughts. I never know, though, most of the time, what she's going to say. I only know that very likely I'm going to find it delightful and inspiring and insightful. I learned all that about her when we were together in Tahiti. Now I see her in her world, looking so incredibly sexy and—okay, I didn't mean to say that, but she is a wonderful armful of woman to hold. I want to *talk* to her, morning, noon and night. With breaks for sleeping and sex, of course."

Joyce's expression hadn't eased one iota. "And why should she care a flying fig how you feel, especially since you disappeared for a year and didn't even send a postcard?"

"That's a very good question. I don't know the answer. All I know is that she didn't find out who I really am. She didn't know that part of me was long dead. My mother killed that part of me and Marissa only knew what was left of the body. And I wanted to bury that part of me at last and not mire her in all of that. I needed to know I wasn't a head case before I came back into Marissa's life. She deserves better than that. If I never got my act together I was going to leave her in peace, at least."

"It sounds as if you've been rehearsing that speech for a while."

"Yes, ma'am."

Joyce gave her a suspicious look. "Turn left up here."

The silence lasted until Linda pulled into parking space next to the elegant BMW. Rain pattered softly on the windscreen. "Marissa may send me away."

"I worry. I'm her mother and I do love her."

"I respect that, Joyce, I really do. You may not know how much."

"If you happen to be around, in my daughter's life, I will remind you that you said that."

Well, it wasn't exactly permission to court her daughter's hand in marriage, but Linda wasn't going to be a stickler about that. "I expect you to."

She watched Joyce drive away and then headed for her motel. She was stopped at a light when she remembered she was providing breakfast in the morning. The rear view mirror told her if she smiled any harder she might break something.

"I wasn't sure what you'd have in the icebox, so I brought a little of everything."

Marissa, wrapped tightly in a purple chenille robe, hobbled back to let Linda pass her. Linda glanced around, noticing signs of cleaning up. She smiled to herself even as she regretted Marissa having to hop around her apartment gathering up papers and dirty clothes.

"I'm on a diet, you know." Marissa slowly followed Linda into the tiny kitchen.

"That's why I have fruit. French bread. Egg substitute. Green peppers. Cooked shrimp. And diet ginger ale for poor woman's mimosas."

Marissa sank into a chair at the tiny table. "I'm buying a condo."

"Okay. Point me toward the knives. I'm actually useful in the kitchen now. Lots of time to cook for myself in Montana."

"All things that cut are in the last drawer on the left. Frying pan below the oven. Plates next to the microwave."

"Ah." Linda found what she needed, including some cooking spray and started on a shrimp omelet. "How is your ankle feeling this morning?"

"Okay. It probably would be better if I hadn't gone out last night but I didn't want to disappoint Philip. He has a lot of friends and family so it was a big, fabulous party with lots of nice gay men to fuss and make sure I had plenty to eat and drink. They rewrapped my ankle."

Linda glanced over, then carried the bowl of egg goo she was whisking over for a closer look. "Ribbon from the presents?"

"Yes." Marissa looked pleased as she surveyed the colorful additions to her ace bandage. "They had a doctor retie the bandage for me, then said he was too butch for the finishing touches. So they had a little contest to pick the biggest Sissy Mary and the winner selected the lavender and orange ribbons to match my Pretty Boy Pink—they said that alone made me an honorary queen—toenail polish. I was so glad I'd gotten my first-time-ever pedicure yesterday."

Linda was grinning as she went back to the stove and poured the egg and green pepper mixture into the hot pan. "Philip sounds like he has some very fun friends."

"He does. It was one of the reasons my dad loved him. He'd spent so much time closeted that Philip's extreme outness never lost its charm. That smells good."

"Thanks—I hope it tastes good." She prowled a few drawers and discovered dried herbs and spices. Basil, salt and pepper would do nicely. "I remember you like a bit of spice in things. Do you have Tabasco?"

"In the fridge. I wish I could help."

"No, you sit and put your foot up."

"I'm trying not to love you again."

Linda lost her grip on the spatula for a moment then went back to moving the eggs around on the heat. "Is it difficult?"

"Yes," Marissa said in a small voice. "It's very hard."

"Good." If her heart could sing, Linda thought it would be belting out "Top of the World." Fighting back a smile, she dished the eggs onto plates, quickly cut the baguette and brought the container of already cleaned fruit to the table with her. "I'm willing to start over, Marissa. I'm willing to let it take time. You, sure of what you feel, are worth waiting for."

Marissa ate a bite of eggs. "Thank you—a hot breakfast is quite a treat."

"You're welcome. For me too."

"Are . . ." Marissa focused on her plate. "Are your feelings certain?"

220

"Do you mean are you still the most fascinating, interesting, touchable, sexy woman I've ever met? Yes, you are."

The blush that stained Marissa's neck was attractive in the extreme. "You don't really know me."

"Then let me be around. Let me make you dinner sometime."

"Okay. Slow. I like slow."

Linda could not help herself. "Yes, I remember."

Marissa looked as if she wanted to fling a forkful of eggs at Linda. "None of that. Not right away."

"Okay."

They ate in silence for a while then Marissa brought up the weather. Weather turned to places Linda might want to rent if the job came through. Discussion of mass transit maps led to theories of city planning and by the time the last wedge of pineapple was eaten they had covered the film career of Gene Wilder, highlighted perplexities of the English language, agreed on global warming and solved many of the world's problems.

Linda was aware that part of her watched their conversation but it wasn't with the detachment of dissociation with which she was so familiar. This was simple wonder that a conversation with Marissa could bring her more laughter and thoughtfulness than any in her life. Being near Marissa made her realize that in many ways, she had not yet begun living.

"The ecotouring people, they are total fascists about leaving no trace but they have to be. We'd build these great fire pits and tell stories. Sing songs. In the morning all the rocks would be scattered, the ashes spread and no trace of us left as we moved on."

"I can see that. Some day I think I'd like to try that sort of thing. Do you get really, really dirty?" Marissa's expression was cautiously intrigued.

"Oh, yeah. As in some of the animals you run across smell better." Linda pictured Marissa's Pretty Boy Pink tipped toes in hiking boots. Boots led to legs to thighs and well, the image worked for her.

221

"It would take some getting used to because I suppose packing around baby wipes on an ecotour is right out."

Linda laughed. "Baby wipes are not encouraged, no."

In one of her lightning changes of subject, Marissa asked, in a low voice, "Was there really a woman in the airport in New Zealand? Did you . . . ?"

Sobering, Linda nodded. "There was. That was the way I used to be."

"I don't know how you could be with someone right after we . . . you know."

Linda didn't flinch. "I wasn't with her. That was the whole point. I was never *with* her. I used sex, flirtation and mystery as walls to end any chance of her possibly touching any part of me that mattered."

Marissa was frowning in concentration. "Say that another way."

Though she'd said it any number of ways in all her talks with Dr. Kirkland, she still had to pick her words with care. "Since I was maybe ten, any time anyone said they thought I was beautiful I wanted to run and hide. But I couldn't do that. So my mind ran away but my body stayed. When I was a little older and boys and girls alike would make sexual overtures, the same thing happened. I could have gone totally passive and let myself be used."

Marissa nodded as tears swam in the corners of her lovely blue eyes. Linda was sorry all over again from bringing pain into Marissa's life.

"But the teenaged me was pretty smart. She realized she had power she could use, which was the very thing that drew people to her. She learned to use the beauty, the schooled charm, eventually the flirtation, to immediately turn any kind of overture to a purely sexual one where she controlled everything. Men were left frustrated. Women were fuc—taken care of. Only rarely would I let someone touch me back and I still controlled it. Some women won't leave until they think they made you . . . you know."

"I'm sorry," Marissa whispered. "To me, that's not sex."

"It isn't," Linda agreed. "It wasn't. There was never a question of them having any piece of me. It was a highly dysfunctional, very successful strategy. And I never want to feel that way again."

"What happens now if someone hits on you?"

Linda tried to hide a nervous swallow. She wouldn't lie to Marissa, not about anything. "At first, that habit of making everything purely sexual comes back. I have to tell myself to turn that off. It takes some effort. I'm getting better at having ordinary conversations with women who clearly think I'm attractive."

Marissa was watching her face intently and yet Linda felt each additional word coming more easily. Marissa was *listening* and that was more than she had hoped for. "I'm finally in a space where I don't take responsibility for how they feel about me. That's their problem. It doesn't threaten me. And sometimes . . ." She paused to smile and was relieved to receive a tentative one in return. "Sometimes, I am willing to consider that they are just being friendly. I *can* and *will* get over myself."

"I still think," Marissa said slowly, "that you are the strongest woman I've ever met."

"I'm not that strong. I make mistakes, and I—"

"You're here."

"I'm ready . . . I don't know how to explain this but thank you, I know what you're trying to say. But I'm ready not to be defined by what I've survived. If I am strong, I want to prove it going forward."

Marissa had a considering look on her face but then she nodded. "Okay." A slow, easy smile spread across her face. "I don't want to be a formerly helpless fat chick. I want to be who I am today and tomorrow—fit, healthy and ready for life."

Linda was grinning as she gathered their plates and carried them to the sink. "Dish soap?"

"Just leave them. You cooked, I wash."

"You should stay off your ankle."

"It's not that bad." Marissa rose as if to prove her point and took a tentative step. "See?"

"Still, let me do this."

223

She hesitated and retied her robe. "I meant to shower and get dressed before you got here but I had rather a lot of wine last night."

"You look ravishing." Linda nearly added, "and ravishable," but she had gotten the Let's Go Slow message loud and clear.

"Sweet talker." Marissa limped into the bathroom and shut the door.

Linda had just finished filling the dish tub with hot soapy water when she heard a distinct thud from the bathroom, followed by a strongly uttered invective.

"Hey in there." She hurried to the bathroom door, but found it locked. "Are you okay?"

"Yes. I just slipped. Dang it all."

"Are you sure?" All Linda could hear now was running water. When there was no immediate reply, she turned the knob with all her strength and the old hardware gave.

"Oh—don't come . . ." Marissa peeked out from under the shower curtains, her shoulders pink and cheeks to match. Her robe and T-shirt were strewn over the commode. "I'm okay. I just slipped getting in. I can shower sitting down. On my own." She followed Linda's gaze and the blush intensified.

With a sense of wonder Linda asked, "Is that my T-shirt?"

"Yes. I didn't know where to send it."

"And so you wore it?"

"Not until last night. Please. Shower?" Marissa let the curtain fall back into place.

Linda retreated and closed the door, relieved the knob would at least function. She'd have to replace the lock.

Grinning broadly, Linda whispered aloud, "She's wearing my T-shirt." The idea was both comforting and incredibly intimate. Go slow, she told herself. Slow.

She finished the dishes and then took her time surveying Marissa's apartment. It was clear that the large number of boxes, labeled with dates going back six years, were the early years of the company. She hadn't had a reason to take them to the office, probably. The apartment had only the one small bedroom, so the living room was further crowded with a computer workstation which was reached only after a stack of boxes was moved. It was the room of someone who had not given much time to more than its functionality of providing warmth, light and shelter. She wondered if Marissa could like the wide open spaces of Montana. Would she really enjoy trekking through mud and heat to see a flower that bloomed for a day once a decade?

"I'm not a slob, really. I'm just short on space."

Turning, Linda tried not to show that breathing was suddenly very difficult. Marissa's robe was not belted as tightly as before, and with her hair damp around her shoulders she looked much like the water nymph of Tahiti. "I understand."

"I really am going to buy a condo—it's a good investment and I'll have more space. Those boxes will finally get out of my life." She limped in the direction of the bedroom, leaving wet patches where her bandage touched the carpet.

"Do you need that retied?"

"I was hoping to preserve the fun ribbons, but now that it's wet I'm not sure it was a good idea." Marissa continued into the bedroom and Linda followed, not sure what Marissa expected.

Marissa was seated on the unmade bed, tugging at the outermost ribbon.

"Let me," Linda said, and without thinking she slid to her knees at Marissa's feet.

Marissa drew in a sharp breath and Linda looked up. Such an expressive face, Linda marveled. She's scared. She wants me to touch her. She doesn't want to want me. She's remembering that night, the next morning.

"Please," Marissa whispered.

Her hesitation was momentary then Linda carefully acknowledged what was happening. She was not afraid. She did not want to control the moment, she wanted to live in it. Marissa was everything Linda remembered of her—and more.

She leaned forward to softly kiss the inside of Marissa's knee.

Marissa was breathing hard. "Linda . . ."

"What is it? What do you want me to do? I'll do it." Linda inhaled the wonderful scent that meant Marissa and closed her eyes with a sense of awe.

"Hold me," Marissa whispered. "I'm frightened."

Kicking off her shoes, Linda pulled Marissa to her on the bed, nestling Marissa's head into her shoulder. "I'm here."

"I keep telling myself I shouldn't feel like this. That I was a fool to let you inside me the first time and I shouldn't let you close again."

"I understand." She's going to send me away, Linda thought with a spasm of pain. So far, every minute with Marissa had been more than she thought she deserved. To be holding her, wrapped in the complex smells of her sheets and her freshly washed hair—it was heaven.

This moment, this woman, they weren't the reasons for her striving to put her life together. She wasn't using the circle of Marissa's arms as an escape from anywhere. Happiness pulsed from the inside of her and the thought blazed behind her closed eyelids, "I didn't run away to be with her but she is still where I want to go."

"Linda," Marissa whispered, and she lifted her mouth to be kissed.

Her body responded before her brain could even decide if this was a good idea. The flash of Marissa's bare shoulder was enough to knock the breath out of her and she kissed the upturned mouth with hunger and heat.

Marissa's hands were in her hair, a feeling Linda hadn't forgotten and hadn't dared to hope she would have again, fingers sifting, then brushing over her temples as their kiss deepened. They explored each other with slow intent and Linda was aware of the heat of Marissa's body.

The hips were smaller, more muscled and compact, but their motion was a limitless rocking that Linda had dreamed about ever since. The robe parted to reveal glorious, full breasts that were as plush and soft as her memory of them. Taut nipples beckoned and with a moan, Linda brushed the nearest with her fingers.

Marissa gasped, her legs parting. Linda felt dizzy. This couldn't be happening—it was like a fantasy, a dream, something she'd wanted so badly she was making it all up. Her hand swept the length of Marissa's curving hip, then around to cup the firm roundness and soft skin of Marissa's backside.

"Oh," Marissa groaned, low in her throat. "No. No, no."

Linda's hand froze but she was powerless to stop her own panting. "I'm . . . sorry."

"No, this is my fault. It's all happening so fast." Marissa pulled Linda's hand to her waist, even as her breast seemed to swell and demand further caresses. "I need some time."

"Shall I go away for a while?"

"No. Yes. How long?"

"A week or two? To give you some air?"

Marissa sat up. She looked down at Linda, her shoulders framed by the open robe, her hair tousled and a glow in her eyes that nearly broke Linda's restraint. "I don't think I could bear it that long. Dinner, Tuesday night, okay? I just need to breathe, Linda. I need to think."

"I understand," Linda said again. She got off the bed and wasn't embarrassed by her groan of loss—it matched the one she heard Marissa make as well. "Should I go?"

"I think . . . you should."

Lightheaded, part of her dancing on air and the rest incredibly frustrated, Linda managed to get her shoes on again and find her keys. "Shall I meet you at your office?"

"No," Marissa said quickly. "At the Opera Café. Do you know where that is?"

Linda nodded. Her motel was across the street. "Seven?"

"Yes, please." Marissa's voice was husky but Linda didn't dare look back. She could picture the yielding legs, the robe falling open, the pink flush on Marissa's neck and face.

It seemed miles to the car. Part of her mind was still in Marissa's bedroom and they had never stopped rocking together on the bed.

She had waited a year to reclaim the wonder of being with Marissa, to see herself again in Marissa's eyes. This time she knew

227

she was the woman Marissa thought she was. If she had to wait another year for Marissa to trust her again, then so be it.

Her mind made up, but her body in a major pout, she drove toward her motel. Job or not, she needed to find a place to live. She wasn't budging from the area unless Marissa told her to go.

Chapter 15

"This is our manifesto: there is someone perfect for you out there." Marissa tried to look as if her ankle wasn't aching as she turned on the overhead projector. It was a good thing she'd gone ahead and dressed as if there would be no one to take this presentation for her, because there hadn't been.

Spending the rest of her Sunday following WebMD's sprained ankle advice while her thoughts went around and around in circles had at least helped her ankle. Her mind was still a mess.

"Your perfect someone is there. Like anything in life, your perfect someone is worth looking for. Why not look smart? Why not let technology help?"

After all, she mused, it found me three and possibly even more compatible women I could have been happy with, most likely. Eventually we'd have went zing in every room in the house, I'll bet. It's possible the world was full of 97s and 98s. It was all Linda's fault that 98 wasn't enough.

"At Finders Keepers we are constantly updating our questionnaire to capture not just who you are today but the changes likely in your life, and match your personality and character with someone who can adapt and grow with you as you adapt and grow with them."

What had all the zing and passion gotten her, anyway? Okay, there were those moments when having a body with nerves in certain places had finally made sense, moments when skin and electricity seemed like the same thing. And okay, those moments were worth months of not feeling that, and okay, zing and passion weren't things she was going to live without.

Dang it all, no sooner did she think she believed one thing for certain than she argued herself into the exact opposite thinking. She could live without zing, without sex, without all the drama but then why bother even dating? A perfectly dispassionate electrical appliance could provide plenty of hum to break up the ho.

"At Finders Keepers, we believe in love. We believe in romance. We believe in first meetings, second dates, third anniversaries and relationships that can last a lifetime."

Sure, a corporation could believe in all those things, Marissa darling, but do you?

The audience, made up of mostly women in the middle years, seemed rapt. Why were they here, Marissa wondered. The questionnaire didn't seem to take into account all that she herself wanted. None of the three women she had called were anything like Linda, and *dangitall*, she thought with undeniable clarity, she wanted Linda.

Dear Self:

Blithering is unattractive.

Love, Marissa

P.S.   Pay attention to what you're doing!

Startled to find herself mouth half-open and not sure what

she'd been saying, she glanced at the screen and tried to play back the last few seconds.

"No computer can really capture the complexity of a human being," she extemporized, silently thanking Helena Boxer. "We are as diverse and complicated as the planet we live on. The universe is in a blade of glass—and in all of us."

Oh hell, where was she going with this flashback to English 1A?

"Your lives are full to the brim already, however. My business partner would kill me for putting it this way but we meet a thousand new people a year and I think we're all too busy to sort the dreck from the gold. So why not let a computer help? After submitting your questionnaire, you would get a profile report like this. Compatibility scores of ninety-five and above, well, they're not dreck. And among those people there is a high probability you will find twenty-four karat gold. All the mystery and magic and frustration of dating and getting to know someone will still have to happen, though. The computer does the analysis—you do the living."

So she had just violated one of Ocky's rules of marketing: she'd focused potential clients on what Finders Keepers *couldn't* do for them. She clicked to the next slide and tried to get back on track.

Her mouth, it seemed, had other plans.

"You could walk out the door right now and bump into someone who is a ninety-seven. You could meet the Perfect Someone stranded on a desert island, even. But if you don't like those odds, then Finders Keepers will help. Three out of four of our clients are still with someone they met through our service as long as three years ago. Many five years ago or more."

That, she told herself, hadn't come out quite right.

She wasn't sure how she got through the rest of the presentation. She gave away a number of business cards but wasn't ready when a woman asked, "Have you filled out your own questionnaire? How did it turn out for you?"

Thinking fast, Marissa said, "I have and I met three really nice people. If anything, it was more choice than I could handle."

The echo of her words—not untrue but far from representing the whole story—stayed with her as she limped to the car and drove back to the office. She tried to drown out her thoughts with Fatboy Slim but she couldn't get the woman's reaction out of her head—that excited, hopeful grin. For a moment she felt like the Take It Off saleswoman, saying whatever the potential client wanted to hear.

Great, just great. She had been ready to move on. Ready to date and find someone and get her life out of aging student mentality into that of a woman ready to grow up and get real.

Then Linda showed up.

Marissa snapped the radio off. "She hauls your heart back into the open air and you feel more alive than you've felt in a year and yet you doubt everything you see and do and ever thought could be true."

"You weren't in love with her," she told her reflection as she brushed her hair that night. "You were in love with how she made you feel. You're in love with the endorphins and the sex and that ridiculous giddy feeling. She hurt you and you can't go back to her like some addict."

She scrubbed regenerating daily serum with UV repair into every last pore on her face. "She's not in love with *you*. She's just feeling the same thing. You make her feel good, that's all it is."

The sleeplessness and emotional turmoil of the previous nights seemed to catch up all at once and her ankle wasn't the only reason she stumbled into bed.

During the night she woke once, heard the sound of the gentle tide hissing over warm sand. A new thought occurred to her. She smiled into her pillow and went back to sleep.

Her ankle was nearly normal-sized in the morning and she made time for a trip to the gym just to do something aerobic that didn't involve her legs. Though the scale wasn't exactly zooming in the right direction after the last weekend, she also wasn't unduly worried she'd suddenly gain ten pounds during a few days where she focused elsewhere.

"How can I hate sweating and enjoy it at the same time?"

The woman at the next station, her tight dreads shining with perspiration, grinned knowingly. "Maybe you have two brains?"

"Yeah, one into cookies and sleeping until noon. The other into pain and thinking sunrise is the coolest time of day." The other woman chuckled while Marissa was chortling inside. Having two brains was making a lot of sense at the moment. Love her, love her not. And it was still not the least bit fair that after her workout she felt more calm and more focused.

"Glad to see you moving a little faster today." Heather handed over the mail.

Marissa leaned on the reception desk. "It's better but it still aches a bit. You look tired."

"I'm nervous about the therapist. Maybe I don't want to know certain things."

"You're still going to go, aren't you?"

"Yeah. I had this nightmare." Heather's appearance was as perfect as always, but her eyes were shadowed. "The kind where you wake up and it's like the most obvious meaning in the world and you think why the heck you had to be asleep to even think it?"

"Okay." Marissa wasn't sure what Heather meant but she was listening.

"I dreamed that I was sitting in the therapist's waiting area and there was a huge tray of Twinkies. I had one, then another and then I couldn't stop eating them. I felt very embarrassed and people were staring—that feeling you get at Mickey D's when you think everyone heard you order supersized fries and they're all thinking 'no wonder she's fat,' you know, even if you haven't had fries in four months?"

Again, Marissa nodded. She wondered how much weight she had to lose before she stopped thinking that waiters were judging her choices.

"Anyway, I couldn't stop eating them and my mouth got all full and so when my turn came I couldn't talk."

Marissa blinked. "Okay, that doesn't take much analysis, you're right."

"I woke up at like four a.m. and I really thought I was going to throw up but I didn't. So. I don't want to know some things. But I can't live like this either." Heather swallowed noisily and looked away.

"You're going to be okay, you know. Whatever happened, it's already done and you're here."

"Keep telling me that, okay?" Heather blinked rapidly, but the tears never slipped over the rims of her eyes. "Thank you for listening to me. I promise not to do this at work."

Marissa reached over the desk to pat Heather's hand. "Yeah, like I can compartmentalize, sure. It's okay—but we can also talk at the gym while we whack weights."

"On the bright, I've had a dozen requests for access to the online registration system this morning. Seems like more than usual."

"Well, it wasn't because I was a ball of fire yesterday." Marissa could hear work calling all the way from her office, but she added, "An old girlfriend showed up last week. I'm all over the place about how I feel."

"Did she treat you badly?"

"Went away for a year. Said she'd get in touch and didn't."

With sympathetic outrage, Heather said, "I hope she was in a foreign prison or something equally unpleasant."

Marissa laughed at Heather's expression. "Some day you are going to have kids and scare off their potential beaus with that look." She sighed. "Not a foreign prison but definitely something equally unpleasant."

"So how do you feel about it all?"

"I understand why she dropped out of the world for a while. But if I trust her again I'm worried I'm a doormat, you know?"

"Well, you always say every situation is different. I wouldn't

234

want you to get hurt again but it's not like she beats you and you think she'll change."

"No, she just tromped all over my heart but had a decent enough reason for her behavior, a reason having nothing to do with me."

Heather made the scary face again. "She gets out of line, I'll have a talk with her."

"Okay." Marissa found herself grinning. "Everyone from Oprah to my mother would tell me not to let her hurt me again."

"It's not their life, now is it?"

"Nope. Which means I can't blame them if I make the wrong decision. Either choice and I might have huge regrets."

"Which stack of regrets will you be sorrier for?"

"Well, that's a good question." She gathered her mail and tested her ankle before putting her weight on it. It was feeling better by the hour but she didn't want to slow down her recovery. "I'm going to give that some thought."

Settled at her desk, she made no special effort to check her e-mail any more quickly than she would have any other morning. She didn't scan the new messages looking for any particular name, either. There wasn't supposed to be e-mail from Linda and there wasn't. Fine. Good.

She made herself focus on work. She'd been putting off studying the feedback from clients who dropped the program without finding someone they liked. The follow-up questionnaire could only provide so much information because if it was too detailed no one would fill it out. Which of the 700 questions didn't ask the right thing? Which comparison didn't screen out why someone hadn't bonded with any of their 95 to 98 percent results?

"Oh, look, she's studying our failures." Ocky dropped into the empty chair, looking pleased. "The cable advertising rep just told me they were lowering rates in a couple of the markets."

"Very cool."

"You have the biggest frown line right now."

Marissa groaned. "Yes, these are our failures. You know, Ocky, where do I—a virtual relationship virgin at the age of thirty-five—get off telling anyone who they are and aren't compatible with? I can't figure it out for myself, even."

"You don't tell anybody anything. Your program gives them potential. That's all."

"None of these people found potential. One of my dates said it was like a mini-therapy session. All I've programmed is an abstract exercise in personality analysis."

"Hey. Don't talk about yourself that way." Ocky sat forward in the chair to put her elbows on the edge of Marissa's desk. "Don't start doubting what you know you know. You told me, when we first started—remember, I was the one with the string of relationships and I thought each one ended for a different reason. First, you pointed out that all my exes eventually held me in contempt for something I did to them. Every relationship ended for exactly the same reason, every time. And, you know, I took the very same exact psych classes you did and you got that point and I never did."

"Maybe because you were having a life and I wasn't. Remember, it was my junior year before I was no longer a theoretical lesbian."

Ocky laughed. "Well, you obviously did something while dwelling in that ivory tower. You got very smart." She crossed one excellent leg over the other. "So first you diagnosed my relationship woes—not that I ever changed a thing but at least now I can see the contempt coming and move on before she boots me out. Then you told me not to confuse anecdotes from real life with the analysis of data. Which at first I thought was the whole problem with logic because life is real and messy."

"Tell me about it." Marissa heaved an enormous sigh. "My work here has acted as if there is no mess in real life. That people will behave like preprogrammed puppets."

"But 'Rissa, we all do. We're all who we are. You figured a way to capture the essence of someone's deep-down programming. Does she laugh when a bucket falls on someone's head? Does he lie to please his mother? Does she want someone who sees her body or her brain? Does he want someone to take care of or someone to take care of him? You give the computer the outline of a puzzle piece and instead of our poor clients wading through the entire puzzle box looking for the possible fits, the computer does it for them."

Marissa lifted one eyebrow. "Even a corner piece has two perfect fits."

"There are puzzles with pieces that have any number of perfect fits and only people who see the big picture ever figure out the right one." Ocky added drily, "Let's not kill ourselves with the analogy."

"I'm all hung up on the perfect fit. I know that ninety-nines are rare and we've never seen a hundred score."

"To my mind, hunny-bunny, it's up to the people involved to take a ninety-five or a ninety-eight and make it a hundred."

Unwillingly, Marissa laughed. "Ocky, I swear you could sell sand to Arabians."

"You work your magic, I'll work mine."

Ocky chatted for a few more minutes then rushed off to a meeting. Sniffing the air for the long-loved scent of Ocky's perfume, Marissa closed her eyes for a moment.

Dear Ocky,

I'm over the crush, but I surely do like you.

Love, Marissa

P.S. Please don't ever change your cologne.

Marissa stirred her iced tea and glanced at her watch. It wasn't quite seven . . . then she knew she should look up because the light changed and she heard surf and yes Linda was right there in the restaurant doorway.

Their gazes locked. Linda smiled as she shook a few raindrops off her hair. The loosely knit tan sweater shot with gold heightened the sparkle in her eyes and for the first time Marissa knew what Ocky meant by legs that went from here to Argentina. Those thoughts no sooner crossed her mind than the limitless smile seemed to pull her right out of her skin and into the warmth of an amber Tahitian sunrise, watching Linda sleep. No moment in her life had been as precious and she wanted more.

Marissa was aware of everything, including each throb of the pulse in her throat and the whisper of air through her nose as she tried to conquer her erratic breathing. Like that last morning in Tahiti, taking in the beautiful wonder that was Linda, this moment was all there was and she didn't want it, or any of the ones that followed, to end.

"I walked over and got a little wet." Linda brushed her hair with one hand.

"Rain will do that." Well, that was inane, Marissa thought.

"Hi," Linda said softly as she slid into the booth across from Marissa.

"Hi." Marissa had never felt more shy.

"You look wonderful. I meant to tell you Sunday. You look so very good."

"Do you like it better?" The question slipped out before Marissa could stop herself. But she did want to know the answer.

"Not better. I find it equally attractive." Marissa knew her skepticism showed because Linda quickly added, "I think *you* feel you're more attractive and that aura of you liking who you are more than ever I find *very* attractive."

"You . . . are still a sweet talker and a flirt, Linda."

"Why thank you. Nice to know that still works." She winked.

They studied the menu. When the waitress arrived Linda ordered a sushi platter while Marissa went for grilled yellowtail with pineapple-mango salsa.

Linda observed, "All we need is something involving bananas, rum and coconut all blended up and served under an umbrella."

"Sunshine and a pristine beach would help."

Linda's gaze traveled from Marissa's hands to her hair to her mouth. "I thought you were gorgeous in the lifeboat. I still think you're gorgeous."

As she fiddled with her napkin, Marissa asked, "That last night? You turned off the light. Why?" She looked up to study Linda's face.

"That was for me. I felt safer, like I wouldn't go away as quickly, in the dark. Because you couldn't see me. Later I wished I hadn't turned it off because I wanted to see your face when you . . ." She shrugged and glanced meaningfully at the crowded nearby tables. "Why did you think I turned it off?"

Oh dear lord, Marissa thought, I'm a goner. She keeps healing the little hurts, even the ones I gave myself. "So you didn't have to look at me."

"Seriously? That's not what I meant at all." Linda's leaned forward, her voice low. "I held the vision of your face in my mind during so many dark hours. Not because you were some kind of unreal saving angel or guiding muse but because you showed me what it looked like to live and *try*. I remembered what you said about contempt and I wanted to be absolutely sure you could respect me, even if you couldn't love me . . . the way you had. So I had to keep trying, because you never gave up."

"Do you want me to love you the way I did? I didn't really know you. Damn." She smiled brightly at the waitress who paused to set down Linda's lemonade and top off Marissa's iced tea. "This might not be a great discussion to have in such a public place."

"Yeah," Linda agreed. One hand uncurled on the table top. "You're too far away."

"Sit next to me," Marissa invited. She scooted over and then half-turned to find herself within the arc of Linda's long arm, which stretched across the back of the booth. Given how Linda's nearness was going to her head she was glad she'd not ordered a drink.

In a low voice, she said, "When you wrote in the book that you weren't sure that you'd fallen in love with 'Ginger' in Tahiti—with me—more than you loved the way I made you feel, you could have been quoting me. I wasn't sure either. I know that I adored how I felt around you. And that I loved it when you smiled, and were happy. Sometimes there were shadows in your face and I wanted to chase them away."

Linda inclined her head and Marissa tried not to focus on how much she wanted to burrow her lips into the pulse point on Linda's throat. "And you did. You did so well that I realized I couldn't live with them anymore. I had to learn to chase them away myself."

"I'm glad," Marissa said earnestly. "I am so glad for you. So glad that you feel whole again."

"Oh, I'm getting there at least. It does feel like parts of me are now all in the same head, working together toward the same goals."

"Such as?"

Linda just stared at her for a minute before saying, "One thing is a career I can not only enjoy but leaves me feeling like I can make a difference." A blinding smile made Marissa blink. "I didn't get the job, by the way."

"But you're happy about that?"

"They offered me another one and I accepted."

"Yeah? Tell me everything." She's staying, Marissa thought. I'll see her again. And again.

"They figured fresh out of school I might be able to study and learn things, so they want me to work on the campaign to raise the amount of open space along the coastline of California and Oregon. Every city, county and of course both states have to agree to take the land over and there are often obligations, expenses, overdue taxes, easements from utilities, which live outside a lot of laws. Is this too boring?"

"Not at all," Marissa assured her. Try as she might she couldn't get her gaze to lift past Linda's lips. "I'm interested."

"Really?" Linda leaned forward, not even an inch, then moved back with a little gasp. "So, um, they need someone to organize the interns and review their work because it's piles and piles of deeds and trusts and so on. It's not very sexy but it's important."

Marissa studied how the light softened and shadowed the contours of Linda's cheeks and all she could think was that Linda would be staying. For a while. Long enough to know . . . to figure it all out. "I get that. Yes, the kind of behind-the-scenes work that nobody really sees but is vital to the process."

The meals were delivered and Marissa cheerfully dug in. "It's a relief sometimes not to think about how many calories is in what I'm eating."

"Do you have a goal in mind?"

"Yes, another twenty pounds."

"Really? Are you sure? You'll be skin and bones."

"Bless you for making me feel like I could ever be too thin." With a shake of the head, Marissa added, "It's still twenty pounds more than those insurance charts say I should weigh but I'm not trying to get into some unrealistic sized clothing or look like—" She directed a glance at the slender, very attractive blonde who walked by their table in jeans no bigger than a pencil. "Like that."

"You're a voluptuous, large-framed woman—to be that thin you'd have to give up your muscle."

"Exactly." Marissa gave a confident shrug. "I'm not doing *The Devil Wears Prada* here. My real goal is having the strength and endurance to do the things I want for the rest of my life. Like climb a cliff when my life depends on it." See the world one step at a time with you, she added to herself, not to mention redefining lovemaking as an aerobic sport.

"I like your muscles. I like your curves," Linda said seriously. "And I'm glad you like them too. You're naturally beautiful." She dabbed wasabi on a slice of dragon roll. "Do you want some?"

Marissa told herself sternly not to cry, even though she was wounded all over again by the knowledge that some of Linda's body wasn't of her own choosing. "Sure—trade you some fish and salsa?"

241

"Yes, please. Scamming some of your dinner was actually my whole goal."

"Greedy."

"Yes," Linda said, not looking at the food.

A hard swallow later, Marissa asked, "And you? Are you liking the body you have more than you did? I was aware, back then, that you were at times uncomfortable about it. I didn't know why."

Linda dabbed at a few fallen grains of rice with her finger. There was tension in her shoulders for a second, then Marissa could feel it leave her again.

Finally, Linda said, "I can't change the past. This is the way I am now. That it wasn't my choice is a big deal, sure. But going forward, keeping this body this way *is* my choice. Therefore, this *is* my body. And I like it."

"So do I," Marissa said sincerely. "And even more, I like the woman who will bash on a coconut for two hours."

After a pause, Linda whispered, "How do you do that?"

"Do what?"

"Say exactly the right thing."

Marissa had no answer but she let her eyes try to speak. Whatever Linda saw in them deepened the tenderness evident in her own gaze. The people around us, Marissa thought, will need insulin shots if we keep this up.

Most of the food was gone before the conversation touched on the issues Marissa could still feel trembling between them.

"You didn't answer my question," Marissa said.

"Which one?"

"Do you want me to love you the way I did?"

"Yes. I mean, I want your love. Whether it's the way you felt before or a brand new way, I don't care. I know that you've changed. I can see it. I've changed too."

"You made me feel like nobody ever had. And when you didn't come back I really missed that feeling." And I missed you, Marissa wanted to add. I missed hearing you laugh and watching you eat and making every minute an adventure. The truth of her feelings was pounding in her heart.

"And now?"

"I've learned how to get the awareness of myself, as you saw me—attractive, sexy, even—"

Linda leaned a little closer to whisper, "Hell, yes. You are so very sexy."

"And you say I'm the one who knows just what to say."

"I speak truth."

Marissa wanted to lean forward three inches and kiss Linda for the next three hours. "I know that I can be interesting and intelligent and I'm worth being loved. It's like I can all by myself finally get enough of the good stuff to make life worth living. I could be content. But when I'm with you . . ." She searched for words.

"It's like megawatts more."

"Yeah. Like that." Marissa put down her fork to hide her shaking hands. "From the beginning I have wondered if I loved you or if I loved the way you made me feel."

"Does the difference matter?"

A helpless smile took over Marissa's mouth. "Middle of the night I asked myself that same question. Does the difference really matter? I don't have to run my feelings through seven hundred questions. People can and do fall in love . . . without . . ." Oh dear, Marissa thought. She wasn't at all sure she should have said that last bit.

"When you look like that I want to kiss you."

Her reflection, the woman she was becoming, was bright and real in Linda's eyes. "When I feel like this I want you to kiss me and never stop." The air in the restaurant was stifling now. "Maybe, just maybe, I love how you make me feel because I'm in love with you. And because I'm in love with you I love the way you make me feel. It's an infinite loop, a Mobius strip, perpetual reflection. God, I'm blithering again."

"You are not," Linda said. One hand, under the table, took hers and squeezed. "You make sense to me, Marissa. You always have."

"I promise," Marissa said in a very low voice, "not to call you beautiful, though I think you are." The heat of Linda's hand quickly increased the already raging firestorm in other parts of Marissa's body.

"I would like," Linda said in a conversational tone, "to pay the check and get out of here."

"And go where?" Marissa glanced outside and was stunned to see that it was raining. Where were the beach and the unending horizon? She looked back at Linda and goodness, she was getting sappier by the minute, she thought, because they were there, in Linda's eyes.

"My motel is right across the street." Linda's gaze was, for a moment, without any kind of intent, then a grin creased her face. "Okay, I'd like to say that I don't mean anything by that, but that would be a lie."

"Why, Ms. Bartok, are you trying to seduce me?"

"God, yes."

"I want you to. But . . ." Marissa waited until the waitress departed with Linda's credit card to continue. "Maybe we should take it slow. Maybe we shouldn't . . ."

"Only when you're ready. I mean that." Marissa saw Linda swallow with effort. "But if you think it's easy not to get down on my knees right now and worship every inch of you, you're wrong."

A wave of heat ran up Marissa's throat and she had to force herself to breathe. They were in Marissa's car, listening to rain pelt on the roof, before Marissa could find enough breath—and brains—to speak. "Before? When I said we should take it slow?"

A streetlight illuminated Linda's face but even so, she looked drawn and intense. "Yes?"

Marissa navigated the broad boulevard before answering. "Do you think that maybe we could have a night of wild, abandoned, meaningless sex before we tried that slow thing?"

She turned into the hotel parking lot and found a spot near the front doors.

"No," Linda said quietly.

"Oh." Marissa blinked in surprise. Had she misread Linda's interest? In the abstract Linda had wanted Marissa but faced with reality, maybe she wasn't feeling that zing?

Linda reached across the car to turn off the engine. "Marissa."

The look in Linda's eyes left Marissa again without words.

"I could never touch you, hold you, kiss you, make love to you and have it be meaningless. I love you. I am crazy in love with you. Every moment with you has meaning and reason. I never want it any other way."

Marissa's mouth formed "oh" again but no sound came out.

Linda's lips curved in the smile that had first caught Marissa's attention. "How about a night of meaningful sex?"

～♥～

The lights were on, all of them. Linda's hands moved slowly over Marissa as she said, "I want to watch you."

Marissa felt self-conscious for a moment then a sensual confidence surged inside her. She knew now that if she did not risk her heart again, she would regret it forever. She stepped back, hands at the buttons on her blouse, and whispered, "Then watch."

Linda kept her hands on Marissa's shoulders but made a wonderful sound as each button parted. When the last button was undone, Linda pushed the blouse off Marissa's shoulders, her gaze so heavy with desire that it seemed as palpable as Linda's hands on Marissa's skin.

Her long arms wrapped around Marissa with ease and one hand mastered the hooks and eyes.

"Thank you," Marissa murmured. She let her bra straps slip down her arms, her gaze not leaving Linda's face. The obvious hunger in Linda's eyes thrilled and aroused her.

"This has changed." Linda ran one finger into the cleft between Marissa's breasts. "Even more alluring."

Looking down, Marissa watched Linda's finger trace the outline of her bra, a new lacey frippery with underwires that felt like steel. She knew she would never be a swimsuit model, never be naturally shaped the way that Linda was, with high, firm and wonderfully round breasts. But she was over finding her breasts an unfair burden. Linda's fingers, closing firmly on one swollen nipple, ended all debate.

Linda kissed her when she gasped, arms winding her close. They fell on the bed with Linda on the bottom and Marissa's bra slipping to her elbows until Linda, with a noise a lot like a growl, pulled it out of the way.

"Watching?" Straddling Linda's waist, Marissa coyly trailed her fingers over her breasts, then lightly stroked her nipples.

"Hell, yes." Linda's hips were moving as both hands slipped under the hem of Marissa's skirt. "Oh . . . these thigh muscles are new."

She'd never have Ocky's long, lean legs but she was more than able to lift, tease and grind herself into Linda in response to the strokes of her hands. Then Linda's hands were between their bodies, putting pressure and heat on the part of Marissa that had been aching for more than a year.

Shivering, she pressed herself against Linda's fingers. "You make me feel wild."

"That's mutual, very mutual." With an intense look, Linda quickly moved her hands back to Marissa's nipples, tugging firmly to pull Marissa down to her. "Is this what you want, Marissa?"

"Yes." The kiss was hot and deep and somewhere during it Marissa found herself on her back, squirming out of her skirt and pantyhose.

"You feel so good in my arms," Linda said in her ear as one still denim-clad knee pushed Marissa's legs apart. "So good against me. I could spend a whole day just holding you. But not today."

"No," Marissa said. "Some other day." Her entire body felt alive now. Ears, lips, knees, toes—all were tingling. She stretched against Linda's body. To her surprise, Linda abruptly rolled off the bed.

"I want to feel your skin," she said as she stripped off the sweater, then stepped out of her jeans.

A square of fabric, too small to be a handkerchief, fluttered to the floor half under the bed and Marissa leaned over to pick it up. It was silk, in an unusual shade of blue. "Don't lose this."

"No, I keep that with me always." Linda took the silk, then lightly touched it to Marissa's face. "I was right. It's the color of your eyes."

Marissa was lightheaded and she didn't know if it was because of Linda's words or the sight of her slipping off the rest of her clothes. Dizzied with emotion and longing, all Marissa could think about was how much she had missed the feel of Linda's skin against her.

She reached for Linda as she returned to the bed, groaning as breasts, stomach and hips pressed together, as her arms went around Linda and Linda's legs pushed hers open.

Leaning back slightly, Linda looked down the length of Marissa's naked body. "There's a valley in Spain where I sometimes stayed for the late summer. Covered in gold, the hills roll." Her fingertips traced Marissa's shoulder, along her upper arm, then into the crook of her elbow. "They swoop, they yield."

Marissa was panting and it was getting harder and harder not to moan every time she breathed out.

"I would watch the sunset most nights and to me it was as if the earth mother was right there before my eyes." Her fingers moved to Marissa's ribs, then slowly swept over her belly and hip. "I would think that I'd never seen anything so womanly in my life."

Marissa closed her eyes and gave herself to the magic Linda was working on her body.

"And then that first morning in Tahiti I woke before you did and you'd kicked off your covers. Your T-shirt was rucked up and you were all golden, curving and yielding, like those perfect, entrancing hills."

Marissa forced her eyes open. Linda was watching her face. She moaned, then, and felt the light scratch of nails on the inside of her thighs.

"The perfect woman, right there before my eyes, and I watched you sleep and wanted you. Holding you is like gathering up all that is female in my arms. It fills me up to touch you." She kissed Marissa softly on the lips.

Marissa shuddered as Linda's hand finally slipped between her legs. "Oh, yes, there."

"That's right," Linda said. "There."

Marissa didn't think even that magic night in Tahiti she had been as aroused and as aware of her own surrender to Linda's sensuality. Linda moved inside her so easily at first, but those caresses grew more firm with each stroke. Linda was fully on top of her now, straddling one leg as her palm massaged outside and fingers pleasured inside, deep inside.

Her arms suddenly limp, Marissa felt like the warm surf spreading in the sun over welcoming sand. She was tensing and melting at the same time, her body anchored to the bed by Linda's while her mind soared and danced, held up by Linda's whispers of adoration and desire.

"Open your eyes, Marissa, please."

She managed, somehow, trembling on the edge of a feeling so unknown she feared she would shake apart. She saw those shining brown eyes, full of passion and tenderness. She looked deep and saw herself, the woman she was, captured there.

Linda was flushed and panting. "That's right. Hold on and we'll fly together. I'm here and I love you and—yes. God, yes."

Release was so powerful, so intense, that Marissa burst into tears as her hips convulsed under Linda's. She let go of the last of her hurt and the empty places it left were filled again with a brimming joy.

There were more tears after that, tears of wonder, of forgiveness and ecstasy. They gave way to laughter cut short by moans. Later, exhausted, Marissa marveled that her own hands could bring so much pleasure to someone else.

In her head she heard her own voice saying, "We believe in love. We believe in romance. We believe in first meetings, second dates, third anniversaries and relationships that can last a lifetime."

Aloud, she said, "I believe."

Linda heaved a deep sigh. "In what?"

She managed to rise onto one elbow, which allowed her to gaze into Linda's face. "No losers, no weepers."

"Not here," Linda said. "Not anymore."

❧

248

"I think we can find the one hundred," Marissa murmured, spooned close behind Linda.

"Hmm? What's that?" The curve of Marissa's arm over her ribs was warm and safe. Sleep beckoned insistently. To call it a full night of meaningful sex was no exaggeration.

"Compatibility score. We don't know what ours is."

"Don't we?" Okay, Linda thought sleepily, she likes to talk after sex. I can get used to that.

After a sigh, Marissa said, "I think my very human computer does know, you're right." She snuggled closer. She sighed again, sounding drowsy. "My heart knows our score."

"So does mine. Thank you."

"For what?"

Linda rolled over so she could kiss Marissa one more time. The lights were now out but the glow of her hair and body were still palpable. "For tomorrow."

Marissa kissed her back and burrowed her head into the hollow between Linda's neck and shoulder. "And the day after that. All yours . . ."

She didn't fear sleep, not these days, and with Marissa now breathing steady and deep, she knew she would wake up wanting to stay right there, within reach of Marissa's warmth and love.

❧

"Dang it all." Marissa patted her pockets. "I left my sunglasses on my desk upstairs."

"Run up and get them." Linda pulled forward again into the parking space. "The groceries are just greens and some fruit—they'll wait."

"In that case," Marissa said shyly. "Maybe you'd like to come up and meet everybody. At least those who haven't left yet?"

"I'd love to." Linda was already out of the car.

Marissa marveled at how right it had felt to find Linda waiting for her when she had left work. The past two weeks had been a series of days and nights that just got easier and easier. It seemed appropriate that since they were having dinner with her mother later at the club that Linda should meet the rest of the people that mattered in Marissa's life.

"Heather, this is Linda." Marissa watched the two women shake hands, then suddenly Ocky was there, with a welcoming, but cautious, expression on her face.

"Hey. It's great to meet you. You two have big plans for the weekend?"

"A hike near Mt. Diablo," Linda answered. Marissa knew her well enough now to see that Linda was aware she was being scrutinized. "And a picnic, complete with small amounts of very good chocolate."

"Sounds romantic." Ocky kept on her 'you're still on probation' face, which Marissa loved her for.

"It's meant to be," Linda answered. "Marissa makes courting her a lot of fun."

Marissa blushed which made Linda look even more pleased with herself. Before they made it to Marissa's office, Linda had met everybody it seemed. Her blush had begun to fade until, behind Linda's back, she saw Bianca giving two big thumbs up. Finally, she got them into her office and was able to search her desk for her sunglasses.

"So this is where the Finders Keepers magic happens?"

"No—that's in the server room. This is just a printer where I can pull results."

"I filled out a questionnaire, you know."

"You're kidding."

Linda shrugged. "It was the day after I made you breakfast. I didn't have anything else to do."

"Did you submit it?"

"Yeah. I thought, well, at the very least I could support your business."

"You're a client? Not anymore you aren't."

"Neither are you then."

Grinning, Marissa agreed. "Done. I'll erase us both from the system when I get back on Monday."

Linda picked up the bendy figure that held Marissa's business cards. "Not even curious?"

"I really think that we should trust our feelings. I know how I feel about you. I don't need a computer to agree with me."

Linda pulled her close for a long, satisfying kiss. "Are you sure?"

"Absolutely."

"Okay then, I don't want to see it either. I want to do things the old-fashioned way. Make mistakes, have a few fights, make up and work things out, all because we're in love and want the future together. Not because we're perfect mates."

"We are perfect mates." Marissa sighed into the comfort of Linda's arms.

"You know what I mean."

"Yeah. I do. Mind reading is one of the signs of our perfect matedness."

Linda tickled her gently. "Ready to go?"

"Sure." Marissa picked up her sunglasses and headed for the door. They were at the reception desk when she smacked herself on the forehead. "I'd forget my head if it weren't velcroed on. My purse . . . be right back."

She hurried through the office, threw herself down into her desk chair, flipped on her monitor and quickly keyed in her administrative override. About thirty seconds later she typed a query. In another thirty seconds the printer whirred into action, spitting out a single sheet.

For a moment her hand hovered over the paper, then she shoved it deep into the recycle pile. She made it as far as her office door before she hurried back to snatch the paper from the bin and quickly glance at the final score.

She smiled.

Epilogue

Still rubbing a small towel over her face and neck, Marissa slipped out of her workout shoes and stripped off her sweat-soaked tank top. The gym wasn't busy and only one other woman was in the process of changing.

She eased down onto the bench to work off her socks and noticed the shorter woman, who probably had a weight loss goal of thirty to fifty pounds, adding dots to the progress graphs she herself knew so well. Even from here she could see that the time spent on exercise had gone up over the last eight weeks, while the weight line had no variance at all. That was the pits.

Planning to shower when she got home—a long, luxurious shower with lots of emollients and conditioners—she pulled on a dry T-shirt and gathered up her things, careful to collect every last sock and sport bra. With a two-week Rocky Mountain hike starting tomorrow, she did not want to return to find something in her locker had spawned a new species. Maybe she could get Linda to join her for their last shower in some time. She paused, for a moment, to savor that idea.

Her gym bag laden, she winked at her reflection, then shut the locker door. She was about to leave when she impulsively turned to the other woman. She waited until she received an inquiring look to speak. "I couldn't help but notice your charts. Plateaus suck. The worst I ever had I ended up changing the order of my—"

"Look, I know you mean well, but I don't need any advice." The other woman frowned as she set her shoes into the locker.

"Oh, I'm sorry, I know what you—"

"What is it with women like you? You don't have a clue."

"Women like me?" Marissa echoed. She was sorry she had opened her mouth but she'd only wanted to help and encourage.

The other woman had obviously reached her frustration limit. "Skinny bitches like you haven't the first clue—"

Marissa couldn't help it. She laughed in the woman's face.

The other woman slammed her locker shut and would have stalked from the room but Marissa quickly grabbed the photograph tucked next to the mirror in her locker door and waved it at the woman.

"I'm sorry, but honest, look. This is me, on a beach in Tahiti, four years ago."

With an exaggerated sigh, the woman looked at the photo. She gaped. "That's you? You're kidding."

"It's me. I keep it right here to remind me why I show up at this place. I read somewhere that even after you empty a fat cell it takes that sucker eighteen months to go away for good. I made my goal weight twelve months ago, so even now I know I can't stop. Not yet."

"How did you do it?" Obviously chagrined, the woman said, "I'm sorry I was rude, really. I've worked so hard and thin people are full of ideas they've never had to live with. They didn't inherit my mother's hips. I snipe about them to hide my envy."

Marissa's eyes stung with sympathetic tears. "I gave up the fad diets, got serious about regular exercise and stuck with it, year in

253

and year out. And I got some really great advice. Here." She scrawled Helena Boxer's phone number on the back of a business card and handed it over.

"Did you ever cry over whether a cracker would undo a week of dieting?"

"Oh, I have been there."

They walked out of the gym together and Marissa waved a cheery good-bye, smiling so hard her face ached.

Dear Dad,

I was called a skinny bitch today. I hope you recognize me when I eventually join you. Not for a good long while, I hope, since I intend to spend at least the next six decades of my life figuring out new ways to amuse and exhaust Linda. I know you know what I mean.

Love, Marissa

P.S. Mom sends Linda and me anniversary cards. Now she's asking where the grandchildren are.

The rock bit into her fingers but the air pumping into her lungs was sweet and powerful. With a final gasp, Marissa pulled herself over the lip of the steep incline, then clambered to her feet to survey the seemingly endless ranges of mountains. The visibility was so clear that she felt she could touch both near and distant peaks.

She tore her gaze from the profound beauty of the landscape. What a dilemma, she thought. The snowcapped Rockies or my lover's eyes? As the luminous topaz gaze met hers she knew, the way she always knew, that she could spend all her life looking into them and never find anything to compare.

"Your turn," she called down to Linda, thirty feet below her. "I know you can do it."

"I love you," came the answer, then Linda began to climb.

OUT OF THE FIRE by Beth Moore. Author Ann Covington feels at the top of the world when told her book is being made into a movie. Then in walks Casey Duncan the actress who is playing the lead in her movie. Will Casey turn Ann's world upside down?
1-59493-088-0 $13.95

STAKE THROUGH THE HEART: NEW EXPLOITS OF TWILIGHT LESBIANS by Karin Kallmaker, Julia Watts, Barbara Johnson and Therese Szymanski. The playful quartet that penned the acclaimed *Once Upon A Dyke* are dimming the lights for journeys into worlds of breathless seduction. 1-59493-071-6 $15.95

THE HOUSE ON SANDSTONE by KG MacGregor. Carly Griffin returns home to Leland and finds that her old high school friend Justice is awakening more than just old memories. 1-59493-076-7 $13.95

WILD NIGHTS: MOSTLY TRUE STORIES OF WOMEN LOVING WOMEN edited by Therese Szymanski. 264 pp. 23 new stories from today's hottest erotic writers are sure to give you your wildest night ever! 1-59493-069-4 $15.95

COYOTE SKY by Gerri Hill. 248 pp. Sheriff Lee Foxx is trying to cope with the realization that she has fallen in love for the first time. And fallen for author Kate Winters, who is technically unavailable. Will Lee fight to keep Kate in Coyote? 1-59493-065-1 $13.95

VOICES OF THE HEART by Frankie J. Jones. 264 pp. A series of events force Erin to swear off love as she tries to break away from the woman of her dreams. Will Erin ever find the key to her future happiness? 1-59493-068-6 $13.95

SHELTER FROM THE STORM by Peggy J. Herring. 296 pp. A story about family and getting reacquainted with one's past that shows that sometimes you don't appreciate what you have until you almost lose it. 1-59493-064-3 $13.95

WRITING MY LOVE by Claire McNab. 192 pp. Romance writer Vonny Smith believes she will be able to woo her editor Diana through her writing . . . 1-59493-063-5 $13.95

PAID IN FULL by Ann Roberts. 200 pp. Ari Adams will need to choose between the debts of the past and the promise of a happy future. 1-59493-059-7 $13.95

ROMANCING THE ZONE by Kenna White. 272 pp. Liz's world begins to crumble when a secret from her past returns to Ashton . . . 1-59493-060-0 $13.95

SIGN ON THE LINE by Jaime Clevenger. 204 pp. Alexis Getty, a flirtatious delivery driver is committed to finding the rightful owner of a mysterious package.
1-59493-052-X $13.95

END OF WATCH by Clare Baxter. 256 pp. LAPD Lieutenant L.A Franco Frank follows the lone clue down the unlit steps of memory to a final, unthinkable resolution.
1-59493-064-4 $13.95

BEHIND THE PINE CURTAIN by Gerri Hill. 280pp. Jacqueline returns home after her father's death and comes face-to-face with her first crush.   1-59493-057-0 $13.95

PIPELINE by Brenda Adcock. 240pp. Joanna faces a lost love returning and pulling her into a seamy underground corporation that kills for money.   1-59493-062-7 $13.95

18TH & CASTRO by Karin Kallmaker. 200pp. First-time couplings and couples who know how to mix lust and love make 18th & Castro the hottest address in the city by the bay.
1-59493-066-X $13.95

JUST THIS ONCE by KG MacGregor. 200pp. Mindful of the obligations back home that she must honor, Wynne Connelly struggles to resist the fascination and allure that a particular woman she meets on her business trip represents.   1-59493-087-2 $13.95

ANTICIPATION by Terri Breneman. 240pp. Two women struggle to remain professional as they work together to find a serial killer.   1-59493-055-4 $13.95

OBSESSION by Jackie Calhoun. 240pp. Lindsey's life is turned upside down when Sarah comes into the family nursery in search of perennials.   1-59493-058-9 $13.95

BENEATH THE WILLOW by Kenna White. 240pp. A torch that still burns brightly even after twenty-five years threatens to consume two childhood friends.
1-59493-053-8 $13.95

SISTER LOST, SISTER FOUND by Jeanne G'fellers. 224pp. The highly anticipated sequel to No Sister of Mine.   1-59493-056-2 $13.95

THE WEEKEND VISITOR by Jessica Thomas. 240 pp. In this latest Alex Peres mystery, Alex is asked to investigate an assault on a local woman but finds that her client may have more secrets than she lets on.   1-59493-054-6 $13.95

THE KILLING ROOM by Gerri Hill. 392 pp. How can two women forget and go their separate ways?   1-59493-050-3 $12.95

PASSIONATE KISSES by Megan Carter. 240 pp. Will two old friends run from love?
1-59493-051-1 $12.95

ALWAYS AND FOREVER by Lyn Denison. 224 pp. The girl next door turns Shannon's world upside down.   1-59493-049-X $12.95

BACK TALK by Saxon Bennett. 200 pp. Can a talk show host find love after heartbreak?
1-59493-028-7 $12.95

THE PERFECT VALENTINE: EROTIC LESBIAN VALENTINE STORIES edited by Barbara Johnson and Therese Szymanski—from Bella After Dark. 328 pp. Stories from the hottest writers around.   1-59493-061-9 $14.95

MURDER AT RANDOM by Claire McNab. 200 pp. The Sixth Denise Cleever Thriller. Denise realizes the fate of thousands is in her hands.   1-59493-047-3 $12.95

THE TIDES OF PASSION by Diana Tremain Braund. 240 pp. Will Susan be able to hold it all together and find the one woman who touches her soul?   1-59493-048-1 $12.95

JUST LIKE THAT by Karin Kallmaker. 240 pp. Disliking each other—and everything they stand for—even before they meet, Toni and Syrah find feelings can change, just like that.
1-59493-025-2 $12.95

WHEN FIRST WE PRACTICE by Therese Szymanski. 200 pp. Brett and Allie are once again caught in the middle of murder and intrigue. 1-59493-045-7 $12.95

REUNION by Jane Frances. 240 pp. Cathy Braithwaite seems to have it all: good looks, money and a thriving accounting practice . . . 1-59493-046-5 $12.95

BELL, BOOK & DYKE: NEW EXPLOITS OF MAGICAL LESBIANS by Kallmaker, Watts, Johnson and Szymanski. 360 pp. Reluctant witches, tempting spells and skyclad beauties—delve into the mysteries of love, lust and power in this quartet of novellas. 1-59493-023-6 $14.95

ARTIST'S DREAM by Gerri Hill. 320 pp. When Cassie meets Luke Winston, she can no longer deny her attraction to women . . . 1-59493-042-2 $12.95

NO EVIDENCE by Nancy Sanra. 240 pp. Private Investigator Tally McGinnis once again returns to the horror-filled world of a serial killer. 1-59493-043-04 $12.95

WHEN LOVE FINDS A HOME by Megan Carter. 280 pp. What will it take for Anna and Rona to find their way back to each other again? 1-59493-041-4 $12.95

MEMORIES TO DIE FOR by Adrian Gold. 240 pp. Rachel attempts to avoid her attraction to the charms of Anna Sigurdson . . . 1-59493-038-4 $12.95

SILENT HEART by Claire McNab. 280 pp. Exotic lesbian romance. 1-59493-044-9 $12.95

MIDNIGHT RAIN by Peggy J. Herring. 240 pp. Bridget McBee is determined to find the woman who saved her life. 1-59493-021-X $12.95

THE MISSING PAGE A Brenda Strange Mystery by Patty G. Henderson. 240 pp. Brenda investigates her client's murder . . . 1-59493-004-X $12.95

WHISPERS ON THE WIND by Frankie J. Jones. 240 pp. Dixon thinks she and her best friend, Elizabeth Colter, would make the perfect couple . . . 1-59493-037-6 $12.95

CALL OF THE DARK: EROTIC LESBIAN TALES OF THE SUPERNATURAL edited by Therese Szymanski—from Bella After Dark. 320 pp. 1-59493-040-6 $14.95

A TIME TO CAST AWAY A Helen Black Mystery by Pat Welch. 240 pp. Helen stops by Alice's apartment—only to find the woman dead . . . 1-59493-036-8 $12.95

DESERT OF THE HEART by Jane Rule. 224 pp. The book that launched the most popular lesbian movie of all time is back. 1-1-59493-035-X $12.95

THE NEXT WORLD by Ursula Steck. 240 pp. Anna's friend Mido is threatened and eventually disappears . . . 1-59493-024-4 $12.95

CALL SHOTGUN by Jaime Clevenger. 240 pp. Kelly gets pulled back into the world of private investigation . . . 1-59493-016-3 $12.95

52 PICKUP by Bonnie J. Morris and E.B. Casey. 240 pp. 52 hot, romantic tales—one for every Saturday night of the year. 1-59493-026-0 $12.95

GOLD FEVER by Lyn Denison. 240 pp. Kate's first love, Ashley, returns to their home town, where Kate now lives . . . 1-1-59493-039-2 $12.95

RISKY INVESTMENT by Beth Moore. 240 pp. Lynn's best friend and roommate needs her to pretend Chris is his fiancé. But nothing is ever easy. 1-59493-019-8 $12.95

HUNTER'S WAY by Gerri Hill. 240 pp. Homicide detective Tori Hunter is forced to team up with the hot-tempered Samantha Kennedy. 1-59493-018-X $12.95

CAR POOL by Karin Kallmaker. 240 pp. Soft shoulders, merging traffic and slippery when wet . . . Anthea and Shay find love in the car pool. 1-59493-013-9 $12.95

NO SISTER OF MINE by Jeanne G'Fellers. 240 pp. Telepathic women fight to coexist with a patriarchal society that wishes their eradication. ISBN 1-59493-017-1 $12.95

ON THE WINGS OF LOVE by Megan Carter. 240 pp. Stacie's reporting career is on the rocks. She has to interview bestselling author Cheryl, or else! ISBN 1-59493-027-9 $12.95

WICKED GOOD TIME by Diana Tremain Braund. 224 pp. Does Christina need Miki as a protector . . . or want her as a lover? ISBN 1-59493-031-7 $12.95

THOSE WHO WAIT by Peggy J. Herring. 240 pp. Two brilliant sisters—in love with the same woman! ISBN 1-59493-032-5 $12.95

ABBY'S PASSION by Jackie Calhoun. 240 pp. Abby's bipolar sister helps turn her world upside down, so she must decide what's most important. ISBN 1-59493-014-7 $12.95

PICTURE PERFECT by Jane Vollbrecht. 240 pp. Kate is reintroduced to Casey, the daughter of an old friend. Can they withstand Kate's career? ISBN 1-59493-015-5 $12.95

PAPERBACK ROMANCE by Karin Kallmaker. 240 pp. Carolyn falls for tall, dark and . . . female . . . in this classic lesbian romance. ISBN 1-59493-033-3 $12.95

DAWN OF CHANGE by Gerri Hill. 240 pp. Susan ran away to find peace in remote Kings Canyon—then she met Shawn . . . ISBN 1-59493-011-2 $12.95

DOWN THE RABBIT HOLE by Lynne Jamneck. 240 pp. Is a killer holding a grudge against FBI Agent Samantha Skellar? ISBN 1-59493-012-0 $12.95

SEASONS OF THE HEART by Jackie Calhoun. 240 pp. Overwhelmed, Sara saw only one way out—leaving . . . ISBN 1-59493-030-9 $12.95

TURNING THE TABLES by Jessica Thomas. 240 pp. The 2nd Alex Peres Mystery. *From ghosties and ghoulies and long leggity beasties* . . . ISBN 1-59493-009-0 $12.95

FOR EVERY SEASON by Frankie Jones. 240 pp. Andi, who is investigating a 65-year-old murder, meets Janice, a charming district attorney . . . ISBN 1-59493-010-4 $12.95

LOVE ON THE LINE by Laura DeHart Young. 240 pp. Kay leaves a younger woman behind to go on a mission to Alaska . . . will she regret it? ISBN 1-59493-008-2 $12.95

UNDER THE SOUTHERN CROSS by Claire McNab. 200 pp. Lee, an American travel agent, goes down under and meets Australian Alex, and the sparks fly under the Southern Cross. ISBN 1-59493-029-5 $12.95

SUGAR by Karin Kallmaker. 240 pp. Three women want sugar from Sugar, who can't make up her mind. ISBN 1-59493-001-5 $12.95

FALL GUY by Claire McNab. 200 pp. 16th Detective Inspector Carol Ashton Mystery. ISBN 1-59493-000-7 $12.95

ONE SUMMER NIGHT by Gerri Hill. 232 pp. Johanna swore to never fall in love again—but then she met the charming Kelly . . . ISBN 1-59493-007-4 $12.95

TALK OF THE TOWN TOO by Saxon Bennett. 181 pp. Second in the series about wild and fun loving friends. ISBN 1-931513-77-5 $12.95

LOVE SPEAKS HER NAME by Laura DeHart Young. 170 pp. Love and friendship, desire and intrigue, spark this exciting sequel to *Forever and the Night*. ISBN 1-59493-002-3 $12.95